EDWARD [illegible]

AND

MR HORSE

COLLECTED SHORT STORIES

VOLUME I

by

Ross Macfarlane KC

ARLAN Press

First Published in the UK in 2023 by

ARLAN PRESS

arlanpress.com
info@arlanpress.com

Paperback ISBN: 978-1-3999-4215-7

Technical assistance in print production by ScottishPrint, Glasgow (www.scottishprint.com)

Illustrations and cover design by

Lesley-Anne Barnes Macfarlane

To Lesley-Anne. Always.

Contents

Introduction

The idea for the character of Edward Kane came to me in a graveyard.

I had written a number of Christmas short stories for both *The Scotsman* newspaper and *The Edinburgh Evening News* and I thought that I'd work on a story about Charles Dickens' visit to Edinburgh in June 1841.

The author's diary recorded that he had visited the graveyard at Canongate Kirk in Edinburgh and was possibly inspired to create the character of 'Ebenezer Scrooge' from an inscription on a gravestone that he read there (the finished story, published in *Scotland on Sunday*, appears as a bonus story at the end of this volume, on page 313).

And then - the seed of an idea. I had been an Advocate – a Scottish Supreme Courts lawyer – for over twenty years. Like our English barrister counterparts, the everyday dress of the Advocate comprised the horsehair wig, the wing collar, striped trousers and a black gown. The Faculty of Advocates – the professional body to which I belonged – had existed since 1532. This garb had not changed in centuries. Many of the Faculty traditions were still in operation into the Twenty-First Century.

I stood among the gravestones. What if…what if…I were to write about a young Scottish Advocate in the time of Charles Dickens, in the middle of the Nineteenth Century? What if our young lawyer was struggling to make a living? What if he had a manservant who had fought at the Battle of Waterloo in 1815?

Thus it was – fully formed – that 'Edward Kane, Advocate' came into being, accompanied by his Cockney manservant – and pugilistic guardian angel – 'Mr Horse'.

At that time, I travelled a great deal by train. So, every day I would get on the train and write solidly for an hour and a half, do my Court work throughout the day, then edit what I'd written on the train home.

I started out with nothing but my two characters (Edward Kane and Mr Horse), the year (1850) and the milieu (Edinburgh, Scotland) – and no plot! Gradually, the story emerged, day by day, and the novel turned into a Victorian 'who-dunnit'. Problem was – I had no idea myself who the murderer was.

Fortunately, in the latter stages of writing, the characters themselves told me.

The fruits of that daily scribbling on those trains became the first Kane novel, '*Edward Kane and the Parlour Maid Murderer*'.

While searching for a publisher for the book, it struck me that it would be good idea to get young Edward 'out there' in the meantime (before anyone else claimed the idea of a Victorian Advocate and his Cockney sidekick!). I wondered if *The Scotsman* would like a wee Christmas serial.

I have always loved Dickens and thought that part of the terrific page-turning qualities achieved in classics like *David Copperfield* were the result of the serialised nature of the storytelling. *The Scotsman* said 'yes', so I started penning the first story in the collection here, '*Edward Kane and the Matter of Honour*'.

So started the annual run of Edward Kane serials at Christmas (accompanied by a couple of stories set at Easter and Valentine's Day).

The response to the characters has been overwhelming. In the play, *Shadowlands*, the writer William Nicholson puts these words into the mouth of the character of C S Lewis: 'We read to know that we're not alone.' I always loved that quote. That's why I write. For you.

So, whether you're reading this in bed, or on a bus, or in the bath, whether reading this in a book or on a phone or on a tablet – you're not alone.

I wish you an easy chair and a glass of something nice and the total immersion into a different world.

And the joy of the company of Edward Kane and Mr Horse.

Ross Macfarlane

Parliament House
Edinburgh

September 2023

Edward Kane

and

The Matter of Honour (2019)

Chapter One

So, the old nobleman closed one eye, took careful aim with his pistol and BANG! Thirty feet away, his young opponent looked dazed for a few seconds – then fell to the ground, his top hat blown into the mud.

The old man nodded and smiled.

Dead? Good. Serves the blighter right…

***

Edinburgh: December 1850

'A duel? Two men fighting a duel??'

Edward Kane, Advocate and his faithful friend, Mr Collins, Advocate, both attired in wig and gown, sat in the Advocates Reading Room, sipping their tea.

Collins furrowed his brow: 'A duel? You mean - with swords and such?'

Kane nodded: 'Collins, you must bring yourself into the modern age. This is the nineteenth century, my friend - the weapons here were pistols.'

Collins considered this. He removed a small square of silk from his waistcoat pocket, removed his horn-rimmed glasses and began polishing the thick lenses: 'Pistols - at dawn, no doubt...'

Kane smiled: 'At dusk, in fact - at the top of Calton Hill...'

Collins continued: 'My dear Edward, there cannot have been a duel in Scotland for…oh, it must be decades.'

'I am simply repeating what I was told, Collins.'

Collins continued to wipe the lenses: 'And what was the point of honour at stake?'

Kane looked up from his teacup: "The point of honour'?'

Collins placed the glasses back onto the bridge of his nose: 'If it was, indeed, a 'duel', Edward, then the gentlemen involved would be fighting over a matter of honour. Without that noble element, it might as well be two Irish navigators engaging in fisticuffs outside the Doric Tavern.' The friends laughed. Collins continued: 'And what is the charge?'

Kane shook his head: 'I am not quite sure. I received a letter of instruction, delivered to my rooms yesterday evening. Consultation is later today. The messenger said that the matter related to a duel. And now you know as much as I do, Collins.'

Collins nodded, but seemed more serious now. Kane marked this: 'You will forgive me for saying that your sudden change in demeanour concerns me....'

Collins, thoughtful, sipped his tea, then: 'Honour or no honour, Edward. Two aggrieved gentlemen travel to a remote spot, armed with pistols, determined to fire those pistols at each other...'

'Yes?'

'In the event of success, then - as a matter of law - one of those men will likely emerge...'

'As a victor?'

Collins put down his cup: '.... as a murderer, Edward, as a murderer...'

***

Was that a drop of snow? Edward Kane looked at the sky. Three o'clock. He pulled on the bell-pull at the door of the offices of Baxter and Bruce, Writers to the Signet, the solicitors who had instructed him. Kane heard the tinkling of the bell inside. After a few moments, the door was opened by a lanky youth, who took Kane's coat, hat and cane and led him through the atrium and into a waiting area. And when he got there, the first thing that he saw was another Advocate, Norval Norris.

Now, Norval Peter Norris ('NP' Norris) was famous (some, of a genteel character, would say 'infamous') for mounting the defence, and often securing the acquittal, of those individuals who - at first blush - were unquestionably guilty of the crime of which they had been accused. Many was the court sheet at the end of the criminal proceedings that had been marked by the Clerk of Court as 'NP' - 'Not Proven' and it had not taken long for the 'NP' of 'Not Proven' to be conflated with the 'NP' of 'NP' Norris, leading to the nickname 'Not Proven Norris'.

Norris rose from his seat: 'Ah, Edward, Edward, my dear young fellow, so nice to see you.'

Kane gave a short bow. Advocates do not shake hands. Norris continued: 'I am glad that they have followed my advice and have instructed you.'

Kane smiled: 'I was not aware of that, Norval. Then, I am grateful to you for the instruction.'

There was no doubting Kane's legal ability (a very good MA, LL.B), but, at this stage of his career, paying work was an elusive occurrence for the young Advocate. He had precious little experience of Criminal Law, and had recently been saved in such a case by relying on the expertise of Norris in the notorious affair that the newspapers had dubbed 'The Parlour Maid Murderer'.

'I'm afraid, Norval, that I have very little idea of what this case is about.' Kane held up his letter of instruction. 'I received this letter only last night, but it is somewhat lacking in detail.'

Norris laughed: 'We are both in the same boat, my friend. I was instructed only yesterday afternoon. I agreed to act as Leader - recommending you as my Junior - and beyond that, I am entirely in the dark.'

'And what is the charge?'

'Didn't they tell you?'

Kane shook his head.

'It would appear that our client, Sir Albert Arthur, has been accused of Attempted Murder...'

And at that point, the lanky lad who had answered the front door appeared and announced: 'Mr Baxter will see you now gentlemen. Please walk this way.'

***

'Of course - I could have killed him, had that been my intention. I am a crack shot, you know...'

Edward Kane, Advocate and his Leader, 'Not Proven' Norris sat in the oak-panelled offices of their solicitors and listened to the facts of the case. Or, at least, the facts as given by their new client, Lord Albert Arthur.

'...could have placed that pistol ball right between his eyes. But showed him mercy. Blew his hat off instead. Saw a great big hole in it afterwards...'

Norris, Advocate, sat listening intently, pulling on his great side-whiskers as he puffed on his pipe. Edward Kane, acting as Junior, scribbled rapidly, attempting to write down the account *verbatim*.

Sir Albert was perfectly affable, but tended to talk around the point. NP Norris, the veteran defender of a hundred accused, brought him to the point: 'Lord Albert, we shall record the *minutiae* of the duel itself in due course, but what interests me at this point - and will be of crucial interest to the gentlemen of the jury - is what was the dispute about?'

The old lord thought for a moment, then: 'I shouldn't like to say, Mr Norris.'

Norris stared hard at Arthur for a moment, then got up from the table. He nodded towards Kane, who was still scribbling, trying to catch up with the conversation, and said: 'Come, Edward. We shall have no business here.'

The solicitor attending the consultation, Mr Baxter (Writer to the Signet), got up from his chair in an attempt to stay Norris' exit: 'Mr Norris, Mr Norris, this is quite outrageous...'

Norris turned on the solicitor: 'No, Mr Baxter, what is outrageous is that you expect the services of two Learned Counsel to take on a case at the very last minute where the accused refuses to provide an explanation for his conduct.' He nodded towards Lord Albert, still sitting at the table. 'If you 'shouldn't like to say', Lord Albert, what the dispute involved, then I 'shouldn't like' to accept your instructions. I must bid you 'Good day'...' Norris bowed '...my lord.'

Norris then nodded to Kane. Kane began to put away his pen and paper. The old nobleman put up his hand: 'Gentlemen, gentlemen, please. Please. Sit down.'

Norris considered this for a moment, then sat down again. Kane, taking this as his cue to remain, replaced the papers on the desk before him and lifted up his pen in anticipation.

The old lord thought for a moment, then: 'It concerned my wife. Lady Arthur. You must understand that she was not born into this life. It might be that her past was more colourful than desired. But I will not have her spoken of in that fashion. This was a matter of honour...'

NP Norris puffed on his pipe and smiled: 'Go on…'

*****

Chapter Two

It was well past eleven o'clock now. Edward Kane, Advocate looked over the papers from that day's consultation. The old nobleman, Lord Albert Arthur had been accused Attempted Murder. Apparently, it was something to do with 'A matter of honour.'

Kane sat in his small set of furnished rooms. Papers were splayed over the table that served as a both a dining table and a desk. He scrutinised his hurried scribbles from the day's consultation and tried to make sense of them. He would present them to his Leader, NP Norris tomorrow morning. So far, he had transcribed:

'I am Lord Albert Arthur. Quite frankly, I fail to see why there is such a to-do about all of this. I quite regularly issue challenges where I feel that my honour has been impugned. I have fought a great number of duels in the past. Simply put, on this occasion, I was attending a social engagement with my wife at The Assembly Rooms. My wife is considerably younger than I am. It is no secret that she did - for a very brief period - have a flirtation with acting in the theatre. As I say, we were engaging in conversation with friends at the social event. This was in the large ballroom area. It was crowded. The parties were separated

into groups of five or six, each group standing in a kind of circle. The punch was being served liberally. I became aware that certain individuals in the group beside us were looking over and sniggering. I recognised young Jack Smith. He served under me in the army. Despite his breeding, young Smith is a 'low' sort of person. I saw him look over and mouth the words 'alleged actress'. This was unacceptable. I handed my drink to the waiter. I approached Smith and demanded an apology. He laughed. I took my glove and slapped his face. I demanded satisfaction...'

Kane's reading of the statement was broken by sound a familiar Cockney voice: 'That you burning the midnight oil again, Mr K?'

It was Kane's manservant, Mr Horse. In the cramped (but cheap) set of furnished rooms, Mr Horse occupied a small room of his own and served as Kane's general *factotum*. Horse pointed to the marble clock on the mantelpiece: 'It's just that I know you, sir. If you burn the candle tonight, then you'll be the devil to rouse in the morning.'

Kane put down the papers and rubbed his eyes. 'I fear that you are right, Mr Horse. However, we appear to have a paying client and I am anxious that I have captured his account accurately and coherently.'

Horse nodded down at the papers: 'Could I have a butcher's, sir? If I can make it out, then...'

Kane handed the papers to his manservant. Horse stood and read them. He looked up: 'Well, Mr K - the whole thing is clear as day, ennit?'

'Your meaning, Mr Horse?'

'Well, sir, if I get his drift proper, then a bunch of blokes are there at some hoity-toity do. And one bloke calls the other bloke's wife a bit of a trollop and the other bloke isn't too happy, so he offers to get him sorted.'

Kane laughed: 'I think, Mr Horse, that the offending gentleman, in fact, called the lady an 'alleged actress', and not a 'trollop' as you would have it.'

Horse rubbed his chin, considering this, then: 'Yes, Mr K - but it's the word 'alleged', ennit? If she was just an actress, then that's fair enough. But an 'alleged' actress - we all know what that means, sir.'

Kane nodded. Horse handed back the papers. Kane looked up from the table: 'And what would you have done Mr Horse? If you had been the husband, I mean.'

Horse thought for a moment, then: 'I find that a swift kick to the whirlygigs usually does the trick here sir...'

***

'But why have we been instructed so late in the day?'

Edward Kane and his Leader, 'Not Proven' Norris, dressed in their horsehair wigs and inky-black gowns were walking up and down the great Parliament Hall the following morning.

Norris gave a little chuckle and puffed on his pipe: 'Do you think, my young friend, that we were the first to be instructed here?'

That fact had not occurred to Kane. NP Norris was frequently first choice in matters criminal. 'Then, who has preceded us, Norval?'

'The larger question might be: 'Who has not?' First port of call was the Dean of Faculty. He soon cried off, pleading conflict of interest...'

This was not surprising. The Dean of Faculty, Robert ('Rab') Lennox - a powerful court practitioner, criminal or civil - was known to be well-connected in the higher echelons of Edinburgh society and it was entirely likely that, given the *dramatis personae* here, Lennox might know some or all of the parties involved.

Norris continued: '...and then there was Freddy Carr...'

Again, a name well-known in the Edinburgh criminal courts. Freddy Carr was a brilliant, if mercurial presence in the courtroom. Passionate and articulate on Day One of a trial, but often muted and (on the face of it) hung-over on Day Two. Norris laughed: '...clash of diary commitments, apparently...'

Kane mused - with Freddy, it was never easy to tell whether the reason given was the real reason, or whether there were other reasons related to the after-effects of late-night gaming, alcohol, or the company of a certain class of woman.

But before Norris could list the entire litany of late lawyers, they became conscious of another Advocate - Charles Cod - an extremely large, cheerful figure standing at the fireplace and motioning over to them to join him. NP Norris nodded back and Norris and Kane walked over to speak to him.

Cod stood there, a sheaf of papers in his hands, the bundle perched on his ample stomach, warming his sizeable posterior by the fire. He greeted Norris cheerfully: 'Norval, Norval - is the rumour true, my friend? Has the errant old nobleman found safe harbour?'

Norris laughed: 'If you mean, do I hold instructions in the case against of Her Majesty's Advocate against Lord Albert Arthur, Charles, then the answer is yes.'

'You do know that you are not the first?'

'Given that the trial is due to commence in fewer than seven days, my friend, I sincerely hope - for Lord Albert's sake - that I will be the last.' Norris indicated Kane: 'Of course, you know my Junior, Edward Kane...'

There existed (and exists) a fiction in the Faculty of Advocates that once an individual had achieved the rank of Counsel, then he was known - and greeted by his first name - by the other Members of Faculty. Even if they had never met before.

Cod looked over: 'Of course, of course. How are you, young fella?'

Kane nodded: 'Very well, thank you...Charles.'

Cod resumed his chat with Norris: 'And you know why old Albert has discarded so many lawyers, Norval?'

Norris smiled: 'If I didn't, then I am sure that you are about to tell me, Charles.'

'Because he's plainly guilty. No defence whatsoever. He's been told to plead again and again, but he refuses. After the duel - when he had blown the other chap's hat off - your man, old Lord Albert, went straight to a police office and told them what he had done. His Second even gave the police a calling card, so that they could come and arrest the old fellow later if required.'

How does he know all this thought Kane.

Norris looked over to the young Advocate and, noting his puzzlement, settled the question: 'Edward, I perhaps ought to have mentioned that our friend Charles here is prosecuting the case for the Lord Advocate...'

Kane nodded. It all made sense now.

Charles Cod puffed out his chest, becoming that bit larger (if that were, indeed, possible): 'Safe pair of hands, that's what's needed here. That's what the Lord Advocate told me, so I agreed do it. Of course, it was an easy decision to take on the task here, given that you have no possible defence...'

*****

Chapter Three

Later in the day, Kane examined his Advocate's Box, where bits and pieces of work would be deposited for the attention of Counsel. Frequently empty - apart from the odd, unwelcome bill - today it held a number of papers bound by a pink ribbon. The papers proved to contain supplementary statements in Lord Albert's case. Kane took the bundle into the Advocates Library and began to study them. Despite being in the handwriting of a legal copyist, the voice of Lord Albert could be heard loud and clear:

'So it was arranged that we should meet at five o'clock in the evening, as the sun was setting, and we should resolve the issue there. At the top of Calton Hill. Near that awful Horatio Nelson monument, the one that looks like the upside-down telescope. I took my Second-in-Command, Captain Harry Street. And as we were drawing up in our carriage, I could see that the blackguard Jack Smith was already there with his own Second (don't know that fellow's name. Think it was his cousin). They had also brought a surgeon, in case one was needed (didn't know that chap either).

'My own Second, Captain Harry Street, went over and asked Smith if he was prepared to offer an apology. Smith refused. Harry retrieved my pistol case from our carriage. It has my initials on it. I

always keep a brace of pistols at the ready for such occasions. Jack Smith and I watched while Harry and the other Second measured out the twelve paces. I took my place and stood facing Smith. We were handed our pistols. The word was given and we discharged the weapons.'

Kane looked up from his papers. He recalled the conversation with Collins the previous day. Two men arrange to meet and deliberately fire pistols at each other. What happens if one of them dies? Does the fact that it's over a matter of honour make it any less of a murder? He continued reading:

'*...and I aimed my shot just above the top of his head. I aimed it so that I might give the scoundrel a new parting in his hair. As I said, I am something of a crack shot. Regarding John Smith: I had nothing to fear. I knew him from the army, and he was a rotten shot. Couldn't hit an elephant with a spade. As I say, I thought I would teach the beggar a bit of a lesson, so I aimed carefully. Bang. Pistol ball hit its mark. Blew his hat off. Gave Smith such a turn - he fainted on the spot...*'

Kane stopped again and considered this. With Smith collapsing after the shot, it must have looked as if he had been shot dead. The remainder of the facts were: a passing clergyman, who had been walking his dog, witnessed the scene ('*...they were pointing their pistols at each other. They discharged the pistols. The next thing I knew, the younger man was lying on the ground...*'; he went over to lend assistance; he watched as the surgeon examined Smith's body for injury; no obvious injury; Smith was revived with smelling salts; honour satisfied, all left the scene. Lord Albert and his Second, Captain Harry Street, immediately called in at the Police Office at the side of St Giles Church and - according to the statement of the desk sergeant, Sergeant Wilson - the following exchange took place:

SGT WILSON: Good evening, Lord Albert.

LORD ALBERT: Good evening, Sergeant Wilson.

SGT WILSON: And how may I assist you, sir?

LORD ALBERT: I am your prisoner, I believe.

SGT WILSON: On what account, Lord Albert?

LORD ALBERT: I have been contesting a matter of honour with an individual named 'Smith'.

SGT WILSON: Ah, a matter of honour. Again. Well, as you will see, sir, we have other, pressing business to attend to at present.

LORD ALBERT: Then I shall leave you my card. It contains my address if that is what you require.

SGT WILSON: Very well, sir. Many thanks.

Sir Albert's Second, Captain Harry Street also wrote his own details on the back of the card. Sir Albert then left the card with the desk sergeant and repaired to his Edinburgh house at Moray Place.

At a later (and it must be said, leisurely) point, police officers attended at the home of Harry Street and they took a full account of the event. They subsequently took an account from Jack Smith. Ultimately, Lord Albert was arrested and received a Petition, charging him with Attempted Murder.

Kane considered the evidence as a whole. In terms of a prosecution, the essentials seemed all in order for the charge. They had the Complainer (Jack Smith); the Accused (Lord Albert); the 'evil intent' or 'wicked recklessness' necessary to make out the Attempted Murder (a man with a grudge arranges to meet another man in a secluded place and fire a deadly weapon at him - aiming so close above his head that it would 'create a new parting in his hair'); and the corroboration seemed plentiful - witnesses: Captain Street; and then Jack Smith's Second, his cousin - whatever his name; the surgeon who treated Smith after his hat was blown off; the clergyman who witnessed Sir Albert at the scene, pistol in hand; Sir Albert's admission to the police sergeant at the police office; even the hole that had been blown in Smith's hat could provide corroboration.

Small wonder that the old lord had been consistently advised - and, no doubt, by good lawyers too - to plead guilty. A guilty plea, and then throw himself on the Mercy of the Court seemed the only way forward.

Kane placed his papers into a neat bundle: *Ah well, as always the burden of proof will be on the Crown - but I shouldn't expect that Charles Cod will be losing much sleep over this one. The problem is the penalty, though. The penalty for Attempted Murder…*

Edward Kane sighed. *Once this comes to trial, honour or no honour, the old man will be destroyed…*

*****

Chapter Four

An early December evening. So dark now, that all the lamps had been lit in the Advocates Library. Edward Kane was sitting at his desk, perusing the latest volume of Session Cases, when the Head Faculty Servant, Mr Manville leaned over him.

'Mr Kane?' Manville whispered.

Kane looked up. 'Yes, Manville?' (Manville preferred the more martial appellation 'Manville' to the more genteel '*Mr* Manville').

'The Dean of Faculty wishes to see you, sir.'

Kane thought for a few seconds. *A request to be seen by the Dean of Faculty?* Was Kane in trouble? The Dean of Faculty, Rab Lennox, brilliant lawyer that he was, was not known to be a welcoming or forgiving individual on a personal level...

Manville cut through Kane's thoughts: 'I think that *now* would be an opportune time, sir. Here, let me assist you...'

And with that, Manville took Kane by the elbow and 'assisted' him from his seat, pointing him towards the Dean's Room.

Once Manville had further assisted Kane into the Dean's Room, Kane looked around. Sitting behind the main desk, in the light of a two-branched candlestick, was the Dean of Faculty himself, looking for all the world like a great, malevolent owl. And then Kane realised that he was not the only one who had been summoned. Also seated in the Dean's room were Norval Norris and Charles Cod. The Dean looked up: 'Come in, young man, come in. Sit down.'

The room had the atmosphere of a headmaster's study, where the cane was about to administered to three naughty schoolboys.

The Dean addressed them: 'Now, I have called you all in here because, this morning, I was approached by the Lord Advocate himself...'

The Lord Advocate? Head of Scotland's prosecution? Why would he...

'...and he is very concerned about all of this nonsense with that old fool, Lord Albert Arthur...'

Norval Norris interjected: 'Dean of Faculty, you will forgive me for interrupting, but it is hardly a 'nonsense' when a man stands accused of Attempted Murder...'

'Oh, Pish posh!' The Dean was not happy at being interrupted. He dismissed Norris with a wave of his hand: 'Come now, Norval. The old booby Arthur is notorious for challenging all and sundry to duels as the whim takes him. I've heard that if you as much as sneeze in the vicinity of his soup, then you find yourself issued with a challenge. This really has to stop. The Lord Advocate wishes to send a shot across Lord Albert's bows. Now, I'm aware of the evidence here...'. The Dean stared at Norris now '...and I presume that Lord Albert will be pleading guilty...'

Norris puffed on his pipe for a moment, then: 'No. Not to Attempted Murder.'

The Dean turned to Charles Cod, the prosecutor: 'Now, Charles, as the Lord Advocate's Depute, you have the authority to reduce the charge, do you not?'

The ample Advocate considered this for a moment, then replied: 'In a matter such as this, I will need to consult the Lord Advocate himself...'

Again, the Dean held up his hand to silence the issue: 'No need, Charles, no need. As I say, the Lord Advocate consulted with me this morning. He is willing to allow you, as the prosecutor in this case, to accept a reduced charge of 'the culpable and reckless discharge of a firearm in a public place."

Again, Charles Cod considered this for a moment, then nodded: 'Well, if that is the will of the Lord Advocate...'

The Dean then resumed his intense gaze on NP Norris: 'And would that be acceptable to the old lord, Norval?'

Norris puffed on his pipe again, then: 'I will take instructions, Dean of Faculty.'

The Dean rose from his chair. The meeting was at an end. 'Thank you, gentlemen. I expect an expeditious resolution to this issue. Keep me apprised of developments. Good evening.'

Kane looked around. Manville was standing at the Dean's door, ready to assist all parties to leave. Kane and NP Norris headed towards the great Parliament Hall to take a walk - and to speak in private.

They walked up and down, side-by-side for a minute or so. Kane said nothing, since Norris appeared to be deep in thought, tugging on his side-whiskers and puffing on his pipe. And then, Norris came to a sudden stop, removed his pipe from his lips, looked directly at Kane - and then let out a hearty laugh.

Given the preceding and intense silence, this sudden jocular outburst took Kane somewhat by surprise: 'Norval - are you feeling quite well?'

Norval looked straight at the young Advocate: 'Of course, of course, Edward - don't you see it?'

Kane shook his head. Norris continued: 'That meeting with the Dean...'

'Yes?'

'That meeting with the Dean was nothing but a charade, Edward. A pure charade.'

Kane knotted his eyebrows: 'But in what sense, Norval?'

Norris puffed on his pipe: 'In the sense, my young friend, that where the prosecution has such a strong case, then why on earth offer to reduce the charge to something so paltry?'

Kane stood perplexed. Norris laughed: 'Oh, no Edward. I can feel it in my bones, my friend. Something has gone wrong with the prosecution case. That is why we now have such a generous offer here.'

Kane stopped in his tracks. 'Then, what do we do now?'

Norris smiled: 'Well, Edward, first we put the latest offer of the Crown to Lord Albert. He will refuse it, of course...'

Kane nodded. 'And then?'

'And then Edward, we wait. We wait until we see that great big hidden hole in the other side's case.'

Norris took out a match and struck it to re-light his pipe. Puff, puff, puff - three puffy clouds emerged from the pipe: 'Now, young fellow - care for a spot of lunch?'

***

'Christmas, Mr K - bloomin' Christmas.'

Edward Kane's manservant, Mr Horse, paused his polishing of Kane's boots for a moment to bewail the coming of the festive season.

'I mean, sir? What's it all about?'

Kane smiled to himself. His father had been a Minister of the Church of Scotland. Many was the time that Kane, as a small child, would sit on the floor of the study, listening to his father read aloud, try out phrases and tinker with the draft sermon for the next Sunday.

Kane looked up from his book: 'Matthew 1:18, Mr Horse, Matthew 1:18...'

'What's that, Mr K?'

Kane put down his book. As a child, he had heard the chapter and verse so many times, that he could repeat the verse by rote: 'Now the birth of Jesus Christ was on this wise. When as his mother Mary was espoused to Joseph, before they came together, she was found with child of the Holy Ghost...'

Horse shook his head. Kane asked: 'Is something troubling you, Mr Horse?'

Horse thought for a moment, then resumed the polishing of the boots: 'Don't know about you, Mr K, but if Mary had been my missus, I would have kept a better eye on her...'

*****

Chapter Five

Lord Albert Arthur was furious now: 'Nonsense - all nonsense! The 'culpable' and 'reckless'...what?'

NP Norris had put to the old nobleman the offer from the prosecution. The Crown would now accept a plea of guilty to the reduced charge of 'the culpable and reckless discharge of a firearm in a public place'.

Lord Albert sat there for a moment, not so furious now, but visibly simmering. Norris continued: 'As a plea, it has much to commend it, Lord Albert. It is a far less serious matter than the original charge of Attempted Murder...'

The old man considered this for a moment, and then he stood up to leave: 'I am sorry, gentlemen, but your endeavours are in vain here. 'Culpable'? A gentleman is never to blame when he is compelled to defend his wife's honour. And 'reckless',' - here he gave a hollow laugh - '...'reckless'? I think not. Far from it. I took great care not to shoot that scoundrel between the eyes. Please convey my decision to those who are determined to hound me. Now, if you will excuse me, I bid you good day, sirs.'

And with that, Lord Arthur got up and left the room.

Edward Kane, NP Norris and their instructing solicitor, Mr Baxter (Writer to the Signet) sat in silence for a while. The silence was broken by Kane: 'And what do we do now?'

NP Norris sat back in his chair, a smile playing on his lips: 'What we do now, my dear Edward, is: we prepare for trial...'

***

Kane's friend, Collins sipped his coffee in the Advocates Reading Room.

'So, the old lord has refused the prosecution offer, then...'

Kane sighed: 'Norval predicted that he would. I confess that I have no idea how we are to mount a defence in this case. The evidence seems overwhelming, Collins. The whole thing appears hopeless.'

Collins considered this for a moment, then laughed: 'Be of good cheer, Edward. Norval does appear to have the ability to produce a very real rabbit from the mere suggestion of a hat.'

The friends laughed. The conversation turned to this and that. Collins adjusted his spectacles and smiled: 'Now, my friend, a far more important question than that of Attempted Murder - are you making your customary annual visit to the Collins household on Christmas Day?'

Kane said nothing for a moment, prompting Collins to develop his submission: 'As you know, my friend, not only will you be able to avail yourself of the company of the vivacious Mrs Collins and my good self, but you will also be treated to a fine festive luncheon of turkey, gravy and mashed potatoes. This will, of course, be accompanied some fine mulled wine and followed by the cook's finest speckled pudding.' Collins' eyes were sparkling now: 'Oh, and did I mention the repeated games of blind man's bluff under the direction the Collins offspring?'

Kane could not help but laugh: 'Collins, my dear friend, I accept your kind invitation. If one o'clock would be suitable...'

Collins raised his teacup as if giving a toast: 'One o'clock would be just capital, Edward. Of course, you have other duties to fulfil in the morning...'

The friends sat in silence now. The atmosphere had changed. More solemn now. Sadder, even. Nothing more was said for a time. Kane looked away and out of the window…

***

The Trial: Day One

'Edward, Edward - what a fine crisp morning, don't you think?'

NP Norris, in cheerful mood, hailed Kane in Parliament Square as they were passing the equestrian statue.

Kane shivered in the December mist: 'Norval, that is a generous analysis. In fact, this cold spell woke me up in the middle of the night.'

Norris laughed: 'Really? I'm bound to say that I was tucked up, cozy and warm and slept like the proverbial log.'

Kane stared at Norris. 'How on earth, Norval, can you get any sleep the night before you defend an Attempted Murder?'

'With ease, my friend, with ease. The cases that keep me awake at night are the ones where there is the slightest chance that there might be a defence. That is not the case here. That old rascal, Lord Albert, is clearly as guilty as sin. We cannot win this case, Edward. Our friend, the prosecutor Charles Cod can only lose it. And, as I say, there is something amiss about the Crown case here. All we can do at this stage is to be vigilant and listen for clues.'

Norris then produced his pipe. He patted his jacket pockets. 'I seem to have mislaid my matches. May I trouble you for a light?'

***

Thirty minutes later, attired fully in full wig and gown, Norris and Kane approached the courtroom and the first thing that Kane became aware of was the noise. The sheer din of several hundred human voices in a state of excited expectation. It sounded for all the world like a crowd at a sporting event. This made him nervous. He glanced at Norris. NP puffed on his pipe: 'Ah, Edward - a full house. Time to make our entrance...'

And with that, Norris and (a somewhat timid) Kane swept into the courtroom. There was a lull now as the ladies and gentlemen (and a few smuggled children) in the public gallery nodded, pointed and gesticulated in their direction.

Norris and Kane made their way to the right of the table at the well of the court, beneath the bench where the judges sat. Norris whispered into Kane's ear: 'Now, Edward, I want you to look across the table. If my prediction is correct, then you should see a nervous-looking prosecutor.'

Kane looked across the table. And there - as predicted - was an uneasy-looking Charles Cod. The portly Advocate was discussing, with some intensity, matters with his own junior. Kane looked back over to Norris and gave a confirmatory nod.

Norris smiled, set his papers down on the table, then called across to his opponent: 'Good morning, Charles.' Cod nodded back towards both Defence Counsel: 'Norval. Edward. Good morning to you both. I'm sorry that we seem to have reached such an impasse here. Still time, of course, for the accused to accept the very generous Crown offer.'

Novak shook his head: 'I am sorry, Charles. Apparently, it's a matter of honour...'

Cod nodded his head, somewhat ruefully, Kane thought.

Looking over at the dock now, Kane saw Lord Albert sitting there, already seated between the two policemen in their stovepipe hats, the brass buttons of their blue uniform coats fastened up to the neck. The old nobleman seemed unconcerned, oblivious to the seriousness of the charge he was facing. To the casual observer, he might have been sitting waiting for an omnibus.

Kane looked up. Coming out through a side door on the raised bench area was The Macer carrying the ceremonial mace balanced on his shoulder. The Court was now in session.

'Court rise!' - a very loud shout from the Clerk of Court.

Emerging from side entrances, three judges progressed to their chairs. Stately in their horsehair wigs, white crosses on their bright red robes, they reached their seats and bowed towards the assembly. All in attendance returned the bow. The judges sat down. The people sat down. Lord Albert tried to sit down, but the police officers in the dock held him up.

The Clerk called the case: 'Call the case, Her Majesty's Advocate against Lord Albert Arthur.' He then addressed the nobleman in the dock: 'Are you Lord Albert Arthur?'

His lordship, determined to remain unimpressed by proceedings, replied: 'I sincerely hope so.' This provoked a deal of laughter from the public gallery, then Lord Albert replied: 'Yes, of course I am.'

The fifteen-man jury was empanelled, and the charge on the Indictment was read aloud to them:

'...that you LORD ALBERT ARTHUR did arrange to meet John Sanders Barrington Smith there and did discharge a pistol at him, wounding him and you did attempt to murder him...'

And Norris stood up and addressed the three judges: 'My lords, I appear for the Pannel in this case. And he pleads…Not Guilty'.

And a hush fell over the room. And the trial began.

*****

Chapter Six

The prosecutor, Charles Cod, rose from his chair and addressed the Court:

'Thank you, my lords. The first Witness from the Crown list is...The Reverend Thomas Paterson.'

At that point, Kane was sure that he heard Norris give a kind of snort. Kane looked up. Norris was already on his feet: 'My lords...'

The three judges looked down at Norris. He was well-known in those courts. It was extremely unusual for Defence Counsel to be on his feet so early - with what already looked like an objection - but it was recognised by all that Norris knew what he was doing, and there was likely to be a valid point in there.

Lord Wallis, in the centre chair, picked up his pen: 'Yes, Mr Norris?'

Norris pointed over at Charles Cod: 'My lords, far be it for me to gainsay the well-known ability of my Learned Friend, the Advocate Depute, but would it not be customary to introduce the Crown Case - for Attempted Murder, mark you - with the evidence of the complainer, some would say 'victim' in the case? Namely...'. Norris looked down and read the name from his copy of the Indictment, '...namely the individual, 'Mr John Sanders Barrington Smith'?'

The judge shook his head: 'Mr Norris as you are well aware, the Advocate Depute, the prosecutor, is the Master of the Instance in this case. In every case. He can call any witness in any order - or none at all. It is entirely a matter for him.'

Lord Wallis smiled down at the prosecutor, Charles Cod, who nodded and smiled back. Norris was not deterred. He pressed on: 'I am obliged to my lord for that. I fear, however, that the gentlemen of the jury,' and at this point, Norris turned towards the jurors and smiled 'may not appreciate being presented with a large quantity of factual material that looks as if it has been cut up and scattered by a jig-saw...'

Some of the jurors smiled at this. Not Lord Wallis. He became a mite testy: 'Mr Norris, Mr Norris - I have made my decision here. Now, I would invite you to sit down, sir...'

Norris ducked the command: 'I am happy to do so, my lord. But I wonder if we could simply ascertain at this early juncture, at what point will we hear from the complainer in this case, Mr John Sanders Barrington Smith?'

Norris looked across the table at Charles Cod. Cod was shifting uneasily in his seat now. Norris had a sudden intuition: '...if we are to hear from that witness at all?'

Lord Wallis looked down at Cod. Cod appeared to be avoiding his gaze. The judge thought for a moment, then: 'Advocate Depute?'

Charles Cod stood up. Lord Wallis continued: 'Advocate Depute, an issue has been raised. One that is easily resolved. Now - at what point do you expect to take the evidence of the complainer, Mr John Sanders Barrington Smith - the injured party here?'

Cod turned over the papers on the desk before him (somewhat shame-facedly, thought Kane) and then replied: 'At no point, my lords. The Crown does not require him...'

Kane saw the three judges - all of whom had had experience of being prosecutors - look at each other somewhat quizzically. Wallis spoke: 'Is Mr Smith under some form of incapacity, then? Have the events narrated in the libel rendered him incapax?'

Cod was perspiring now. 'No my lords. I understand that he is currently out of the country.'

'Has he been cited personally to appear?'

'No, my lords. Personal citation proved impossible, since...'

Lord Wallis picked it up: '...since Mr Smith is out of the country.' Again, he looked around at the other judges, then back at Cod: 'Then, how do you intend to proceed, sir?'

Cod, spoke now giving the impression that the absence of this main witness - the man whom it was alleged had almost been murdered - was not going to be a problem. Cod addressed the judges with the appearance of ease and confidence, every inch the experienced prosecutor. He indicated Lord Albert in the dock: 'Oh, my lords, the evidence against the Pannel in this particular case is overwhelming. And there is a great deal of it. I am confident that I will be able to demonstrate a clear sufficiency here, despite the absence of Mr Smith.'

The judge nodded: 'Very well, Advocate Depute.' He turned to NP Norris: 'Mr Norris, are you content to proceed?'

Norris stood up: 'Yes. I am obliged to the Court for clarifying that the individual who claims to have been the victim of an attempted murder should not trouble himself to turn up at the trial...'

Some of the jurymen laughed. Lord Wallis could no longer contain his annoyance: 'Sit down, Mr Norris. That remark - and before the gentlemen of the jury - was quite uncalled for'. He turned towards the jury members: 'Please disregard what you have just heard, gentlemen.' Then, turning to Cod: 'Call your first witness...'

Norris sat down and grinned at Edward Kane. Kane whispered over to Norris: 'How can they disregard the fact that the victim hasn't 'troubled himself' to show up?'

Norris smiled: 'Oh, they can't, Edward, they can't...'

***

'And what is the name of your dog, sir?'

Charles Cod was examining his first witness, the Reverend Thomas Paterson (D.D.), the clergyman who - when he was walking his dog - had witnessed the duel.

The clergyman replied: 'The dog is called 'Ezekiel', sir.'

Cod turned towards the jurymen: 'No doubt because of his interest in bones...'

Some of the jury members laughed. Others, who did not recognise the Biblical allusion laughed anyway at what was obviously meant to be a humorous comment by the prosecutor.

Kane watched Charles Cod, an experienced Advocate at work. Oh, yes - Charles Cod knew how to play to his audience. Confident and clear. Taking the evidence with a very sure touch. Letting the story unfold. The men in the jury looked intently at Cod. Here was a man who could be trusted. Cod continued: 'And so, you came upon a duel...'

Norris leapt to his feet: 'Don't answer that question...'

The clergyman seemed startled by Norris' loud objection and looked towards the three judges for guidance. Lord Wallis looked down at the witness with a kindly smile:

'Reverend Paterson, forgive the interruption but Defence Counsel has an objection.' The judge turned to Norris: 'Yes Mr Norris?'

'I am objecting to my learned friend's last question. It is a leading question. The words '...and so, you came upon a duel' are entirely leading. They tell this witness precisely what the evidence is - before he gives it.'

This objection seemed so entirely reasonable that even the jurymen began to nod. Norris continued: 'Further, the prosecutor's question 'you came upon a duel' alleges a course of criminal conduct not in the charge. Duelling is, of itself, an offence. But he is not accused of that. The wording of the charge is very specific: '...you did arrange to meet...' - no mention of a duel there.'

The judges began nodding now. Lord Wallis turned to Cod: 'Advocate Depute?'

Presenting as ever-reasonable, Cod held up his hands: '*Mea culpa, my lords. Mea culpa.* Of course, my learned friend is entirely correct. I will withdraw the question.'

And then Cod smiled over at Norris. Both of them knew exactly what had just happened. The prosecutor had just informed the jury that Sir Albert had turned up to fight a duel. Despite the judge's acceptance that this evidence was not admissible, Charles Cod had now placed that image into the minds of the jurymen.

Lord Wallis said: 'Thank you Advocate Depute please continue.' And picked up his pen again. Cod continued his questions:

COD: And what did you see?

PATERSON: I saw that gentleman, there [at this point, the witness pointed at Lord Albert in the dock]. He was standing about twenty paces away from the other chap. They were both holding pistols and pointing the pistols at each other...

There was a slight pause, and in the silence, Lord Arthur was heard to say in a very loud stage whisper: 'Well - sounds like a duel to me...'

*****

Chapter Seven

Norris was in the middle of his Cross-Examination of the clergyman, Reverend Paterson. It was not going well…

'Now, Reverend, you have told the court that you saw Lord Albert there,' - Norris pointed to the old nobleman in the dock - 'and another gentleman with pistols.'

'Yes, sir.'

'But for all you knew, they were possibly engaging in a spot of target practice.'

'Not unless they were using each other as targets sir...'

A guffaw from the public gallery.

Norris decided to take a different tack: 'You gave a statement here, did you not?'

'Yes.'

'And you were telling the truth?'

'Of course.'

Norris lifted up a piece of paper from the desk and studied it for a moment: 'And in that statement, you said 'The next thing I knew, the younger man was lying on the ground'.'

'That is correct, sir.'

'I am curious about the phrase '...the next thing I knew...''

The witness looked puzzled. 'I regret to say that I do not follow you, sir?'

Norris turned to face the jury, but continued his questioning with his back to the witness: "...the next thing I knew...' - does that not suggest that your attention was diverted for a time?'

The clergyman knotted his eyebrows and considered this. He said nothing for a while, then: 'What you must understand, sir, is that I am climbing a hill with a puppy...'

This was news to Norris: 'Ezekiel the dog is a puppy?'

'Yes...'

NP saw his opening: 'And like many puppies - energetic and boisterous?'

'Yes.'

'And you are how old? If you do not mind me asking?'

'Fifty-seven, sir.'

'And on that hill, I dare say that the puppy was off the leash for a period?'

'Yes, sir.'

Norris placed the fingers of his hands together, like a little steeple. Kane had seen him in action a number of times and knew that Norris was now formulating a question that would likely blow a great hole in the prosecution's own hat.

'So,' Norris continued, 'you - a fifty seven year-old man are climbing a great hill while, at the same time you are managing an energetic and boisterous young puppy - off the leash, mind you. Correct?'

'Correct, sir.'

'It is fair to say, then, that your full attention was not always on the men with pistols?'

No answer.

'Is that fair?'

The clergyman paused, then nodded: 'That is fair, sir.'

Norris pressed on: 'Thus, when you say '...the next thing I knew, the younger man was lying on the ground...' you did not, in fact, see him being shot. That is accurate, is it not?'

Reverend Paterson thought for a moment, then: 'Yes, sir.'

'At no point did you see anyone shoot anyone else, correct?'

'Correct.'

'And when you went to assist the young man lying on the ground, there was found to be no injury to him, was there.'

'That is correct.'

'And the only treatment that he received was the application of some smelling salts.'

'Correct.'

His work done, Norris gathered up his papers from the table before him, but - unbidden - the witness then volunteered: 'But, apparently, there was a hole blown in his hat, sir.'

Norris put his papers down and turned on the witness: '...'Apparently'? 'Apparently'?? Again, sir, your very wording betrays your lack of direct knowledge here.'

The clergyman fought back: 'Well, I was told...'

Norris cut him off: "I'm afraid that 'I was told' is not acceptable evidence here. You have come to this court today and you have given sworn evidence that you saw someone being shot - and that was not true. You then talked about a gun-hole in a hat, a hat - it transpires - that you have never even seen. Are you familiar with the Ten Commandments, Reverend Paterson?'

'Of course I am, sir, I am a Man of God...'

'Then you can perhaps remind us of the Ninth Commandment?'

The witness responded immediately: 'Thou shalt not bear false witness against thy neighbour.'

'You seem to know the Commandment, sir,' Norris collected his papers from the desk, 'all that I would ask now, is that you follow it...'

And Norris sat down.

Kane saw a number of the jurymen nodding. There was a moment of silence, and then Lord Wallis looked towards the prosecutor, Charles Cod: 'Any re-examination, Advocate Depute?'

***

Kane was banging on his own front door: 'Mr Horse, Mr Horse...the door appears to be blocked...'

A Cockney voice from inside: 'Give us a minute, sir...'

A certain amount of huffing and puffing from inside Kane's rented rooms, then a small fellow in a cloth cap appeared. He tipped his hat to Kane as he passed - 'Sir' - before making his way down the stairs.

Kane entered the hallway - *What are those? Pine needles?* - and then the sitting room. Horse was sitting by the window, a wide grin on his face, admiring their new acquisition: 'Well, Mr K, what do you think?'

And there, standing in the middle of the room was an enormous, bushy Christmas tree.

Kane struggled to find the words: 'I think, Mr Horse, I think...it's awfully...*big*...is it not?'

Horse beamed: 'Yes, sir - she's a beauty, ain't she!'

Kane stood there, unsure of what to say next. Horse waxed on: 'I'm glad we had that little chat the other day about Christmas and all, sir. Made me realise that I was being a bit of a grump. And so...'. He pointed to the tree.

Kane had to laugh: 'And so...it is enormous, Mr Horse...'

Horse surveyed the tree with pride: 'As the gentlemen would say, sir - it is 'all the rage'. I half expect Prince Albert hisself to pop out of it.'

Kane smiled: 'Well, it cannot remain in the centre of the room, Horse.'

'I'll stick it here by the window.' He crouched down and began to shuffle the tree gradually across the floor. 'Ooh, it's a whopper, sir. Took two of us to get it up the stairs...'

Kane repaired to his bedroom. He saw that Horse had already prepared the wash basin and had laid out Kane's clothes for the evening.

And when Kane emerged refreshed, Horse had placed the tree by the window and was standing admiring it: 'I'll go down to the Lawn Market tomorrow, sir, and get some ribbons and the like.'

He brushed his hands together, shaking off the tiny pieces of brown bark: 'Now, Mr K, I'll get the dinner on. I got us a nice chop for tea. And then you can tell me all about today.'

Chapter Eight

The Trial: Day Two. NP Norris was already waiting for Edward Kane, smoking his pipe before the statue of Walter Scott in Parliament Hall: 'It's a bad sign, Edward. It's a bad sign.'

'I'm sorry, Norval, I don't quite…'

'Not a wink, Edward. I could not sleep a wink last night. Always a bad sign.'

Kane shook his head: 'But yesterday seemed to go so well…'

'That's the problem, my friend – it appears that we now have something to lose...'

***

Police Sergeant Wilson pointed to Lord Albert in the dock: 'Yes, sir. That's Lord Albert there.'

Charles Cod was taking the evidence of the police Desk Sergeant who had spoken to the old nobleman directly after the event, when the confession was tendered at the police office.

The sergeant continued: 'So he came in with his man, Harry Street, and he said he wanted to report a crime. And I say: 'What is it then, Lord Albert?' And he says: 'I've just fought a duel with Jack Smith.''

Cod smiled, looked at the jury and repeated: 'Lord Albert said: 'I have just fought a duel with Jack Smith'. And what happened then?'

'Then, he gave me his card. But we knew where to find him, because...'

At this point, Charles Cod put up his hand to silence the witness. This was to stop the policeman giving evidence of all the other reports to police of the many duels involving the old nobleman.

The witness realised why he had been silenced and continued: '...because, sir, we knew where he lived anyway.'

Cod smiled. Problem averted: 'So what happened then?'

'Well then Lord Albert's man, his Second Harry Street came and he wrote his own details on the back of the card.'

The prosecutor lifted a calling card from the table and handed it to the Bar Officer, who handed it to the witness: 'Is this the card?'

The officer examined the calling card: 'That's the one, sir.' Sergeant Wilson was an experienced witness for the prosecution. He lifted the card up for the jury to see: 'See - it's got Harry Street's writing on the back.'

Cod smiled. - 'Thank you Sergeant Wilson. I have no more questions for you.' - and sat down.

Lord Wallis looked down at Norris: 'Mr Norris?'

Norval Norris rose from the Defence side of the table. He was holding two sheets of paper in his hands. He addressed the police officer cordially: 'Good morning, Sergeant Wilson.'

'Good morning, Mr Norris.'

NP continued: 'Now, I should begin by saying that this is not the first time that you and I have had the pleasure of facing each other in court, is it?'

The sergeant replied: 'I've given evidence in these courts a number of times, Mr Norris...' The witness broke into a broad grin: '...and I always seem to get questioned by you at some point, sir.'

The jury members laughed.

Norris continued: 'Then you will be aware that many of the people that I choose to represent are found to be innocent, Sergeant Wilson.'

The policeman smiled, thought for a moment, then nodded: 'Certainly - they have not been *proven* to be guilty. But I'm not sure if that is the same thing, sir.'

Jury laughed again. NP Norris was notorious for securing a 'Not Proven' verdict in the unlikeliest of cases.

Norris smiled: 'Thank you, Sergeant. Now, I would like to ask you about the statement that you gave in this case. I am aware from our previous meetings that you do not like others to prepare your statement, but that you tend to prepare the statement yourself. Is that still the case? '

'Yes, sir.'

'Again, I, of course, recall the reason for that, but you can perhaps tell the gentlemen of the jury the reason yourself.'

Sergeant Wilson turned to the jury; 'Well, I found that when you let someone else prepare the statement, then they can miss things out. So I always do it myself. In this case, I wrote out my statement the same night that Lord Albert came into the station.'

'The very same night?'

The witness turned back to face Norris: 'Yes, sir.'

'So you are confident that the statement contains the full and accurate account of your dealings with Sir Albert that day - word for word - when he came into your police office.'

'Yes, sir.'

'Nothing added and nothing left out.'

'Precisely, sir.'

Norris paused for a moment, and held up one of the sheets of paper: 'Then let us have a look at that statement now, shall we?'

He handed the sheet to the Bar Officer, who handed it to Sergeant Wilson. Wilson read through it and looked puzzled. He held the paper down for a moment, lifted it up, then read through it again. He began to frown. Norris saw his chance. He turned to face the jury, but spoke to the witness: 'Sergeant Wilson, you will forgive me for saying so, but it will be apparent to all - especially the gentlemen of the jury - that you seem vexed, sir.'

The witness looked at the piece of paper, then he held it in front of himself, reading it again: 'This is not how I remember it, Mr Norris.'

'This is a record of your conversation with Sir Albert at the police office on the day in question, is it not?'

Wilson studied the paper: 'Yes.'

'Prepared by your own hand.'

'Yes.'

'On the very day it took place.'

The witness nodded. Norris smiled: 'Word for word - nothing added and nothing left out?'

The witness was frowning now and saying nothing. Norris pointed to the great clock on the wall of the courtroom: 'That was your sworn evidence to me at three minutes past eleven, sergeant. Is your sworn evidence now different - at four minutes past?'

The witness was silent again. Obviously not happy.

Kane, watching this, noted that the men in the jury were sitting, paying close attention now. This witness was clearly in trouble and had all the appearance of a child's balloon - in the process of deflating.

'You see' Norris pressed on, 'when one looks at your statement, and the *verbatim* conversation with Lord Albert - the word 'duel' does not appear, does it?'

The witness considered the paper again. 'No, sir.'

'Nor is there a mention of a 'Jack Smith'...'

Sergeant Wilson tried to retrieve his position: 'There was talk of an individual named 'Smith', Mr Norris...'

'But not 'Jack Smith'...'

'No.'

'And certainly not John Sanders Barrington Smith.'

'No.'

Kane was forming the impression that the witness would now say anything to get off of the witness stand.

'Because - and to be fair to you, Sergeant Wilson - you have no idea how many 'Smiths' there are in Scotland, do you.'

'No, sir.'

Norris pointed to the fifteen men in the jury: 'For example, how many of these men are named 'Smith'?'

The Sergeant replied, weary now: 'I have no idea, sir.'

Norris turned to the jury to make the point. The jurymen mistook this as a question as to how many 'Smiths' there were in the jury. Four of them raised their hands.

Norris smiled and turned back to the witness, pointing at the jurors: 'In fact, the 'Smith' referred to could have been any of these gentlemen, could it not?'

The slow leak continued: 'Hypothetically, that must be correct, sir.'

'Or one of their wives, perhaps?'

'You don't fight a duel with a woman, sir...'

Norris sprang on this answer: 'But there was no mention of a duel, was there?'

Sergeant Wilson studied the paper again: 'No, sir...'

'Nor, in fact, whether the 'individual' in question - and that is the word that you have recorded here - is a man or a woman?'

The witness nodded.

'So we do not know if the 'Smith' in question is a porter in Portobello or a milkmaid in Musselburgh, do we?'

The jurors laughed. The witness was now entirely deflated: 'No, sir.'

Norris folded in half the piece of paper in his hand and gave a small bow to the witness: 'Until we meet again, Sergeant Wilson...'

The witness bowed: 'Until then, Mr Norris...'

Norris smiled and sat down. Job done. For now…

*****

Chapter Nine

T*he Trial: Day Three.* 'What in blue blazes is going on here???'

The Dean of Faculty's face was a crimson beacon of anger. The Dean's Room was filled with the Advocates involved. Again.

'I make a simple request - a SIMPLE request - that this matter should be resolved quickly and without further ado and what do we get? Nothing less than a common and vulgar pantomime.'

He turned on NP Norris: 'And you! What is this I hear about making fun of a police officer - '...a costermonger in Corstorphine' or some such nonsense....'

Norris removed the pipe from his mouth: '...a porter in Portobello' as I recall it.'

The Dean fumed on: 'I don't care if it was a barber in...in...'. The Dean struggled to find the match '...Prestonpans....'

Silence for a moment. They were in the midst of the severe dressing-down, but each Advocate in attendance found himself disappointed that the Dean could not locate a decent piece of alliteration.

NP Spoke up: 'Dean of Faculty, you do us a great wrong.' He nodded over to the sullen-looking prosecutor: 'Charles here has been handed a witness list that appears to have been consumed by moths...'

Norris nodded towards Kane: 'While young Edward and I are saddled with an old rascal who is convinced that he has done nothing wrong. What would you have us do, Dean of Faculty?'

The Dean thought for a moment, then turned to Cod: 'Charles - there must be a further reduction available here? A lesser charge, perhaps?'

Cod shook his head: 'It has been tried, Dean of Faculty. Lord Albert has refused 'culpable and reckless'....'

They Dean looked over at Norris. Norris puffed on his pipe and said nothing. The Dean looked back at Cod: 'Then offer something better...'

'But the Lord Advocate...'

The Dean was shouting now: 'Are you deaf, man? Are you deaf? I told you - I have spoken to the Lord Advocate. Fix this, Charles - fix it.'

The Dean stood up. The Advocates stood up. Charles Cod looked anxious: 'I would require more time...'

Rab Lennox, Dean of Faculty, sighed: 'I will have word sent to the judges. There will be no evidence today.' He stared at Charles Cod - 'Fix this...'

***

Well, Mr K - what do you think?'

Mr Horse, extremely pleased with himself, pointed to the Christmas tree at the window.

Kane stood and admired their recent over-sized acquisition.

Picture-perfect, it stood. Busy and ungainly, but now a joyful splash of colour. And at the Lawn Market, Horse had picked up some bright red ribbon, and had fashioned a number of festive bows. And dotted among the green pine needles now were white paper decorations and a host of large angels - made of macramé.

Kane stood and admired Horse's handiwork: 'Those are some very intricate bows, Mr Horse.'

Horse smiled: 'Learned to tie a good number of knots in the army, sir. Make sure them French prisoners didn't escape on us'

Kane laughed. Horse fumbled in his pockets: 'Oh, and I've got another thing here for you, sir. Picked it up last night.'

And with that, Horse reached into his pocket and produced a beautiful ladies' cameo brooch. He handed it to Kane, who took it and ran his fingers around its outside: 'Is this gold, Mr Horse?'

Horse shook his head: 'No, Mr K - most likely a bit of the old Pinchbeck brass, but I thought you'd enjoy the picture, sir.'

Kane studied the picture on the brooch. Shell or coral had been hand-carved into a raised illustration of Michelangelo's Pieta. There was the Virgin Mary, cradling the body of Jesus on her lap.

Kane recognised the image. A similar engraving had hung on the wall of his father's study. His father, a clergyman, had always wanted to visit Rome to see that great marble masterpiece for himself, but that hadn't happened. How long was it that his father had been dead now? Three years? Four?

Kane's reverie was broken by Horse's Cockney brogue: 'So, Mr K, I thought that it might come in handy for a Christmas gift or the like. You know. For Christmas morning and your visit to…well, your visit and such...'

Of course. Before going to the Collins household, Kane had another visit to make.

'Mr Horse, this is very impressive. May I offer you some money for it?'

Horse shook his head: 'Put you hand back in your pocket, sir. We can square up the next time you get paid.'

Kane admired the brooch again. 'It is beautiful, Horse. Where on earth did you get it?'

'I won it last night, sir. At cards...'

***

The Trial: Day Four

'This whole case...this whole case is going to pigs and whistles!'

Lord Wallis was bellowing now. Prosecutor Cod stood. Cowed.

The jury had been removed from the court for the time being so that the judges could shout at the Advocates.

The judge turned on NP Norris: 'And you, sir, with your allusions of milkmaids in Portobello and the like...'

Kane mused to himself: *Have none of the senior lawyers ever heard alliteration? Milkmaids in Musselburgh was much better...*

'...this courtroom is not a place for levity, Mr Norris. This is a trial for Attempted Murder. You would do well to remember that, sir.'

NP Norris remained seated, but gave a bow in acknowledgment. Wallis turned to back to Cod: 'And you sir, on day four of the trial, seeking yet another adjournment...'

Cod could do nothing but sigh,

Wallis harrumphed and lifted up his pen: 'And what is the basis for *this* Crown motion to adjourn?'

Cod looked down at his papers: 'Certain difficulties with Crown witnesses, my lords.'

Lord Wallis threw down his pen. He looked as if he were about to explode: 'Again? Again?? You are already conducting you case without the benefit of a complainer, sir. Apparently, the gentleman, one John Sanders Barrington Smith has decided to be abroad for these proceedings.' Lord Wallis looked at the other two judges: 'And one can only envy him....' He turned back towards Cod again: 'What is the issue now?'

Cod lifted up his papers and read from them: 'It would seem that we have not been able to cite Mr Smith's Second, his cousin, a certain Mr Charles Smith.'

Lord Wallis was writing now. He looked up: 'Why not?'

'Because he is also abroad.'

The judge shook his head and continued writing. Charles Cod continued, as calmly as he could: 'And as far as the surgeon at the scene who treated Mr Smith is concerned, he...he is...'

Lord Wallis looked up wearily: 'Let me guess. He has emigrated to the Isthmus of Panama...'

'He is unable to be traced, my lords.'

Lord Wallis sighed and shook his head. NP Norris got up to address the court, but the judge waved him away. 'Sit down, Mr Norris.'

Lord Wallis then summoned the judges at his sides to come and speak privately. The three judges stood in a huddle, their backs to the lawyers and the main gallery. Much nodding and gesticulation. Then they returned to their seats. Lord Wallis addressed the prosecutor:

'We appreciate the learned Advocate Depute's difficulties here, but an adjournment of another full day would, we feel, be excessive. Thus, Advocate Depute you can have until two o'clock this afternoon. Who is your next witness?'

Cod sighed with relief: 'That would be Captain Harry Street.'

'And what is he to speak to?'

'Captain Street was the gentleman who assisted the Lord Albert at the...' he thought about saying the word 'duel', but thought the better of it '...at the event in question. He will confirm the identity of the accused, the identity of the complainer, Mr Smith, and he will speak to the accused here firing the bullet at Mr Smith's head.'

Lord Wallis looked around him and the judge on each side nodded. Wallis closed his notebook. 'Very well, Advocate Depute. Two o'clock, then. And I would be very grateful if you could ensure that this witness does not emigrate in the meantime...'

*****

Chapter Ten

Norris and Kane walked up and down Parliament Hall. Norris puffed on his pipe and pulled at his side-whiskers: 'Well, Edward - what say you?'

Kane shook his head: 'I fear that the next witness will prove to be the end of our case. This is the cast-iron witness that the Crown has been waiting for. He assisted Lord Albert as his Second in the duel, he can identify both our client and the complainer and he saw the shot being fired. He is the complete witness, I fear.'

Norris and Kane continued to walk up and down. Inspiration was not forthcoming. Then they noticed Charles Cod waving them over. Norris greeted him cheerfully: 'Charles, dear chap. You look anxious. What is the matter? Is the next Crown witness on a ship to Timbuctoo?'

Cod laughed good-naturedly: 'I confess that I would be tempted to join him…'

Norris and Cod laughed. Here were two friends who were often on opposite sides of one another, but who shook off the results of each case and renewed their friendship each time. Cod got to the point: 'Now, I have reviewed the papers. And despite the Dean's - how shall I put it - 'encouragement' to reduce the charge here, I regret that I cannot see any scope for that, Norval.'

Norris nodded: 'Quite understand, Charles. This is the High Court of Justiciary. You cannot exactly reduce a charge from Attempted Murder to a *Breach of the Peace...*'

They both laughed…

***

Kane checked his Advocates Box. No work. Kane joined his friend Collins and they sat, sipping their coffee in the Advocates Reading Room. Kane took out his pocket watch, noted the time and sighed: '…and thus, at 2 o'clock today, my friend, our carefully-constructed house of cards will tumble down.'

Collins laughed: 'Ah, Edward. *Fiat justicia* - though the heavens tumble.'

'Indeed, Collins, indeed.'

Collins smiled: 'But you will be able to regale your children and grandchildren about the notable case of the old nobleman and the matter of honour...'

Kane laughed in spite of himself. Collins continued: '...a music hall entertainment in which a pretty young wife was called an 'alleged actress' by a blackguard who fled the country with his Second so that they could avoid prosecution themselves for taking part in a duel in which the only real casualty was an expensive top hat...'

Kane laughed again. But then frowned. He began rubbing his temples. Collins studied him, concerned: 'Are you quite well, my friend?'

But then Kane covered his mouth: 'Oh, Collins, Collins, my friend - you are quite simply a man of genius.'

And with that, Edward Kane, Advocate, dressed in full wig and gown – ran out of the room.

***

The courtroom was hushed now as Captain Harry Street took the stand.

The word was out: here was the witness who would finally sink the chances of the old nobleman, Lord Albert Arthur.

It was well-known that Captain Harry Street was Lord Albert's dearest friend, but it was also known that Street was a man of honour who would never lie under oath for anyone or anything. And so, Harry Street was sworn in. And the prosecutor got to it: 'Now, Captain Street, you are a friend the accused here – Lord Albert Arthur?'

Lord Albert gave Street a cheery wave from the dock. The witness smiled back and was about to answer - but Norval Norris had bolted to his feet: 'Don't answer that question.'

This took everyone by surprise - not least the judges. Lord Wallis looked down: 'Mr Norris, we do expect objections from you, sir, but, I venture, not *quite* so early in the examination...'

Norris addressed the court: 'Thank you, my lords. I concede that the objection is early but, as I will demonstrate, not premature...'

Lord Wallis looked over at prosecutor Charles Cod, and motioned for him to sit down. Cod, with a rueful sort of grin on his face, shook his head slowly. Then eased down into his chair.

The judge picked up his pen: 'Yes, Mr Norris?'

Norris continued: 'It is trite law, my lords, but law none the less, that no man, when giving evidence, is obliged to incriminate himself.'

Lord Wallis nodded: 'Of course, Mr Norris. And what is the issue here?'

'This witness,' Norris pointed to Harry Street 'is being asked if he knows the accused...'

The judge interjected: 'Mr Norris, despite Lord Albert's undoubted failings, I am quite sure that the act of knowing him does not constitute a criminal offence...'

Much laughter from the public gallery. And a broad smile from the old man in dock.

Norris smiled: 'Not ordinarily, my lords. But in this case, the witness is being asked the question with the intention of showing that the witness knows the accused and then actively assisted the accused - acting as his Second in a duel - in what is alleged to be an attempt at murder.'

Lord Wallis was silent for a moment. He then nodded, and started writing.

Norris continued: 'The simple fact is this: any person who took part in such an event is liable to be prosecuted. Why do we think that the so-called 'victim' Mr Jack Smith is not here today?' Norris smiled down at Edward Kane. 'As my Learned Junior reminded me, only this afternoon: the alleged 'victim' of the offence, and his own Second and even the phantom surgeon who was there to treat any wounds...'

All three judges were listening closely now.

'...the allegation is that they were all there for the same reason. To participate - each according to his own role - in the duel. The duellists, the men helping them, the surgeon...if one of them is guilty of Attempted Murder...'

Lord Wallis nodded and finished the sentence: '...then they are *all* guilty of Attempted Murder, given the common purpose here.' The judge leaned back in his chair and considered this: 'I see your point, sir. As in an act of robbery, the man who acts as a look-out is no less guilty than the man who robs the victim...'

Norris nodded: 'Precisely, my lord. The principle of Art and Part applies. Thus, when Captain Street here is being questioned,' Norris pointed to the witness, 'then my lord requires to inform him that he does not require to answer *any* question that may incriminate him. Even a question that appears to be the most innocent one.'

Lord Wallis looked at the ceiling for a moment, then looked around at the other judges. Again, all three judges got up out their chairs and formed a huddle with their backs to the lawyers. Much discussion - then back to their chairs. Lord Wallis addressed Charles Cod:

'Advocate Depute, you have heard Mr Norris' argument. As a matter of law, it must be correct. I intend to give the relevant warning to this witness.'

Cod bowed: 'I have anticipated the issue, my lords. The focus of my questions is what this witness *saw*, not what he *did*. Thus, there should be no impediment to his answering.'

Wallis nodded: 'Very well.' He turned to the witness: 'Captain Street, if you are asked any question that you feel might incriminate you in any way, then you are not obliged to answer that question. Do you understand, sir?'

The witness considered this for a moment, then: '*Any* question, my lord?'

The judge nodded: '*Any* question.' He turned to the prosecutor, inviting him to continue: 'Yes?'

Charles Cod asked the question: 'Now, Captain Street - you know Sir Albert Arthur, do you not?'

The witness thought for a moment, then: 'Sorry, sir. I shan't answer that.'

Cod smiled: 'I merely ask if you know the gentleman in the dock, sir?'

The witness smiled back: 'Well, that would be telling, wouldn't it, sir. Sorry - not answering that one.'

Cod got testy: 'On what basis, sir?'

Captain Street cocked his thumb in the direction of the judge: 'What *he* said.'

Cod huffed and puffed somewhat: 'I merely ask if you know Sir Albert Arthur. As I understand it, and it is well-known, you served in the army together...'

The witness thought for a moment, then pointed at the judge again: 'What *he* said...'

Charles Cod, Advocate Depute stared at his papers...

*****

Chapter Eleven

'Breach of the peace? Breach of the Peace?? What does that even mean?'

Norris puffed on his pipe: 'It means, Lord Albert, that the prosecution have offered to reduce the charge from one of Attempted Murder to one of Breach of the Peace.'

Inside the offices of Baxter and Bruce (Writers to the Signet) Norval Norris puffed away, Edward Kane took notes, and Lord Albert looked even more puzzled than before: 'It simply makes no sense. We were on top of a ruddy great hill with no-one else there. Whose 'peace' were we 'breaching', then?'

'The Queen's peace, Sir Albert, the Queen's peace.'

The old nobleman shook his head: 'I have had the great pleasure and privilege of meeting Her Majesty on a number of occasions, and I can assure you that she has no interest in gun-play at the top of Calton Hill.'

Norris continued: 'Given that the original charge was one of Attempted Murder, Lord Albert, then we appear to have had a sizeable mountain reduced to a barely visible molehill.'

The old lord thought for a moment: 'What would *you* do?'

NP Norris puffed on his pipe: 'Lord Albert, I have spent hundreds - perhaps thousands - of hours in courtrooms. The only thing of which I am certain, is that it is impossible to predict the outcome with any jury. The Crown offer here is very, very reasonable...'

'And what is the likely penalty?'

'A fine, perhaps. You have no previous criminal record. Admonished, possibly. Or the Court could defer sentence for a period for good behaviour...'

The old nobleman sat back in his chair and considered this: 'And what is the maximum penalty?'

'The maximum penalty?'

'For Breach of the Police, or whatever the devil it's called...'

'For Breach of the Peace?' At this point, Edward Kane noted that Norris had begun pulling at his side whiskers. Something that he generally did when he was nervous: 'I have told you the likely penalties, Lord Albert.'

The old gentleman was irate now: 'Don't play the lawyer with me, sir. I asked for the maximum penalty here. For Breach of the Whatever-it's-called...'

'Well Lord Albert,' Norris nodded, 'in the High Court...the maximum penalty...for Breach of the Peace...that would be Life Imprisonment.'

Lord Albert looked stunned for a moment. Then burst into peals of laughter: 'Oh Mr Norris, Mr Norris - the whole affair would make a stuffed bird laugh...'

***

The consultation was fruitful, if only because Lord Albert gave clear instructions: first, that the Crown offer of the reduced charge was refused. Second, that the Lord Advocate himself should be stuffed.

***

The Trial: Day Five

When Kane arrived at Parliament Hall that morning, he found Norval Norris waiting for him again, smoking his pipe before the statue of Walter Scott.

'Ah – Edward!' Norris smiled: 'Apparently, the Dean would like to speak to us. Both of us. Shall we go in together?'

***

Rab Lennox, Dean of the Faculty of Advocates said very little. He stood with his back to the others, looking out of the window. He reminded Kane of a condemned prisoner, looking out at the last sunrise.

Charles Cod was finishing his account of the current state of play: '...and the further offer to reduce the charge has been refused.'

The Dean continued to look out of the window, his back to the Advocates: 'I told you to fix this, Charles.'

Cod stole a glance at Norris and shook his head: 'It would appear that some things are beyond repair, Dean of Faculty.'

The Dean turned to face them: 'Well, earlier this morning I had the Lord Advocate in here. And the Lord Advocate himself...'

***

'...and the Lord Advocate himself has reviewed the evidence in this case...' Charles Cod was standing up and addressing the three judges on the bench, '...and has, in his discretion, decided that there should be no further proceedings in this case. In fact, the whole matter was raised as a warning to the lieges at large that duelling in public will not be tolerated and will invariably result in prosecution.'

And with that, the large and stately Charles Cod lowered himself into his chair (with as much dignity as he could muster in the circumstances).

Lord Wallis looked around at the other judges at his sides. All were smiling now. He turned to the old nobleman in the dock:

'Lord Albert Arthur, stand up.'

Lord Albert stood up.

'The Crown has withdrawn the libel against you. We find you Not Guilty of Attempted Murder. And Lord Albert...' the judge smiled, '...Lord Albert - don't do it again!'

And with that, there was a great laugh and a cheer from the public gallery. The last thing that Kane saw was the old nobleman being surrounded by well-wishers almost shaking his hand off, and then Sir Albert leaving the courtroom – arm-in-arm with Captain Harry Street.

*****

Chapter Twelve

Edward Kane's manservant, Mr Horse, stared into the fire and shook his head.

'But don't you think, Mr K, that some people are just born lucky?'

Kane sat in his wing-back chair by the fire, cradling a glass of port: 'It certainly helped that the so-called 'victim' in the case was plainly as guilty as the accused, Mr Horse.'

Over dinner, Kane had told Horse all about the events in court that day. As always, Horse listened had listened carefully, but said nothing, just nodding occasionally. Then: 'Well, it sounds as if your man, Mr Norris, done a good job, sir.

'I do marvel, Mr Horse, at his ability to spread a thick fog over the clearest landscape'

Horse went to the pantry: 'Well, sir, as me old nan used to say: you might hear the footsteps, but you never know who's comin' up the stairs.' Clinking from the pantry. 'Would you like some more port, sir?'

'Yes, please, Mr Horse.' Kane began to muse, almost to himself: 'It has to be said, Horse, that we must stand in awe at Mr Norris's feats of legerdemain...'

Horse had emerged from the pantry with a decanter and glass. But he stood still, a puzzled look on his face. One of the words was too big. Kane noted this and looked up: 'Mr Horse, it means when someone is nimble with the hands...'

Horse continued to look puzzled. Kane explained: 'You know. For example, when someone does a card trick and things begin to disappear...'

Horse grinned and nodded now: 'Ah, got it, Mr K. Got it. I had a friend done that. The Old Bailey gave him eighteen months...'

Kane laughed. Horse stoked the fire with a poker. He gave a great yawn: 'Well, sir. Time to hit the hay.'

'And how are preparations progressing for tomorrow, Mr Horse?'

Kane mused that what with all the fuss and focus on the fate of a quarrelsome old nobleman, it had been easy to forget that tomorrow was Christmas Day.

'Well, Mr K, like you asked, I went down to the Lawn Market and I got a good price on a nice bottle of port for your chum, Mr Collins.'

'Excellent, Mr Horse."

'And a pretty box full of sweet things for his nippers.'

'Capital, Mr Horse, capital.'

Horse looked a little sheepish now: 'But I didn't get you nothing, sir. Seeing as I gave you the brooch and all. But everything has been wrapped, Mr K. You know, for your *other* visit. The early morning one...'

Kane smiled: 'Mr Horse, you have done me a great service with the brooch. I am sure that it will be much appreciated.' He got up from his chair. 'Now, I also have something for you in the way of a gift. You will forgive me that it has not been wrapped...'

Kane got up from his chair and went into his room. He emerged shortly afterwards, holding something behind his back: 'So, I had a quiet word with the court Bar Officer in Sir Albert's case and asked him what was to become of the items lodged by the Crown. Apparently, if they are not claimed - as they were not here - then, they are deemed abandoned, and they belong to her Majesty the Queen. But one can only wonder how Her Majesty would have any use...' and Kane produced the item from behind his back '...for a top hat with a hole blown in it.'

Kane handed the top hat to Horse. Horse was speechless.

'As you will see, Mr Horse, it is of good quality, made of silk and - perhaps with a discreet patch just above the brim - it will provide you with a splendid piece of head-gear for any occasion.'

Horse's eyes were open wide: 'Mr K, Mr K - this must be worth a bloomin' fortune, sir.'

Kane smiled: 'Try it on, Horse...'

Horse placed the top hat on his head. Perfect fit. Kane laughed and handed Horse a looking-glass. Horse examined his reflection: 'I'm thinking, Mr K, that all it needs is a new headband to cover the hole and all, and then...' he began to admire himself, turning his head left and right, '...and then, sir, your man Horse will look very spruce...very spruce indeed, Mr K.'

Kane smiled: 'And have you finalised your own arrangements for tomorrow, Mr Horse?'

'Like I said, sir, I told the barmaid at the White Hart that I'd go with her to see her nan, sir. So that's me sorted, Mr K.'

And when Horse retired to bed (still wearing his new hat), Kane sat on for a while in his chair. And he smiled at the great tree at the window, all red ribbons and bright angels. And the memories returned of Christmases long past. When he would wake up as a child in the sheer, breathless joy of Christmas morning. With father, puffing on his pipe, expressing delight at the smallest gift from Edward. Or mother, always warm, always there. A smile in her eyes as she watched Edward remove the wrapping paper, sharing in her son's joy at those bright red toy soldiers or the wooden animals of Noah's Ark. Ah, those days, those days. Where are those days now? And the mantel clock struck midnight.

*****

Chapter Thirteen

Christmas Morning

It was not so much a hospital ward, as a sort of dormitory that housed ladies of a certain class.

Clutching the (beautifully-wrapped) pieta brooch (*Thank you, Mr Horse*), Edward Kane walked along the middle of that long room. Beds on each side, Kane gave a little bow to some ladies, smiled at others, and to others he wished 'Merry Christmas'.

And, in a bed at the end of the room - there she was. Sitting up and smiling in his direction. His mother, Emily Kane. She held out her arms to greet him: 'Edward, my own Edward.'

Kane smiled: 'Mam*a*.'. He leaned over the bed and embraced her for the longest time, '...my own Mama...'

She looked better today. Not so hollowed-out. The dark rings around her eyes disguised by the careful application of make-up. And nothing, nothing could dull the warmth in those eyes. Nothing. Not even serious illness.

Emily Kane gave a girlish giggle. 'And what, Edward, would Christmas morning be without an exchange of gifts?' She reached under the top blanket of the bedclothes and retrieved what - judging by its shape and size - was likely to be a book, and a thick one at that.

Kane laughed - as he handed over his own gift to her. 'What indeed, Mama, what indeed?'

Mother and son sat happy in each other's company as they examined the festive packages. Emily Kane was excited now: 'Open yours, Edward. Oh – I always loved to watch you open your gifts.'

Kane tore the paper. It was, indeed, a book. 'Oh, Mama. Thank you ever so...'.

It was a copy of '*David Copperfield*'.

The mother smiled: 'I am rather proud of myself, Edward. Heard that it was published as a book last month, so I sent word to our Mr Thin in Infirmary Street, and he was able to secure this copy from London.'

Kane opened the book and smiled: 'And such marvellous illustrations.' He nodded towards his own gift: 'Your turn.'

Emily Kane's eyes sparkled. She took the little package and shook it, teasing him: 'Let me guess. Is it an orange?'

Mother and son laughed. She proceeded to tear open the paper delicately, enjoying the anticipation of what the gift might be: 'And so beautifully wrapped, Edward.'

'That was my man, Mr Horse, Mama. A man of unexpected talents, it would appear.'

And when the gift was opened, and she saw the contents, Emily Kane uttered a little squeal of delight. A cameo brooch. Michelangelo's pieta. Mary cradling the adult Jesus in her arms: 'Oh, Edward, Edward - it is...beautiful.'

Kane beamed that the gift had been so well received: 'I'm afraid that is not gold, Mama...'

She laughed: 'Oh, Edward, stuff and nonsense. Look at the quality of the carving on the shell. The whole thing is quite exquisite...'

Kane's mother examined the image for a long time, and Kane could see a range of emotions playing on her face now: 'Your father had this very picture hanging on his study wall…'. Her eyes studied the coral carving. She gave a little laugh '…and he could never understand what the artist meant…'

'How so, Mama?'

She ran her finger over the carving: 'Your father said that the picture made no sense. Look closely, Edward. The face of Mary is the face of a young girl. Fifteen years old, perhaps? But here she is, cradling the body of her son - a man of thirty-three years…'

Kane examined the image more closely now. 'At first, your father thought that it must be a mistake. You'll recall that he would often say 'Even Homer nods sometimes…"

Kane laughed. 'But, Edward, when you consider the image, it is simply that of a mother holding her baby. Mary was just a slip of a girl when Jesus was born. And here she is now, a young girl once again, holding her baby in her arms. For the last time…'

The mood had shifted now. The surface gaiety with the exchange of the Christmas gifts had evaporated. Emily Kane seemed exhausted, as if she had just grown older before her son's eyes. Kane looked at her hands. They seemed almost transparent now. His mother placed the brooch on her lap and leaned back on her pillow: 'Oh, Edward. Pay no attention to me. I am such a silly goose sometimes…'

Kane took his mother's hand. She turned to face him. 'Will you read to me, Edward? As I used to for you when you were small...'

Kane smiled: 'Of course...'

'Will you read to me? Until I sleep?'

Kane smiled and nodded.

Emily Kane motioned to the well-worn Bible that sat on a chair at her bedside. Kane picked it up and looked at her. *Where from?*

She gave a slight wince and leaned further back into her pillow. And Kane saw on his mother's face something of the pain that had been her companion for many months: 'In honour of Christmas, Edward, let us have Luke. Luke, Chapter 2...'

The reading had been an annual favourite in the Kane household at Christmas. And Kane opened up the book and he read of the shepherds abiding in the field, and of the angel of the Lord, and the babe wrapped in swaddling clothes, lying in a manger, and the multitude of the heavenly host praising God.

'And all that heard it wondered at those things...'

And Kane looked up at his mother, and Emily Kane had tears in her eyes.

She looked down, took her son's hand and smiled, then lay back on her pillow and said, almost to herself: 'But Mary kept all these things, and pondered them in her heart...'.

She smiled, and studied the image on the brooch: 'Poor Mary.' She closed her eyes. 'I think I should like to sleep now...'

*****

Chapter Fourteen

Christmas Afternoon.

Edward Kane's friend, Mr Collins, Advocate, exclaimed in triumph: 'Yes, Edward - '*David Copperfield*'!'

Collins was praising himself for the gift that he had just handed to Kane. Kane stood in the Collins household, contemplating the book that had just been given him. The second copy of '*David Copperfield*' that day, another one having been given to him that very morning by his mother.

Collins enthused: 'I know that you are a fanatic for Mr Dickens' work, Edward. For my own part, I find it all rather sensational. But, my friend, as they say: 'It takes all sorts...''

Kane looked at his friend's shining face, but said nothing of the fact that he already had the book - and with a feigned surprise: 'What can I say, Collins? I shall read it twice...'

And then the five Collins children, shepherded by the vivacious Mrs Collins, were brought into the room and were lined up at the side of the dinner table. They stood there, from eight years to four years old. They reminded Kane of a line of little dogs begging for scraps at the table, getting gradually smaller and smaller as the table progressed.

Collins stretched out his hand: 'And now, my dear friend, I hand you over to the less-than-tender ministrations of the Collins offspring.'

Kane addressed his tiny audience: 'Well children - what would you like to play?'

A common clamour filled the air: 'Swat the Blind Man! Swat the Blind Man!'

Mrs Collins put her hand to her lips to stifle a laugh. Kane turned to Collins: 'Not a game with which I am familiar, I'm afraid.'

Collins laughed: 'Simple, my friend. We are all blindfolded and we proceed to bash each other over the head with pieces of paper...'

Kane had the fleeting thought that this sounded very much like appearing in the Appeal Court...

'You'll soon get the hang of it, Edward. In fact, it's rather like fighting a duel.' Collins smiled: 'But please don't breathe a word of it to the Lord Advocate. I would hate to see the children in the dock...'

***

And later that night, when the games were over and Kane's gift of port had been opened, sampled and much praised, Kane bid his hosts goodnight. He made his way through the snowy streets of the Old Town of Edinburgh and returned to his furnished rooms.

After seven o'clock now. The rooms were empty, and more than a little chilly. Kane lit a candle. He took off his wet shoes and placed them near the fireplace. *Ah, Mr Horse has left the fire made up – requiring only a match.* Taking a box of matches from the mantelpiece, he struck one, knelt down and lit the papers in the fireplace, and soon the kindling began to crackle and flame. He sat down, and before long he was basking in its warmth.

What was that noise in the street? *Children? At this time?*

Kane got up, opened the window and looked down. And there in the street was a group of children involved in their own duel - squealing and chortling and throwing snowballs.

Kane rested his elbows on the windowsill and watched them for a time, smiling. And in the fading winter light, the whole scene was like some flickering magic lantern of the past, of his own childhood, gone these many years now.

Kane smiled and closed the window. Then, with a blanket on his lap, and cradling a glass of rum and milk, he sat down before the fading embers of the fire.

He opened the book that his mother had given him. Only now, did he realise that it had been inscribed:

'To my precious son, Edward.
Always remember: you are the hero of your own life.
Merry Christmas.
With much love from your adoring Mama
Edinburgh
Christmas Day
In the Year of Our Lord, 1850'

And the young Advocate smiled and nodded to himself, and turned the pages of his book. As outside, a gentle blanket of snow began to cover the long, winding streets of the Old Town of Edinburgh.

*****

Edward Kane

in

No Bunnies in The Bible

1851. Edinburgh. Good Friday

'Mr Horse - what on *earth* is that smell?'

Edward Kane, Advocate, yawning, and still dressed in his nightgown and nightcap, stood in the doorway of his bedroom and peered at the marble clock on the mantelpiece. Just after 6 o'clock in the morning.

Mr Horse, Kane's Cockney manservant, gave a shy grin: 'Apologies, Mr K, apologies, sir. I got this big batch of eggs on the cheap and I think one or two of 'em might be off...'

Kane walked into the sitting room. He looked at the fireplace. And there, on top of the open fire, on a metal frame, sat a large pot of bubbling, boiling water. Kane looked into pot. Bobbing around, were - what looked like - twenty or so eggs. And the water was blood red. Kane looked up.

'Horse …what on earth...this looks like a witch's cauldron...'

Horse grinned: 'Happy Easter, Mr K. Happy Easter, sir...'

Kane began to come round, and remembered that today was Good Friday: 'Happy Easter, Mr Horse.' He nodded towards the bubbling pot on the fire. 'But what...?'

'Remember, sir. You said that you was seeing your friend, Mr Collins today, and Mr Collins has got the five little nippers, so - like we said – I've got some eggs to take with you, sir.'

Kane looked again at the pot: 'But why is the water all...all *bloody*?'

Mr Horse lifted up a piece of red onion skin: 'I'm giving the eggs a bit of colour, sir. For Easter. With red onions and some beetroot. Give them twenty minutes, Mr K, they'll be a nice shade of red. I already done the green ones with the periwinkle.' Horse pointed to a pile of eggs on the nearby table - all bright green.

Kane stood there. Not quite awake yet. Mr Horse went into the larder - 'I'll get another pot on the fire, sir. Get some more hot water and we and have a brew. And then you can have a wash and a shave.' He nodded towards the bubbling pot: 'Can't use the water in there, Mr K. You shave in that and you'll look like a human beetroot....'

***

Quarter-past ten now, and Edward Kane and Mr Horse were making their way through the crowds along Edinburgh's Lawn Market towards Calton Hill.

'Well, I feel like a right, ponce, sir...' Horse's Cockney accent cut through the din.

'Chin up, Mr Horse, chin up. Remember - the basket was your idea.'

Oh, but it was a beautiful, fresh morning. A very jolly Kane strode along dressed in top hat and cape, swinging his cane before him. And at his heels, lagged a less-cheery Mr Horse - carrying a basket of coloured eggs and bright flowers. To the casual onlooker, the image brought to mind a gorilla. Carrying a handbag.

The Lawn Market was crowded today. Mothers and fathers dressed in their finery. Children carrying tiny baskets overloaded with coloured eggs.

And the cries of the lawn-merchants, bellowing at the market stalls: '*I don't want a florin, I don't want a shilling. No, ladies and gentlemen, this silk handkerchief - a tanner!*'

At another stall, two elderly sisters were inspecting a piece of cloth, holding their spectacles against the fabric to interrogate the quality of the weave.

And there, at the side of the road, sits a stony-faced farmer, guarding his baskets of eggs and rolls of cheeses from a group of rowdy young boys.

'Mind your back, mind your back!' A carriage of fresh fish, with the fishmonger barking his warning to the folks before him on the cobbled road.

And now a group of police officers, a blue blur of stovepipe hats and brass buttons, are spilling out of the Police Office at the side of St Giles Church, pushing their way towards the troublesome youths.

Kane pointed towards them: 'Ah, Mr Horse , our noble police officers. On hand to quell those lads and employ the Rule of The Law.'

'If it was up to me, sir - I'd employ the boot up the arse...'

Kane had never seen Calton Hill so populated.

From a distance, the bright, holiday clothes of the Easter revellers on the green grass made the hill look like a Christmas tree with migrating decorations.

Kane and Horse began to climb the hill. Kane consulted his pocket watch: 'Almost eleven o'clock, Mr Horse. I told Mr Collins that we would meet him under the Nelson monument.'

They looked up. There, at the top of the hill was the great monument, the upturned telescope dedicated to the late admiral.

Horse grunted as they climbed the steep incline of the hill: 'Never understood that monument, Mr K. You got Admiral Nelson - a bloke with one eye - and you give him a monument of a telescope. Is that a joke, sir?'

Kane smiled: 'Read your history books, Mr Horse. It was the Admiral himself who said: '*Sometimes we have a right to be blind*'. Ah, I see them…'

And looking up, they saw Kane's friend, Mr Collins, standing at the foot of the great telescope. And standing beside him was the vivacious Mrs Collins, all smiles and bows and ringlets. And there were two exhausted-looking housemaids, stick-thin girls in their early twenties, standing guard over a hamper that they had just lugged up that hill.

And, of course, the five young Collins children, jumping up and down now, squealing and clapping their hands at the prospect of rolling those coloured eggs down the hill.

Kane gave a low bow. Mr Collins bowed: 'Good morning, Edward. And a very Happy Easter to you.'

Kane smiled: 'And to you, Collins, and to you.'

The vivacious Mrs Collins gave a small curtsey: 'Good morning, Mr Kane.' Then – 'The Lord is Risen'.'

Kane - the son of a clergyman - thought that since this was Good Friday, there would be no question of any rising from the dead for a good two days yet. But no point in being discourteous: 'He is risen indeed, ma'am.' Kane beckoned to his manservant: 'Mr Horse?'

Horse handed Kane the basket. Kane produced a bunch of flowers and presented them to Mrs Collins. She blushed: 'Oh, Mr Kane. Easter lilies. How thoughtful...'

Then Kane looked down at the expectant faces of the five children: 'And what have we here? I don't suppose that any of these virtuous little boys and girls are at all interested in...' Kane pointed to the contents of the basket '...the rolling of Easter eggs?' Much jumping and squeals followed: 'Oh, me, sir...oh, please, Mr Kane...'

Kane held the basket down and let the five children pick out eggs, and in a matter of moments, those coloured eggs were being rolled or thrown down Calton Hill to the sound of much gleeful chortling, the girls encouraging the eggs down with their little wooden spoons, the boys thwacking them with twigs and branches.

And stumbling behind them, Mr Horse, minding his footing, who, in an act of gallantry, had volunteered to carry the enormous Collins hamper, so that the housemaids '*…don't hurt them lovely little hands of yours…*'

Crowds near the bottom of the hill now, as a number of other families had laid out their picnic blankets and were sitting down, laughing and drinking and peeling the coloured eggs for eating.

Mr Collins nodded towards a grassy space: 'Here! This is a nice spot.' Horse put the hamper down with a grunt. The housemaids reached in and took out some large tartan blankets and started to arrange them on the ground. Then they began to unpack the hamper contents: some bottles of brown lemonade, a large square of toffee and a great number of hot cross buns.

Kane invited Mrs Collins to sit down. She did so. Collins and Kane then sat down beside her. The five Collins children sat separately on a blanket nearby with the two housemaids and with Mr Horse, who appeared to be entertaining them. Collins nodded over: 'Your man, Mr Horse, is very adept at entertaining the children, Edward.' Kane laughed: 'I fear, Collins, that if you are not careful, will find him very adept at entertaining your housemaids…'

The friends laughed. And then something caught their attention. Nearby, an elderly gentleman wearing a clerical collar was setting up what looked like a wooden box to stand upon. After two or three false starts, the old gentleman finally fixed it into the ground and now he was rummaging through his bag. After a short period, he produced a large, black, leather-bound Bible. The aged clergyman then mounted the box, somewhat unsteadily, thought Kane, and began to address the holidaymakers - now his unwitting audience:

'Turn ye away! Turn ye away from these Pagan rituals!'

Men, women, children and servants were all turning their heads now, looking up at the figure standing on the box: 'You are not rolling eggs down a hill - you are rolling your children into Hell...'

It's fair to say that the preacher had caught the attention of his audience, whether they liked it or not. He began to wave the Bible above his head: 'Study the word! Study the word! There is no 'Easter' within these pages. There are no eggs, no rabbits...'

At this point, Mr and Mrs Collins looked over at Kane for confirmation or otherwise. Edward Kane's father had been a Minister of the Church of Scotland. He was meant to know these things. On this occasion he didn't.

The passionate preacher continued. Two directly opposite things happened: some families re-stacked their picnic baskets, folded their blankets, grabbed their children and moved to a nearby spot less theologically-intensive. On the other hand, some others stood up and began to surround the speaker. Kane noted that those surrounding the old man now included some of the rowdy boys who had been spotted earlier that morning at the Lawn Market. Kane could hear a great deal of laughter now as the boys challenged the speaker:

'Shut yer pie-hole, you silly old fool.'

The old man's voice cut through the cat-calling: 'You are the unwitting slaves of the Pagan gods. 'Eostre' - goddess of fertility - and her symbols: the egg and the rabbit...'

A tall boy with red hair hooted: 'And you - the mad March hare...'

And the mocking hilarity began to spread through the crowd. Many were jeering openly now. He was not quite sure why, but Kane rose from the comfort of his blanket and began to make his way towards the speaker and the hostile mob. He was stopped when Mr Horse, jumping up, reached out and held an open hand against his chest: 'Where you going, Mr K?'

'I am simply going to remind those boys of their manners...'

Horse exhaled: 'I wouldn't do that, sir. I know some of them lads. They've got the devil in them, Mr K. I would just...'

But Kane, undaunted by the warning, swept past his manservant and made his way to the front of the crowd.

The preacher was in full flow now: 'You are the unwitting apostles of Ashtoreth. The Pagan goddess Astart-e...'

The lanky youth with bright orange hair at the front of the crowd had emerged as the ringleader. He shouted: 'Well you can shut up for a-start-e...'

Edward Kane approached the youth: 'You! Yes, you, young lad...' The tall youth looked down on Kane, not at all chastened. He took a bite out of the hot cross bun that he was holding and answered as he chewed: 'What?'

Kane pointed his finger: 'Stop it. Stop it now. This is no way to treat your elders and betters.' The boy kept chewing: 'And what if I don't?'

Kane stood there, staring at the lad. The lad stared at Kane. And then, very deliberately, the lad tore off a piece of his bun and threw it at the old preacher. The five or six boys around him, taking this as a cue for more mischief, tore off pieces of their own buns and began to shower the bemused old man with them.

Kane raised his voice: 'I told you to stop.' The tall ginger lad turned round, lowering over him again. 'And who's going to make me? Are *you* going to make me?'

Everything was still for a moment. Not a sound from the crowd. Even the preacher appeared to be holding his breath. And then, out of nowhere, a full bottle of lemonade hurtled towards the lanky youth's face and caught him square on the nose. The boy, blinking heavily, fell to the ground, moaning. And then, emerging casually from the crowd, walked Mr Horse. He picked up the bottle, wiped the blood off the bottle and onto his sleeve, and addressed the rest of the tall lad's friends: 'Any of you other lads fancy a taste of this? Who's next, then?' And the remainder of the boys appeared to evaporate into the throng at that point, each one weaving through the crowd, head-down. The tall, ginger boy lay on the ground, holding his bloody face and moaning softly. Horse bent over him: 'Would you mind keeping it down, son? I'm trying to hear the bloke what's on the box. He says we're all going to Hell...'

***

Six o'clock in the evening. Back in the rented rooms, Mr Horse was pulling off Kane's boots. Kane leaned back into his wing-back chair by the fire: 'I'm bound to say, Mr Horse, that while your method of dealing with that young ruffian proved highly effective, it was not very Christian.'

'I thought there was enough religion going about already, sir. Anyway - don't it say somewhere - in the Good Book, I mean - if the eye is giving you a bit of gyp - you gouge it out.'

Kane laughed: 'I never took you for a Bible scholar, Mr Horse.'

'When I was a boy, Mr K, I had to read it to me old Nan. When she was going blind...'

'Then you will have seen the part about turning the other cheek?'

Horse grinned. 'Must have skipped that bit, sir.'

Boots off, Horse boiled some water on the open fire and made them both a cup of tea. He handed Kane the cup and saucer, then sat at the table and drank his own tea from an old tin mug. Horse produced a long, clay pipe from his jacket, struck a match and carefully lit the tobacco in the bowl of the pipe. Master and man sat in contented silence for a while. Then Horse spoke:

'Mr K, you know all that stuff the old fella on the box was raving on about - no 'Easter' in the Bible, no eggs, no rabbits. Is all that true, sir?'

Kane thought for a moment, then: 'I suppose it was largely accurate, Mr Horse. I can't recall anything significant about rabbits in the Bible - except, perhaps, 'Don't eat them'.'

'Then that makes us both sinners, sir!'

Master and man laughed. Horse pressed on: 'But what about the eggs down the hill and the like, sir? Was that not, like, when your man Jesus was rolling away the stone?'

Kane shook his head: 'Unlikely. Apparently, the stone covering the tomb was shaped like a coin...'

Horse took the pipe from his mouth: 'Hold on a minute, sir. If there ain't no 'Easter' in the Bible, and there ain't no bunnies and there ain't no eggs to speak of, then why are we chasing all them bloomin' eggs down Calton Hill?'

Kane thought for a moment, then: 'To be perfectly honest, Mr Horse - I have no idea.'

And then, Mr Horse started to laugh. He laughed so much that he began to cough. Kane looked up: 'You seem to derive a great deal of pleasure from the absence of scriptural authority, Mr Horse.'

Horse coughed into his hand: 'Oh, I'm sorry, Mr K, but I was thinking about what you was saying about the Admiral Nelson and the monument. All these people running up and down the hills with their eggs and their bunnies – and all about something what was never in the Bible anyway? What did the Admiral say again? '*Sometimes we got the right to be blind*'? Old Nelson must be looking down and laughing his head off. I mean, what's the point?'

Some days, Kane, as a Son of the Manse, felt exhausted by a life exposed to theology. He began to feel that now. But he could not let the conversation rest there: 'The point, Mr Horse…the point is not what happens on the Friday. It's what happens on the Sunday. Today, when that young ruffian – the one, as you said 'had the devil in him' – when he was challenging me to a fight, and no-one was coming to my aid…he must have thought at that point that he had won. But come Sunday, he will wake up with a black eye, a headache and fewer teeth. And *that* is the point of Easter, Mr Horse. It's when the Old Tempter thinks that he was won the fight on the Friday, but Jesus comes back and the Devil wakes up with a bloody nose on the Sunday. That's the point, Mr Horse.'

Horse puffed on his pipe for a moment, then nodded: 'You would have made a wery good preacher, Mr K.'

Kane smiled: 'Thank you, Mr Horse. Now – do we have anything in the larder for supper?'

'How about a nice green egg, sir?'

Kane shot Horse a look. Horse sat there grinning: 'Happy Easter, Mr K'

Kane chuckled: 'Happy Easter, Mr Horse…'

Edward Kane

in

A Promise is a Promise

Chapter One

E*dinburgh, Capital of Scotland. 1851*

'Is it me, or is it particularly chilly today, Mr Horse?'

Edward Kane, Advocate was sitting at the table, waiting for breakfast. A breakfast being prepared by his manservant, Mr Horse.

Horse pointed toward the window, and the snow piled up on the windowsill outside. He answered in his Cockney brogue. 'It's these old win-durs, Mr K. Well past their prime. I think the landlady must have got them off Noah and his ark, sir.'

Kane sighed: 'I don't suppose you could have a word with her. The landlady, I mean, Mr Horse?'

Kane noted the expression on Horse's face. The rent had not been paid for three weeks: 'Perhaps not, Mr Horse, perhaps not.'

Horse went over to the open fireplace and lifted an enormous frying pan from the stand above the flames. Kane looked over and saw the two fat sausages sizzling in the pan. Horse carried the pan over to the dining table. He scooped the sausages onto the plate before Kane: 'There you go, sir. Get them down you.' He pointed to the teapot on the table: 'And the tea is nice and mashed now, sir and I'll get the toast on. The milk is still good, Mr K - I left it on the windowsill overnight. It froze, but I broke it with a hammer, sir.'

Kane poured himself a cup of tea and some icy fragments from the milk jug as Mr Horse sat holding a long, two-pronged fork, toasting a thick slice of bread.

Kane took a sip of the tea. His eyebrows shot up: 'Well, Mr Horse, the strength of your tea is undiminished this morning. I wager that we could possibly cut it into slices...' he looked out onto the snow and ice '…and furnish me with an overcoat.'

Horse beamed: 'Thank you, sir.'

Mr Horse, a veteran of the Battle of Waterloo, was a man of many skills. His tea-making was a particular source of pride to him. 'Strong on the inside is strong on the outside...' he would say. His many martial abilities came in useful for facilitating the affairs of a young, impecunious Advocate like Edward Kane. Cooking, washing, ironing, the cleaning of boots (and where necessary, 'the cleaning of clocks', as

Mr Horse would have it) were among his duties. Importantly, Mr Horse was the Keeper of the Purse Strings. No mean feat, where there was often nothing in that purse.

'There you go, Mr K,' Horse came over and dropped the toast onto the side-plate, 'get a bit of butter on that and you'd never know that that bread was two days old...'

Kane raised his teacup to acknowledge receipt of the toast. Horse sat down on his stool by the fire, and drank from his old tin mug: 'So, Mr K - what does the day hold for you today, sir?'

Kane chewed slowly, allowing the tea to soften the toast in his mouth: 'Much of the same, Mr Horse, much of the same. I shall dress in wig and gown and I shall parade up and down Parliament Hall until some needy individual hails me - like a common cab in the street.'

Horse drank the rest of his own tea, tilting his old metal mug towards the ceiling as he finished it, then a long, satisfied sigh: 'Aaaaah. I got a feeling Mr K, that today is the day. Today is the day that some great big, juicy dripping roast of a case will just fall into your lap...'

Kane laughed: 'Your metaphor sounds somewhat messy Mr Horse - but I applaud the general sentiment...'

'And in the meantime, Mr K, I'll see what I can do to plug that window frame sir. Talk about a draught? You could fly a bloomin' kite in here.'

***

The great Parliament Hall in Edinburgh was virtually empty today. Monday. The judges don't sit on a Monday. It struck Kane that he had a head full of learning and a larder full of nothing. Dressed in wig and gown, he took a solitary stroll along the Hall. No life today in that great space. He stood again by the fire and mused: *Mr Horse predicted a day of success, well, Mr Horse, I regret to inform you...*

But at that point, Kane became aware that a young lad, a messenger, a shock of red hair, possibly aged eleven, had dashed into Parliament Hall. The lad looked up and down the Hall and fixed his eyes on Kane standing before the fire - then ran over: ''Scuse me sir, I'm looking for an Advocate...'

Kane smiled: 'Of course, which one?'

The lad was out of breath. 'I don't rightly know sir...'

'Then your task becomes more difficult...'

'I got a letter here sir. In my bag somewhere...'

The messenger boy rifled through his satchel, produced an envelope and handed it to Kane. Kane looked at the letter.

There was a blank space where a name should have been, with the word 'Advocate' written underneath. This was common, where no Advocate had been specified to do the work and any Advocate could be instructed for something that was essentially a formality.

Kane handed the letter back: 'I should think that any Advocate could accept these instructions.'

The lad breathed a sigh of relief: 'Thank you, sir. Thank you. This is my first day on the job, you see. Now - where do you think I can find an Advocate, sir?'

It struck Kane that since he (Kane) was standing in the middle of Parliament Hall, next to The Advocates Library, and dressed in full wig and gown, that the lad before him might not have finished dux of his school.

'I am an Advocate, young sir.'

The boy looked even more relieved: 'Then I'll leave the letter with you, sir. Sorry, sir. I thought you were one of the judges or some such thing.'

Kane gave a short bow: 'Then I am happy to accept your instructions, my young buck.'

And after the lad had written down Kane's surname (after several aborted attempts, and with a surprising degree of variation, given there were only four letters available), breathless, he ran off to the next task.

Kane took the letter into the Advocates Library, sat down and studied its contents. The more that Kane studied the papers and the law, the more he realised that this was a matter that would be decided upon the facts of the case, but that there was insufficient factual information in his letter. Best that the lawyers instructing him be told this. Kane took out his watch from his waistcoat pocket and looked at the time. Fifteen minutes past two. The address of the law agents? Just around the corner.

***

As Kane was climbing the narrow stair on his way up to the offices of solicitors Messrs McAllister and McAdam, all that he could hear was shouting. A woman's voice. Not young. And obviously not happy.

And when Kane reached the first floor landing, and looked though the open door of that lawyers' firm, he was faced with the sight of a lady, possibly in her seventies, in the act of assaulting a small ginger-headed boy.

*****

Chapter Two

The old lady had the boy's head inside the crook of her left arm, and she was twisting his ear. Kane angled his head to get a better look at the boy's face. This was the self-same lad who had delivered that morning's instructions!

It appeared that the boy's first day at work was not going smoothly.

'Ow...ow...OW!'

Kane, rather than trying physically to interrupt the punishment being meted out, cleared his throat instead. 'A-hem...'

At this, the old lady looked up. It struck Kane that she now looked like a cat that had just been interrupted in the licking of its hind quarters.

'I apologise for the interruption, madam...'

'Yes?'

'I was looking to speak to a Mr McAdam...'

'Do you have an appointment?'

But before Kane could answer, the captive child looked up and pointed: 'That's him, ma'am! That's him!'

The old lady looked at the lad for a moment, and then looked at Kane: 'Could I have your name, sir?'

'I am Edward Kane, Advocate.'

The lady nodded: 'Ah, so it's you, sir.' She pointed to the messenger boy, still trapped under her arm: 'This...this fop-doodle lost the piece of paper with your name on it. All that he could remember was that your name had something to do with cattle...'

Kane racked his brains for a moment: Ah - 'kine' - a good old Scottish word for 'cattle'...

'So Mr...Kine...'

The young Advocate corrected her: 'Kane...'

'So, Mr *Kane*, how can I be of assistance, sir?'

It struck Kane that this discussion with the old lady could be more efficiently conducted if she were to stop throttling the boy in her grip. Kane raised his eyebrows and nodded towards the child.

The captive was released: 'Get away wi' ye. Get back to your sister in the cash room...'

The boy rubbed his neck. 'Thank you, Mrs McAdam.' He bowed to the young Advocate: 'Thank you, Mr Kine.' and dashed off.

Despite her rough treatment of the boy, Kane thought that he detected a note of fondness in the old woman's voice as she watched him go: 'Oh, that lad. We only let him work here because his sister begged us.'

Formal introductions then took place in the less-combative atmosphere as the woman introduced herself as Mrs Morag McAdam, mother of the solicitor Murray McAdam. Her son was conducting business nearby and would return before long. Some tea in the meantime?

As Kane was being led to McAdam's office, he passed a small, windowless room. Looking in, he saw an extremely pretty girl – mid-twenties, perhaps - immersed in clacking through a large abacus before her. The girl looked up and caught Kane's eye. She smiled. Kane blushed. He smiled back and doffed his hat. Then Kane noticed, sitting behind the girl, was the wee lad whose ear had been so recently abused. *Ah - the cash room - the cash girl - the cash girl's brother!* The resemblance was obvious now, except the redness of the hair was just another lovely feature in her, and, where the boy's face was a study in blank vacancy, the girl's face radiated softness and gentleness and a kind of long-suffering patience.

Murray McAdam, bustled in. A burly, brisk man in his mid-50s. The conversation was brief. McAdam got straight to the point: 'So no hearing tomorrow, then. That is what the other side wanted. I shall send word immediately. The other side's Advocate can appear for both sides. You are released from your instructions, sir.'

Kane nodded, somewhat wistfully. Because of his diligence, some paying work had just evaporated. McAdam noted this: 'But you will, of course, be paid for your day's exertions.' McAdam proffered a pen and a piece of headed notepaper across the desk: 'If you would detail your fee on this, then I will arrange for immediate payment. Would cash be preferable?'

Cash? Oh happy day! Kane sat and detailed the work that had been undertaken. McAdam studied the note: 'Seems very reasonable, Mr Kane. Very reasonable.' He studied the note again, then gave what sounded like a little snort: 'I wager you will not die rich, sir, if you continue to under-value your services thus. Come - we can settle this immediately'.

And with that, McAdam rose from the table and beckoned to Kane to follow him. They entered the small cash room and Kane again noted the presence of the pretty cash lady and her brother. McAdam barked: 'Rose?' The girl, who had been submerged in totting up a column of numbers on the ledger before her, looked up with a start. Re-surfaced, she gave a compliant smile: 'Yes, Mr McAdam?'

'This Mr Edward Kane, Advocate...'

The girl stood up and gave a little curtesy. Kane bowed in response.

'...and he has a fee note here that he should like to be settled today. In cash. Immediately, if you please.'

The girl knotted her eyebrows: 'Oh, Mr McAdam, begging your pardon, sir, I don't know that we have sufficient cash for the fees of an Advocate...'

McAdam laughed: 'You will see the terms of the note, Rose. I venture that the *petty* cash will be sufficient.'

Rose looked at the note and nodded: 'Of course, Mr McAdam. I will just prepare a receipt for Mr Kane to sign.'

McAdam turned to the girl's brother, who was sitting on his hands, staring into space and swinging his legs to and fro. 'And you, young sir. I have a letter here for Baxter and Bruce in Castle Street. Do you know where that is, boy?'

The boy nodded and jumped down off his chair. He reminded Kane of a puppy scratching at a door to get out: 'Aye, sir, aye, sir.'

McAdam shook his head, somewhat fondly now, Kane thought, and handed the letter to the boy. The solicitor pointed to a figure in the adjoining room: 'Take it to my mother. Tell her to make two copies. One copy will go immediately to the address on the envelope. Is that clear?'

'Aye, sir. Straight away, sir.'

And with that, the boy snatched the draft letter, ran into the adjoining room and presented it to old Mrs McAdam.

McAdam shook his head and turned to Kane: 'I understand that the boy made a pig's ear of your letter of instruction today?'

Kane caught a glimpse of the cash girl's face. He thought that he detected an imploring look in the girl's eyes: *Please don't make it any worse.*

'Not at all.' Kane smiled. 'Master Timmy was extremely courteous, and I am sure that – given time - he will prove an asset.'

The receipt having been prepared and signed by Kane, he was handed his fee in cash: two guineas! Kane bid his goodbye to McAdam and - as he was passing the little cash room - looked in again at the cash girl. Initially absorbed in her numbers, the girl looked up, gave a sad little smile and mouthed the words: 'Thank you...'

***

As Edward Kane turned round the corner, smiling and jangling the two guineas in his pocket, he noticed that a crowd had formed near the entrance to his furnished rooms. Everybody was pointing up. But at what? Snow was falling now, and Kane shielded his eyes as he looked up. He made out a figure. It was a man standing, swaying on the window ledge. It was the window ledge of Kane's apartments. It looked all the world as if this man was about to jump.

Chapter Three

Kane rushed into his set of rented rooms: 'Mr Horse, Mr Horse!'

Kane barged into the small sitting room to see Mr Horse sitting at the table, smoking a long pipe and leafing through a newspaper. Horse got up: 'Mr K - you're home early, sir...'

Kane nodded towards the window frame: 'Mr Horse - why is there a man who appears to be intent on suicide hovering at our windowsill?'

Horse looked over: 'Ah, sir...'

The apparently suicidal figure appeared to be on his back now, hanging half-in and half-out of the window. Horse nodded towards it: '...that's my friend, 'the monkey'.'

'The 'monkey'?'

“‘Macpherson’ - ‘The Monkey Macpherson’, we likes to call him...’

Kane studied the figure half-in/half-out of the window. The fellow appeared to be whistling tunelessly as he braved the heights and was patting around the windowpanes.

‘You was complaining of the draught from the window this morning, Mr K, so I sent word and The Monkey came round to fix it. He says that the putty on the outside is all mardy, so he’s sorting it all out for you.’

Kane stood, taking it in: ‘The monkey...Macpherson...’

‘That’s what they calls him sir. A dab hand at windows with his swinging in and out. He can clean them an’ all. Inside and out. I’ve seen him hanging out of the best windows in Edinburgh, sir. Proper rich people. Advocates like yourself, or solicitors, sir. And you should see him up on the roofs, Mr K. He looks like one of them pet monkeys you can get at the docks. If you could spare ten bob that is...’

Kane was lost for words. Horse took Kane’s hat and cloak: ‘Shall I make us a brew sir?’

***

Mr Horse, tin mug in hand, sat and listened to the events of the day.

‘Well, Mr K, to my mind, you done the right thing, sir. Telling them lawyers that there was a problem and all.’

Kane back sat in the wing-back chair and nursed his glass of rum and milk.

'I hope so, Horse, I sincerely hope so. Though, I confess that I was rather put out by the comments of the solicitor, Mr McAdam...'

'What? That you was going to die in the gutter, sir...'

'Well, he did not exactly say...'

'That you was bound for the poor house, Mr K...'

'...not...quite...'

'...sleeping in a dirty grubber, and lying famished across an old rope...'

'That is not precisely...'

Horse laughed: 'Next time, sir, just charge him double what the work is worth. That'll learn him.'

'I can't do that, Mr Horse. That would be...that would be wrong.'

Horse was silenced by this. A line had been drawn in the sand. Edward Kane might be an Advocate today, but he would forever be a Son of the Manse, the son of a clergyman. Time to call a halt to the conversation. At least in this for the time being.

Horse stood with his back to Kane and was looking out of the window. He examined the windowpanes: 'Well, at least The Monkey done a good job with the windows, sir.' Horse went to the table and lifted up the candle in its candlestick holder. He took it over to the window and held it in front of the panes of glass: 'Look sir, see that? Barely a flicker, sir. Barely a flicker. A wery useful man is the Monkey Macpherson.'

Kane nodded: 'And did it cost much, Mr Horse?'

'I just gave him a nip of your rum and the thruppeny bit in me pocket, Mr K, and he was well happy with that. He'll do anything for a swallow of rum, will The Monkey.'

Kane had a fleeting - but alarming - picture of Macpherson swinging over the Edinburgh rooftops in a state of significant inebriation.

That image was interrupted by a knock at the door.

Kane and Horse froze. Kane looked at the clock on the mantelpiece. Ten past six pm. It was around this time that the landlady, the Widow Thomson, did her rounds for the collection of the rent. Horse put his finger to his lips, then whispered: 'We'll just keep the bone-box shut, Mr K, and she'll get tired and move on.'

They waited in silence. Nothing. Then more knocking. More waiting. More silence. Then a wee piping voice:

'Mr Kine. Mr Kine - are you in there, sir?'

Horse frowned and looked at Kane. Kane relaxed: 'I suspect that I know this person - let him in, Mr Horse, let him in...'

Horse went into the hallway and opened the door. Standing at the door was a little red-headed lad aged around eleven. The boy noted Horse's broken nose. And gulped: 'Oh...oh...I'm sorry, sir. I was looking for a Mr Kine, the Advocate, sir. I should have known that he wouldnae live in a stair as manky as this....'

Horse stood there and said nothing. The boy turned on his heel. But before the lad could make his escape, Horse grabbed him by the scruff of his neck. The boy squealed: 'Don't kill me, sir. Don't kill me. I might dress posh, but these are my work breeks. I've nae money, sir, nae money....'

Horse lifted the boy up and started to carry the dangling lad into the sitting room.

'I've got *some* money, sir...*some* money...I've got a couple of farthings, but I'm saving up for my old age...'

Horse carried the boy into the sitting room where Edward Kane was sitting before the fire. Horse lifted the boy further up off his feet and presented him to Kane, as a cat might present to its owner a tiny, squirming mouse.

Kane peered at the boy's face for a moment, then: 'You can put him down, Mr Horse. I know this lad.'

The manservant lowered the messenger boy to the floor. The boy grabbed the bottom of the jacket he was wearing and pulled it down in an attempt to present a more business-like appearance. Kane smiled: 'Mr Horse, this is Master Timmy...I am not sure if I was ever made aware of his surname...'

The boy piped up: 'Timmy Thomas, sir, Timmy Thomas...'

Kane nodded: 'This is Master Timmy Thomas. Newly-appointed messenger boy for the firm of law agents, McAllister and McAdam.'

The boy gave a low bow. Kane continued: 'And Timmy, I think that you have already made the acquaintance of my man, Mr Horse...'

The boy, still in the low bow, could be heard to mutter: "Horse'? That man is as strong as an ox...'

Kane laughed: 'Now Master Timmy, how may I assist you?'

The boy stood up straight, cleared his throat, and then tried to remember his prepared address to the Advocate: 'Ahem. Mr Kine, the firm of McAllister and McAdam presents condiments...'

Horse looked at Kane. Kane smiled and looked at Horse, then spoke to the boy: 'I think that you mean present '*compliments*'...'

The boy nodded. A grave look on his face: 'Aye sir. That's it. Whatever that means. I've just got to say the thing - then give you this letter sir...' And with that, Timmy Thomas produced a (by now, somewhat crumpled) letter from his jacket and handed it to Kane. 'And I've got to wait for a reply.'

Kane took the letter and opened it. It was indeed from McAllister and McAdam and it did indeed present compliments. The letter invited Kane to accept instructions in a new matter and to consult the following forenoon at eleven o'clock at the lawyers' offices. Was that convenient?

Kane read the letter aloud and Mr Horse listened closely. Horse put his thumbs up: 'What did I say, Mr K? What did I say? Today's the day, sir. The tide is a-turning...'

The boy frowned, viewing Horse with some caution, perhaps fearing that Kane's Cockney manservant would lift him off his feet again.

Kane spoke: 'You may inform the law agents that I am delighted to undertake any task in furtherance of their instructions and I will attend at the appointed hour.'

The boy looked blank. Kane leaned forward in his chair: 'Tell your masters - the answer is 'yes'.'

The boy almost swooned with relief: 'I'll do that, sir. I'll do that. My sister will be so happy...'

'Your sister? The girl...'Rose'...who works in the cash room?'

Timmy nodded: 'That's her, sir. She said you would be good for the case. You see, sir, Mr McAdam didn't want you. He said he thought you were a bit of a drip...'

*****

Chapter Four

'A wee drop of milk, Mr Kane?'

Kane smiled and nodded: 'If that's no trouble.'

Sat there in the outer offices of McAllister and McAdam, at ten past eleven in the morning, Kane was being served tea by the elderly Mrs McAllister. She poured the milk from the jug, put the jug down, then lifted up a plate adorned with small biscuits: 'And a wee biscuit, Mr Kane. I cannae drink tea myself, unless I have a wee biscuit with it, sir.'

Kane took a biscuit, and a small bite: 'These have a very pleasing flavour, Mrs McAdam. Lavender isn't it?'

Mrs McAdam nodded: 'They were made by Wee Rosie in the cash room there. She made them, but it's *my* recipe, sir.'

'Then, they are a tribute to the art of collaboration, madam.' And he took another biscuit.

The lady smiled: 'And we gave her the lavender an' all, Mr Kane. We like to look after our people, sir. It's only Christian charity. And, as the Proverbs say, 'Charity begins at home'...'

Kane smiled and nodded. The old lady's reference was wrong. Not from Proverbs. But what was the point of correcting her? Kane's father was a Minister of the Church of Scotland, so the young Advocate knew his Bible. *'Charity Begins at home.' Definitely not Proverbs. Where was it again? St Paul, perhaps? One of the letters to Timothy?*

'...and she's nice lassie, Wee Rose. We like to treat her as family. It's just a husband she needs, sir, but, of course...well...'. Mrs McAdam shook her head '...my son should be back at any minute, Mr Kane'. The old lady's pensiveness was broken by the door of the room being swung open and the appearance of a very small barking dog.

The unexpected entrance of the creature immediately caused Kane to pull his knees in sharply. He covered the top of his teacup with one hand and the bottom of the saucer with his other.

Mrs McAdam laughed: 'You are not a lover of dogs, Mr Kane?'

Kane relaxed: 'I apologise, madam. I was startled for a moment. In fact, I love all animals.'

The animal sat down before Kane and cocked its head to one side. Kane noted that it was a mongrel. Brown and white. Sharp, pointy ears, and a very winning disposition. It looked up at Kane as if to say: Am I not unspeakably bonny?

Mrs McAdam scooped up the animal and began to ruffle its neck with her fingers. The old lady's lips made an 'oooh' shape as she cooed over the pup: 'Oooh, Dash - good boy - mummy's little darling...'

Dash? And then the door opened wide. There stood Murray McAdam, dressed in hat and coat. He saw his mother fussing over the dog. He looked over at Kane and rolled his eyes: 'Oh, Mr Kane - I see that you have met my mother's favourite son.' He turned to the lady, who was still fussing over the animal: 'Mother, mother - we have company...'

The old mother, immune to rebuke, was holding the animal face-to-face now. She gazed into its eyes. She puckered her lips and spoke: 'I know - but he is SO beautiful...'

McAdam shook his head: 'Mother - give that infernal creature to Rose and bring more tea to my room.'. He beckoned the young Advocate: 'Mr Kane, follow me, if you please.'

Kane made a small bow and left the old lady - who, by this point was encouraging the animal to lick her face.

***

Kane sat in McAdam's office. Piles of paper everywhere. Piles of paper on McAdam's oaken desk, piles of paper on the top of each cabinet and chest, piles of paper in various stacks on the floor.

The solicitor looked across the desk at Kane: 'As you'll see, Mr Kane, we do not lack for instructions in this firm. If all goes well with this case, then you can perhaps help us with a great number of others...'

What was it that Horse had predicted yesterday? '...some great big, juicy dripping roast of a case into your lap...'

McAdam continued: 'Now - and I do not mean to be impertinent, sir - but I trust that you can keep a secret?'

'Of course.'

McAdam sat back in his chair: 'You see, the matter at hand is...how may I describe it...a delicate one...and very near to the reputation of this office.'

Kane smiled and said nothing, waiting for the explanation to unravel at its own pace. McAdam rose from his chair and went to the window. He began searching through the piles of papers on the floor. 'I had a fair copy made of her statement. It's here somewhere. Ah! Here we are.'

The solicitor produced a bundle of papers from the pile and examined each page for a moment. Then he looked up at Kane: 'The case, perhaps unusually, involves both affairs of the heart and contractual matters. Are you confident of your abilities in these fields?

Kane smiled: "'Contractual matters', of course. However, regarding 'affairs of the heart', I fear I am likely to be as foolish as any other man.'

McAdam stared at Kane for a moment. Unsmiling. Then: 'Ah, I see. A humorous response. Well, I do not consider this to be a matter of levity, Mr Kane. Here....' and he handed Kane the papers.

Kane nodded, somewhat chastened, and took the papers. He attempted to diffuse the now tense atmosphere in the room. 'And will the client be joining us today, Mr McAdam?'

McAdam walked round and sat at his desk: 'She is already here. Read the papers, Mr Kane. Let me have your preliminary view.' McAdam pointed to a small bureau at the window. 'You may use the smaller desk.' He began to study a set of papers on his own desk. 'In the meantime, sir, there is much work to be done. I really must employ a clerk. Let me know when you have completed your perusal of the papers and we will discuss further at that point' And then McAdam seemed to vanish into the paperwork before him.

Kane walked across the room and sat down at the small desk. He reached into his briefcase, took out his notebook and pen and laid them in front of him. He took the sheaf of papers that McAdam had given him and began to read:

'My name is Rosemary Daisy Thomas. I am known as 'Rose' or 'Rosie'. I am 26 years of age. I am employed by Messrs McAllister and McAdam, Solicitors and Notaries, Edinburgh and I work in the Cash Room....'

Kane looked up from the papers. *Of course, this is the pretty girl in the cash room. Lovely sister of the errant Master Timmy...*

'I am an orphan. My mother, Violet Thomas, died in childbirth with my wee brother, Timothy. Timmy is now aged eleven. I have been asked to talk about my dealings with one Thomas Tack, Esquire. I am very embarrassed by the whole matter. I did not know that anyone could be so heartless.

*****

Chapter Five

'I first met Thomas Tack around six months ago. It was in The Meadows area, here in Edinburgh. Part of my employment is to take the dog for a walk. The dog belongs to Mrs Morag McAdam, the mother of my employer. Her dog is a little mongrel named 'Dash'. He can be very lively.'

Kane smiled. He read on:

'We were just getting to the Hope Park end when the dog 'Dash' ran off. I tried to catch him, but my skirts made that too hard. When I caught up, Dash had stopped at another dog and they were sniffing each other. The fellow with the other dog - he saw that I was chasing Dash to catch up - had taken a hold of Dash and was keeping Dash there until I got there.

'I thanked the gentleman and we had a very pleasant conversation. It turned out that he was also walking a dog, a poodle, for his own employer. The fellow's name was Thomas Tack. He was a Writing Clerk for the firm of lawyers, Fergusson and Fergusson. He said that his duties were mainly copying documents, visiting the tobacconist and walking the dog for his employer, 'Old Man Fergusson' (or 'The Old Tyrant', as Thomas later called him). The dog was a miniature poodle named 'Minnie' (I think that is short for 'Minerva' and not 'miniature'). Thomas was very poorly paid, but would do anything to retain that employment - otherwise he feared that he would find himself and his mother on the street.

'And after that day, Thomas Tack and I would meet every day, Monday to Friday, at the same spot at the same time. And the dogs loved each other. Dash and Minnie would run all around The Meadows, each other's best. And Thomas and I would just walk and talk. We talked about the fact that I was an orphan and had a difficult upbringing. And that, after my mother died, I had to bring up my brother Timmy since he was a baby. Thomas Tack was very understanding about that. For his own part, he was very solicitous of his own mother, who was an invalid and required to be conveyed in a bath-chair. We also talked about our dreams for the future. I was seeking a stable home for Timmy and me. Thomas Tack wanted to gain promotion and become a proper Articled Clerk, to raise a family and continue caring for his mother.

'And then, after a period of seeing each other almost every daily, our feelings grew. Thomas began to call me his 'spaniel.' He would hand me little notes that he had written while at work and addressed to me - 'To my own Spaniel' or 'Dearest Spaniel...' He would scribble little humorous sayings or poems and I would read them and laugh.

'And one day, Thomas looked serious as he passed me the note. I can see it in my mind's eye even now. I remember the headed notepaper, 'Fergusson and Fergusson'. And the note read: 'My Dearest Spaniel. I love you with all my heart. Would you do me the honour of being my wife. We shall build our own little dog house for Mama, Timmy and our own little puppies. With deepest love and affection. From your own Spaniel. Thomas.' I immediately accepted and - I am somewhat embarrassed to say - we embraced in public at that moment. Thomas promised that we would be married by Christmas. But then the problems began...'

Kane looked up from his papers. It made sense now what Master Timmy had said last night. Timmy's sister, Rose, the cash room girl, had been allowed to select Kane in this matter, because it was actually her case. And Rose Thomas had, no doubt, chosen Kane because of Kane's kindness towards Master Timmy.

His thoughts were interrupted by the voice of McAdam: 'Mr Kane - you are neither reading nor writing. Have you encountered a problem, sir?'

Kane turned round to face the solicitor: 'I am merely digesting the facts, Mr McAdam. I had no idea that the...the 'subject-matter' - if I may call it that - was likely to be so...so close to home, sir.'

McAdam took his pen and pointed it towards Kane's papers. 'She is a good girl, Rose. She is a good worker.

Reliable. Always trying to improve herself. Her mother died in childbirth, you know, giving birth to that half-wit brother of hers. Poor Rose has required to raise the boy ever since. Hence, her particular solicitude for the lad.'

'It is to her credit...'

'It was my mother's idea to take her on. As you have seen, Mother has a fondness for waifs and strays.' And with that, McAdam dipped his pen in the ink-well and started writing again, silent, and directing his attention exclusively to the papers before him.

Kane turned back to his own papers. He could hear Rose's voice in his head now:

'...the problems began. One day, around six weeks ago, Thomas did not appear at the appointed place. I waited with Dash for some forty minutes. I assumed that Thomas had been given some other, more urgent task and had been called away that day. This had happened on one or two occasions in the past, and so I thought little of it. I attended the following day at the same time and place, and again – no appearance from Thomas. After four such days, I wondered if my darling might have fallen ill, and so I sent a little note to the offices of Fergusson and Fergusson. The following day, I received the note back with a reply written on top of it [Reference is made to Pursuer's Production Number One]...'

At this point, Kane filed through his papers until he found the bundle marked 'Productions' and examined them. He found the note from Rose Thomas. The note, in

Rose's gentle hand, had now been cut through with a large swipe of red ink and, at the bottom, in large red letters had been scrawled: '*Kindly desist from further communication with Thomas Tack....*'

Kane raised his eyebrows, taken aback by the response. After the gentle narrative from the young lady, the red ink that scarred the paper seemed to sneer at any prospect of romance. His thoughts were interrupted again by McAdam: 'You have stopped reading again, Mr Kane. I wager that you have now come upon the red-ink response?'

Kane looked round again: 'Yes. There seems to be a certain brutality in the reply that I was not expecting, sir.' Kane held up the papers. 'This Thomas Tack, with his humorous sayings and poems, struck me as something of a sensitive soul - but his response here...'

McAdam shook his head and laughed: 'Oh, Mr Kane, Mr Kane. Can you not read between the lines here?' He nodded towards the papers: 'Young Thomas Tack had nothing to do with that response...'

*****

Chapter Six

'Oh, Mr K - what a load of old codswallop, sir'

Mr Horse, Kane's manservant, stood at the table, stirring the leaves in the teapot.

Edward Kane sat in his wing-back chair by the fire: 'I don't agree, Mr Horse. A promise is a promise...'

Horse took a cup and saucer from the larder and fetched the old tin cup for himself: 'So what you're telling me is this: a bloke takes his dog out, so that the mutt can 'water the flowers', if you take my meaning, and he comes back with a wife on his back?'

'Mr Horse, the matter is quite simple. There has been a breach of promise to marry here. Thomas Tack made a proposal of marriage. The young girl, Rose, accepted. Mr Tack has reneged on that proposal and so must face the consequences'

Horse poured the tea into the teacup: 'And what did the young madam have to say for herself, sir?'

Kane pursed his lips: 'I attempted to consult with her directly, but she quickly became upset. We got as far as the phrase 'Thomas had such beautiful penmanship', then she burst into floods of tears.'

Horse stood, shaking his head. Kane looked up: 'You can shake that head of yours all you like, Mr Horse, but a promise is a promise. And Mr Thomas Tack Esquire is in breach of that promise.'

Horse poured the tea into his tin mug: 'What is the world coming to, Mr K? When a man takes a dog out for a bone - and he comes back with a new rib...'

***

Despite the solicitor's reservations on the small nature of Kane's fee, the sum was enough to clear the outstanding rent on the set of furnished rooms and to 'feather the nest' (as Horse had it) for the following weeks. More paid work followed. The drafting of the Summons in the case now known as Miss Rosemary Daisy Thomas against Thomas Tack, Esq was complete and sent to the solicitors. Also, the firm of McAllister and McAdam threw Kane - what Horse described as - 'a few juicy bones'.

***

Kane was sitting in the Advocates Library biting the feathers on the top of his pen, when a voice whispered his name: 'Edward?'

Kane looked up. It was James Sim.

James Sim, Advocate - known to all as 'Jim Sim' was a popular figure at the Bar. Jim Sim had what could only be described as an infectious cheerfulness. A 'good egg', Jim Sim. Always pleasant, always fair.

'Jim - good morning. How are you?'

'In fine fettle, my friend, in fine fettle.' He nodded towards Parliament Hall: 'Do you have a few moments to spare, Edward?'

***

The great Parliament Hall was then - and is today - where Counsel of all vintage would walk up and down, dressed in wig and gown to discuss their cases. Sim got to the point.

'I've just polished off a set of Answers in a case, Edward. I believe it's one of yours. The one about the dogs...'

Kane smiled and then frowned: 'If the action has a dog as its focus, then I a fear that it is not one of mine, Jim.'

Jim Sim laughed: 'Apologies, Edward. The dogs were perhaps minor players in the drama where the principal *dramatis personae* were the two young lovers - a certain Miss Thomas versus a certain Mr Tack...'

Kane smiled: 'Of course, my Breach of Promise case....' He thought for a moment, then looked at Jim Sim: 'So, you have prepared a defence, Jim. And what precisely, pray, does that amorous - if faithless - lover, Mr Tack deny?'

'Oh, he denies nothing, Edward, nothing at all. In fact, my hand became quite cramped as I required to write the word 'Admitted' again and again.'

Kane stopped in his tracks: 'Then Thomas Tack will simply concede the case against him?'

Jim Sim laughed again: 'Oh, no Edward. Thomas Tack admits everything, but the case against him will never succeed.'

'But there will be evidence that he wrote a letter proposing marriage.'

'Yes?'

'On solicitors' headed notepaper, no less.'

Jim Sim smiled: 'Of course. And have you seen that letter for yourself, Edward?'

Kane thought for a moment, then: 'No. You're right, Jim. Now that I think of it, the letter was not among my papers. I suppose I was expecting...' Kane stood trying to process the situation: 'I take it, then, Jim, that you will strenuously deny that such a letter ever existed...'

Jim Sim interrupted him: 'Not in the least, Edward. As you will see from my Answers, both the letter and its contents are admitted...'

'Then I do not understand the basis of the defence, Jim.'

'Study the letter, Edward, study the letter...'

***

'What do you mean 'The dog ate the letter'?'

Edward Kane stood in the offices of McAllister and McAdam, jaw dropped. Murray McAdam, solicitor, looked somewhat chastened, was silent for a moment, then turned towards the main office and barked: 'Mother!'

Mrs Morag McAdam came into the room: 'Murray, son, whit a noise. Ye don't have to shout sae loud. I'm just in the next room.'

McAdam pointed towards Kane. 'Mother, Mr Kane would like to see the letter.'

'The letter?'

'The proposal, mother. From Thomas Tack. You remember. The letter in which Thomas Tack proposed marriage to Rosie. You know. The letter that is essential to her case.'

The old lady's face flushed. She turned toward Kane: 'The letter...the letter... was destroyed, sir.'

McAdam nodded and raised his eyebrows to encourage his mother to continue her narrative: 'And how, mother, did that valuable piece of evidence come to be no more?'

Mrs McAdam nodded towards a pile of papers in the corner of the room. 'You see that pile, Mr Kane? That pile is called 'the scrap pile'. It's just old bits of paper we can scribble on or we use to clean up. For example, when my wee dog Dash does his business in the office by mistake, we clean it up from paper. From the scrap pile. I was giving Dash a wee treat - some raw liver, sir - and I didnae want to stain the rug, so I took some paper from the scrap pile and put the liver on that. Dash ate the liver and the paper an' all.'

At that point, the solicitor McAdam went to the window. He put his fingers through the circular brass holdings at the bottom of the window frame and yanked the window open. Kane saw a brick on the window sill outside. The weight of the brick secured a large envelope. McAdam lifted up the brick with one hand, picked up the envelope with the other and brought it inside. He opened it. Kane detected the smell of rotting meat. McAdam placed his thumb and index finger together and produced a document, holding it up as he might hold a dead rat by the tail. Kane could see the printed heading 'Fergusson and Fergusson' at the top, and the ragged, chewed bottom.

McAdam held the item at arm's length and looked at Kane: 'As you will note, sir, the letter is now rotten. Rotten as the proposal itself...'

Chapter Seven

The White Hart Inn in the Grassmarket was crowded to bursting now. The din of a lively crowd on that happy voyage from a hard day's work to a lubricated oblivion. And at one of the tables sat Mr Horse and the Monkey Macpherson - a great number of now-empty glasses before them.

Horse got up: 'Well, my friend, time to hit the hay.'

Macpherson was struggling.

Horse laughed: 'I think, my friend, that you are well squiffed. Get your hat. I'll make sure you get home.'

Macpherson nodded: 'Aye, I'd better. I've got thone big windows tae clean in the morn. Frederick Street. And Old Man Fergusson is a right...a right...'

Horse stopped him: 'Fergusson? Fergusson the lawyer?'

The Monkey looked up with a bleary eye and nodded. Horse smiled: 'Then, my friend, you can do your old pal, Horse, a turn here...'

***

Jim Sim, Advocate, had to cover his face to stifle the laugh: 'Oh, Edward, Edward...the dog ate the letter? Priceless!'

Sim and Edward Kane were promenading up and down Parliament Hall again, discussing the case. Despite his predicament, Kane had to laugh: 'I fear, Jim, that should I produce the document, it will be readily recognisable on account of the vultures circling around it.

They laughed again. Then Jim Sim - always amenable - said: 'Well, it's never been denied that the letter was written by Thomas Tack. In any event, I have instructed that Fergusson and Fergusson should lodge an example of their headed notepaper.'

Kane raised his eyebrows: 'That's very decent of you, Jim...'

'However,' Sim continued, 'I assume that you will lodge the other letter - the one with the great red-ink scrawl warning off the fair Rosemary?'

Kane nodded: 'I confess that I found it surprising that a sensitive soul like Thomas Tack could bring himself to pen such a brutal missive.'

Jim Sim stopped: 'Oh, Edward, wake up, my friend. The poor penmanship alone in the red ink should tell you that this was not the work of Thomas Tack.'

'Then....?'

Jim Sim laughed: 'Tack's employer - Old Man Fergusson - the old man's paw-prints are all over this mess. Saints preserve us from dog-lovers...'

Kane stopped to consider this. Jim Sim put his hand on Kane's arm. Deadly serious now: 'Edward...Edward, please don't think me impertinent...'

Kane knotted his eyebrows: 'Yes...?'

'... and I say this respectfully - don't you see what this case is really about?'

Kane was puzzled. The friends stood in silence for a time.

***

Frederick Street. Outside the offices of Messrs Fergusson and Fergusson.

'There's an awful lot of windaes - I'll take the front, son, and you can make a start on the back.'

Armed with buckets, rags, ladders, and a tiny, nine year-old boy - to deal with any work that entailed crawling up a chimney - 'the Monkey' Macpherson stood outside the offices of Fergusson and Fergusson, assessing the scale of the work before him.

'But go inside first and see if there's a 'Mr Tack' aboot...'

***

When Edward Kane checked his work box that morning, he noted that a bundle of papers had been placed there. It was the Inventory of Productions Jim Sim had promised. Kane untied the pink ribbon. The first item was, as promised, a blank sheet of headed notepaper bearing the heading 'Fergusson and Fergusson'. *Good old Jim Sim - always true to his word.* Kane paid this formal production scant attention, since there were other, more puzzling items in that bundle of productions. A neat and carefully scribed copy of what appeared to be some old Parish records - mostly Baptisms and Deaths - easily a decade old. Kane shook his head. And all in Latin, to boot. And why the names of flowers? Is that 'hyacinth'?

***

Nine year-old boys are not generally held out as the example of as assiduous time-keeping. This concept was not lost on Monkey Macpherson. But that lad had been in the office area now for a good five minutes or so - and no sign of him - or Thomas Tack, for that matter. The Monkey decided to take a chance and leave his cleaning paraphernalia inside the front entrance, while he investigated the missing assistant. Now, the Monkey MacPherson was not a man given to shock, but it must be recorded that he did feel a great measure of surprise when the first thing that witnessed in that office was an elderly gentleman pick up a small dog with both hands and hurl the poor creature in the direction of a young clerk writing at a nearby desk. The dog hit its target, and the clerk seemed stunned for a moment, but then placed the animal gently down onto the floor. And then the clerk resumed his copying of letters. The old man, seething, yelled a single word: 'Despoiled!' and left the room. The little dog limped over to a large wicker basket in the middle of the office. The Monkey peered over and saw that the basket contained...

***

'...puppies?'

'Yes, Mr K - that's what the Monkey seen, sir. A basket full of puppies. Five of them, he says'

Edward Kane, stood there processing the news: 'Breed?'

Horse continued: 'He says he don't know, Mr K. And when it comes to dogs, sir, the Monkey knows his onions. A mix breed, he says. But 'beautiful', he says. Beautiful little mongrels they are...'

***

McAdam slammed the papers down on to his desk: 'And what in the blue blazes is this about?'

Kane was again sitting in the offices of McAdam and McArthur, knees together, holding the cup and saucer and weathering the storm. He motioned to the discarded papers on the table. 'It's a diversionary tactic, Mr McAdam. The other side say that there is something legally wrong with our case, and so they wish to debate it before a judge.'

McAdam sat back in his chair: 'This is Old Man Fergusson being…Old Man Fergusson. The chap is insufferable. I have told him so to his face. This is just probably…I don't know…'

Kane studied McAdam's face. For the first time since they had met, Kane noted that McAdam looked nervous. The young Advocate continued: 'Well, I have re-read all of the papers in this case, Mr McAdam. I have drafted the standard Summons. I am confident that our case has been pled in a competent and relevant matter.' He pointed to the discarded papers on the table: 'This motion is a mystery to me. Unless, of course, there is something that you are not telling me, Mr McAdam.'

The solicitor sat silent and brooding. Then: 'Don't be ridiculous, Mr Kane ...'

*****

Chapter Eight

'Liver and onions alright, Mr K?'

Later that night Kane was sitting in his less than salubrious rented rooms in Edinburgh's Old Town, crouching over the dining table that served as his makeshift study.

He leaned back in his chair and stretched: 'That would be a welcome distraction from the mysteries of this case, Mr Horse.'

Horse placed a large frying pan on the metal frame on the fire. He put a slab of lard in the centre of the pan and watched as it melted and started to sizzle: 'You still working on that marriage and mutt malarkey, sir?'

'If you are referring to the case of 'Rose Daisy Thomas versus Thomas Tack Esquire', then you are perfectly correct, Mr Horse.'

Horse stirred the pan with a wooden spoon, spreading the melted lard around the edges. 'Begging your pardon, Mr K, but I thought you said that the spaniel case weren't coming to court for a good few months, sir.'

Kane nodded and held up the sheaf of papers: 'Ordinarily, yes. But my opponent, Jim Sim, has lodged this bundle of papers and I can't for the life of me work out why. He claims that there is something wrong with our case...'

Horse stirred: 'Of course, there's something wrong with your case, sir - a bloke sends the young girl a bit of a flirtation, and he ends up handcuffed, and halfway down the aisle with a mother-in-law in tow. Bloomin' liberty, if you ask me...'

Kane shook his head: 'I venture, Mr Horse, that you are employing your own perspective and - perhaps - your own experience here in what a clear beach of promise in this case.'

Horse murmured to himself and kept on stirring.

Kane pressed on: 'And - for the avoidance of doubt here - there would be no acquisition of a mother-in-law by the groom. That poor lady, Rose's mother - Violet Thomas – expired on the birth of her child, Timmy Thomas, and the fragrant Rose has required to be the boy's 'little mother' ever since.'

More murmuring. More stirring. Kane stared at the papers: 'Jim Sim is an entirely agreeable fellow, but he is no fool. He claims that there is something wrong- *legally* wrong - with our case and he wishes to debate that before a judge. But, what any defect might be...'

Horse took a large knife from his waistband and scraped some onions from a wooden chopping board into the frying pan. He put down the knife and the chopping board and began to wipe his hands on a ragged old cloth: 'So, what is it that's in them papers that's causing you so much grief, Mr K?'

Kane sat back in his chair: 'That's the problem, Horse. I can't find anything of any moment here. The answer must be in these old parish records somewhere. But of what relevance they could be to a case that has been raised over a decade later? I am flummoxed.'

Horse put down the dish-cloth and motioned over: 'Can I have a swatch, sir?'

Kane proffered the papers: 'Be my guest, Mr Horse.' He laughed: 'But be careful the papers don't end up in the liver and onions there. We have already lost one essential production to a culinary fate.'

Horse took the papers and began to read. He screwed up his eyes and followed the text by moving his finger down the page. Kane saw Horse's lips move as he read. Horse looked up: 'Well, it's all Greek to me, sir...'

'More precisely, Latin, Mr Horse. Parish records. Apparently, a certain 'Father Patrick Flanagan' preferred to make certain entries not in the Queen's English, but the dead language of Vergil and Cicero.'

'And how are you meant to read all this, Mr K?'

Kane smiled: 'With difficulty, Horse. With great difficulty.'

'But if it's the church record, all wrote in Latin, then you'll need to get a priest to read it, eh sir?'

Kane nodded: 'My thoughts exactly, Mr Horse. Fortunately, we have some months before the hearing itself, so I am confident that we will be able to find that particular man of the cloth and interpret these Classical runes.'

Horse pointed at the papers: 'It's something about bells and flowers by the looks of it. But this one here - why is there no writing on the first page, sir?'

Kane smiled. 'That was at my request. No need to interpret that. That is an example of the headed notepaper where Thomas Tack was employed. It's the office whence he wrote the letter. It is a standard type of lawyer stationery, containing details of their address and the like.'

Horse ran his finger across the type as he read aloud: 'Fergusson and Fergusson, Frederick Street, Edinburgh…'

'That sort of thing, Horse. A formal production at best, requested by me. It simply confirms the address of Thomas Tack's employer. But it does add credence to the account of Rosemary Thomas.'

Horse read on, moving down, following the type with his finger and mouthing the words as he looked at the small printing at the bottom of the letter.

Kane continued: 'Of course, the original letter with the written proposal has been partially destroyed, eaten away by a hungry 'mutt' - as you would have it.'

Horse nodded, said nothing and stared at the paper. Silence. No sound but the sizzling of the onions.

Kane nodded over to the fire. 'Mr Horse, may I suggest that own offices would be better employed by immediate attention to our supper? Bound to say, I'm starving.'

Horse, deep in the papers in one hand, almost without looking, turned to the fireplace and with his other hand lifted the sizzling pan from the fire and lowered it carefully on to the grate on the floor.

Kane raise his eyebrows: 'Horse, I did not mean for your interest in this case to distract you from your usual duties...'

Horse cut across him: 'Mr K - you says that the boy Tack proposed to the girl Rose with one of these letters...'

'Yes.'

'Identical to this one.'

'In every way, Horse. That is why a sample has been lodged. It is, I confess, the mainstay of our case.'

'And you've read this letter?'

Kane motioned over: 'Not that one. That one is completely blank. Look at it - no writing, Mr Horse. It was the other...'

Horse interrupted again and pointed to the page: 'But it's got writing, sir. It's got 'Fergusson and Fergusson' and the like.'

Kane resisted the temptation to sigh. He started to explain more carefully now, as if to a child: 'The printed writing on the headed paper merely gives the name and address of the firm, as you can see, Mr Horse. It confirms...'

'But what about the other bit?'

What 'other bit'?'

Horse moved his finger along the bottom of the page. 'The bit what says: 'Nothing in this comm...commun...'

"Communication'?'

Horse read on: "Nothing in this ...com...munication shall be con...construed as constitu...constituting a contract...'?'

Despite the promise of liver and onions for supper, Edward Kane, Advocate experienced a sudden loss of appetite. He motioned over to the letter: 'Could I...could I see the letter again, please...'

*****

Chapter Nine

Any experienced Court practitioner will tell you this: Only one thing is certain in Court. Nothing is certain in Court...

In the courtroom, Kane and Jim Sim were sitting waiting for the legal debate, attired as usual in horse-hair wig, black gown and white bow tie. Jim Sim whispered over: 'I say, Edward, this pen is provoking awfully leaky - I don't suppose you have a spare one there, chum?'

Kane produced a fresh pen and handed it over to Sim. 'Many thanks.'

They sat and waited for the judge to arrive. Sim whispered again: 'I take it Edward, having seen the papers, you now understand why we are here.'

Kane nodded: 'It was the letter, wasn't it. The legal disclaimer.'

Jim Sim smiled: 'That's the one. Nothing promised in the letter has any legal effect. It says so. Explicitly at the bottom. I confess I was surprised that you didn't notice it.'

Kane had to laugh: 'Possibly because a certain animal had scoffed a good part of the letter for its dinner...'

Sim covered his mouth to stifle the laugh. Kane, too, was overtaken with the absurdity of his position. Arguing a hopeless case. Where a dog had eaten the evidence.

'Court rise!' The Macer entered the Court, the ceremonial mace slung over his shoulder. The judge shuffled on, bowed, and sat down. Everyone in court mirrored the bow and then sat down.

Jim Sim got to his feet: 'My lord, may I mention the case: 'Rosemary Daisy Thomas versus Thomas Tack..."

Kane looked up at the bench. Lord Lambert. Ah! This put a different complexion on matters. Andrew Lambert - 'Liquid Lambert' had been a widely-respected Counsel in his day. He possessed that rare gift of reaching into the body of a case and seizing its beating heart. His legal understanding was lightning quick, but, as with many gifted people, this meant that he could be impatient with others who were slower on the uptake...

Jim Sim continued: 'My lord, to start at the beginning...'

Lambert – eyes tight shut – interrupted him immediately: 'No, Mr Sim, this is my Court - today, we'll start at the end. I've read the papers. What is your final submission?'

This unexpected interjection unbalanced Jim Sim, who now stood silent.

Now, while Lord Lambert's impatient demeanour was, perhaps, sometimes justified, the old judge had other faults that were not so easily excused. For one, he did enjoy his brandy of an evening. Copious amounts of it. This, of itself, was not an issue, but the after-effects could be problematic the following morning. On those days, the demeanour of the judge could be construed as less than forgiving. Supplies of magnesia and peppermint water were kept in Lambert's chambers to combat such indisposition. And where those remedies failed - there was always more brandy.

Jim Sim ploughed on. The judge growled: 'Be assured, I have your submission, sir. Your client - an idiot by the sound of it - writes a letter and proposes to an innocent young lady. She accepts the proposal. And now that same idiot claims that there was no proposal because the letter in question says that nothing written there can be deemed a proposal.' He leaned forward and glared at Sim: 'Do I have you correctly?'

Jim Sim nodded. Liquid Lambert, one hand nursing his throbbing temple, was ferocious now: 'Sit down, Mr Sim. Your point here is that some nicety of the law should protect this young blackguard...'

Jim Sim stood his ground: 'With the greatest of respect, my lord, the letter gives a clear indication...'

Lambert barked: 'The only 'clear indication' here is that this young philanderer is attempting to hide behind the law, and he is using a firm of law agents to assist him in the process. This is a disgrace, sir. Do his employers know that they are harbouring a lothario?'

'They are fully supportive of his defence, my lord.'

Liquid Lambert had his head in both hands now. The magnesia and peppermint were wearing off. He turned to Kane's papers. He studied the Summons for a good three minutes. Silence. Then, with all the warmth of a storm cloud, he looked down at Sim: 'Have you read the Summons, Mr Sim?'

'Of course, my lord'

The judge was icy: 'Turn to Article Three of Condescendence...'

Jim Sim turned to Article Three.

Weary now: 'And, unless I am in sudden need of eyeglasses, the Article contains the words: '...did by the said communication written at his employers' offices *and* by subsequent conversation propose marriage to the Pursuer...''

'Yes, my lord...'

The old judge smiled, but there was no warmth in his eyes: 'Then - Mr Sim - presumably, you know what the word 'and' means, don't you?'

Sim was struggling.

The old judge continued: 'It *means* that your opponent here...'. The judge nodded down towards Kane '...is likely to lead evidence over and above the letter to prove his case.' The same crocodile smile. He looked down at Kane now: 'Isn't that right, Mr...Mr...'

Kane bobbed up: 'Kane, my lord, Edward Kane. Yes, that is correct...'

The old judge eased back in his chair: 'And there we have it.' He addressed Sim: 'Sometimes, sir, a lady requires to 'shake the tree so that the fruit will fall', as it were. That is commonly understood. Now, when is the evidential hearing in this matter?'

Kane was still on his feet: 'It is some three months hence, my lord.'

Liquid Lambert rubbed his troublesome temples: 'Three months? Three months??? Pish-posh! A child could decide this matter in three minutes. What about three days, sir? We can have the hearing in three days.'

The judge looked down at the Clerk of Court. The Clerk looked up and nodded. Liquid Lambert smiled: 'Then it is decided - proof hearing three days hence. Should occupy all of an hour. Get this nonsense off the Rolls.'

Jim Sim spluttered: 'But my lord, no witnesses have been cited to appear...'

The judge sighed: 'As I understand, there are only four witnesses here. A Rogue Romeo, a Jilted Juliet and two dogs. I shall ordain them to appear. The lovers, I mean. Not the dogs. Can't bear dogs. Slobbery animals...'

*****

Chapter Ten

'So - you live to fight another day, then Mr K.'

Kane sat in his wing-chair before the fire, sipping his tea: 'Heavens be praised, yes, but that other day is precisely three days hence. No doubt about it - his lordship was being pursued relentlessly by the Blue Devils this morning.'

Master and man laughed. Horse drank from his own battered tin mug: 'I suppose that gives you a couple of days, sir, to find that priest – 'Father Flanagan' - the one what wrote all the Latin.'

'Oh, the Latin is their problem now, Mr Horse. It is for them to find a translator, not us.'

Horse was silent for a moment, then: 'What church was it again, sir?'

Kane looked at the papers: 'Chapel of St Mary's.'

'That'll be the one off Queen's Street, sir.'

Kane raised his eyebrows that Mr Horse should know this so readily. Horse grinned: 'That's where my little friend Bridget – the barmaid at the White Hart – that's where she puts on her scarf of a Sunday.'

Horse got up and took Kane's cup and saucer: 'But you do look done in, Mr K. Time to hit the hay, sir.'

'I confess that I am somewhat drained by the events of the day...'

'Well, tomorrow is another day, sir.'

Kane, stiff, got up from his chair: 'Indeed it is, Mr Horse, indeed it is. And tomorrow, I will pay another visit to McAdam and MacArthur and attempt to speak again to the fragrant Rose.'

'And I'm going to church, sir.'

'Church???'

'St Mary's. See if I can't find Flanagan. I got a feeling, sir…'

Kane laughed: 'Be careful, Mr Horse. Don't find yourself in one of those confessional boxes. Knowing you, it may be some time before you are released...'

***

But the following morning, when Kane climbed the stairs and arrived at the solicitors' offices, he found the doors shut. A note was pinned to the door: 'Due to the Indisposition of a Family Member these Offices will be closed until Tomorrow.'

***

'Can I help you, my son?'

Mr Horse had waited until Mass had finished and the worshippers had streamed out of the front entrance of St Mary's Chapel. This took some time, since a great many of the parishioners - all women - had congregated at the front, chatting to each other as they waited for 'Father Pat'. One elderly lady was holding a plate covered by a dishrag, obviously the gift of cake for the parish priest, Father Patrick Flanagan.

Horse shook his head: *What is it about women and priests?*

And then the good Father emerged. But this was not what Horse was expecting. Tall, handsome - and all of twenty-four! Horse sighed to himself: *This here devil-dodger was probably still at school when those parish entries were made.*

After an age, and after the young Father had granted benediction to his throng of admirers, the priest noticed that Horse had been waiting patiently.

The young Father spoke with a gentle Irish brogue: 'Can I help you, my son?'

'I was looking for Father Flanagan...'

'I am Father Flanagan.'

'Yes, but, eh, Father Patrick Flanagan.'

'I am Father Patrick Flanagan'

'The one what writes all the Latin and the like.'

The young priest smiled: 'Ah - that would be *Old* Father Flanagan...'

'Is he still about?'

'Old Father Flanagan died these seven years ago.'

Horse looked crestfallen. Seeing this, the young priest laid his hand on Horse's shoulder: 'But the Church that he served is eternal. What is it that ails you, sir?'

'I got some Latin what the old Father wrote in the parish register and I need to get it..get it...' Horse searched for the word.

'Translated?'

'That's it - 'translated'.'

Flanagan smiled: 'That will not be a problem, Mr...Mr?

''Horse'. They calls me 'Horse'.'

Young Father Flanagan held out his hand: 'Just give the document to me, Mr Horse, and I will be happy to translate it for you.'

And then it struck Horse at that moment that he had brought no such document with him.

The young priest interpreted Horse's silence and noted that his visitor was empty-handed: 'Ah - you have forgotten it....'

'Just some old papers. I can run up and get them, sir.'

'I'm afraid that I have other, pressing duties to attend to today, Mr Horse. Perhaps another time? Sunday? After Mass? Would that suit?'

'I would need it by tomorrow night, sir.'

'Then what about tomorrow evening? I will be carrying out my home visits, in any event. Nine o'clock? Would that suit?'

Horse nodded, still feeling somewhat remiss.

The young priest gave a gentle smile: 'And don't vex yourself that you forgot those papers. Remember: *Errare Humanum Est...*'

Horse looked blank.

''To err is human', Mr Horse, to err is human...'

***

'I confess, Edward, that I was tempted to go straight home and have a stiff drink myself...'

Jim Sim and Edward Kane were walking up and down Parliament Hall, revisiting Sim's recent roasting by the old judge, 'Liquid' Lambert.

Kane laughed: 'I did wonder if there was a medicinal cure for being savaged by a lubricated Senator?'

Sim smiled: 'There is indeed: reclining in a dark room, applying a cold compress - and issuing an enormous fee-note!' They laughed. 'My instructing solicitor, Old Man Fergusson, in any event, seems to enjoy being in a state of near apoplexy the majority of the time, so I thought that I would help him along with a substantial fee of several guineas.'

The friends laughed and walked on again for a moment, then Kane asked: 'Jim - what is this case actually about?'

Sim smiled: 'You tell me, Edward your lady is the Pursuer here...'

'No, no, I mean. The whole sorry affair. The withdrawal of Thomas Tack. The awful letter scrawled with red ink and the like....'

'You will have gathered by now, Edward, that the red letter was, in fact, written by Old Man Fergusson.'

Kane frowned: 'But why should Fergusson take the slightest interest in the romantic affairs of a lowly writing clerk. It makes no sense.'

Sim nodded: 'It makes sense, Edward, when you understand that the old man does not approve of mixing the thoroughbred with the mongrel...'

Kane blinked in surprise: 'Jim! I am shocked at the sheer indelicacy here. Young Rosemary Daisy might be an orphan, but...'

Sim held up his hand: 'The dogs, Edward. The dogs. It transpires that Rosemary Thomas and Thomas Tack were not the only lovers at play here.'

Kane stood and processed this while Sim continued: 'And if you seek proof of any amorous - if canine - congress here, Edward, then would I invite you to attend at the offices of Fergusson and Fergusson and see for yourself a hearty litter of five young pups. Apparently an unusual cross-breed - half-miniature poodle, half-mongrel. So, how do you think that came about, my friend?'

Kane thought for a moment, then: 'So this whole bad feeling has nothing to do with Rosemary Daisy Thomas or Thomas Tack...'

'The historic animosity between my agent, Old Man Fergusson, and your own solicitor has not helped, Edward. The issue relates to pure breeding.'

Sim placed his hand on Kane's arm: 'In any event, study the church papers, Edward. It will soon become clear that your lady, the fragrant Rose, will not survive cross-examination in the matter. Indeed, you may find something of a mongrel in your own basket...'

Chapter Eleven

'Disappeared.'

'Disappeared???'

Edward Kane, Advocate stood, hat in hand, in the offices of MacArthur and McAdam.

The solicitor McAdam glowered behind his desk: 'We only learned this morning, Mr Kane. You'll recall that the office was closed yesterday, sir - bad oysters on my part, I'm afraid. And then Rose simply did not arrive for work this morning. Sent word to her lodgings. Cleared out. All of her belongings - gone.'

'And what of her brother, Timmy?'

'No sign. Vanished without a trace. The two of them.'

'But, Mr McAdam, the hearing is tomorrow...'

Kane now realised that he could hear the sound of sobbing from the adjoining room. McAdam nodded towards the door: 'That's mother. She is inconsolable. She treated that girl like the daughter she never had - and this is how she re-pays us. It all started after the other side lodged all of that foreign mumbo-jumbo...'

Kane looked into the other room and saw old Mrs McAdam sobbing, her face buried in the dog on her lap.

Kane frowned: 'Then, the case...the case tomorrow...'

'Speak to the chap on the other side...what was his name...'

'James Sim.'

'Yes. He seemed reasonable. Tell him that we will not proceed with our case if they do not insist on the expenses. That blasted girl has had enough of our charity for one lifetime...'

Kane ventured that the problem might not be Jim Sim - it might be the truculent old solicitor, Thomas Tack's employer, Old Man Ferguson.

McAdam looked up: 'Tell him that we accept that Old Fergusson has won this round. That might shut the old man up...'

***

'Look at that snow, Mr K. Wouldn't like to be out on a night like this I tell you. Good job we got them old windurs sorted eh?'

Mr Horse was standing at the window, looking out at the swirling snowstorm in the streets below. Kane gave a feeble nod in response. Horse looked round: 'Ah, but you looks mighty weary, Mr K...'

'You know, Mr Horse, I often wonder that I do not wake up in the mornings with a shock of pure white hair.'

Horse pointed to the kettle on the fire: 'A nice cuppa tea, sir, that's what you need. A nice, strong, cuppa tea...'

The kettle had been placed on the fire. And master and man waited for the kettle to peep. But at that point the silence was broken by a gentle knock on the door. Kane looked up. Horse looked at the mantel clock: eight-fifteen. 'Well, if that's the priest, sir, he's early. I'll just get my knife, Mr K, in case...'

First, Horse wrapped his hand around an old cloth and took the kettle off the fire. Then he picked up his long-bladed kitchen knife, tucked it into his belt and went to answer the front door. Then Kane heard a soft, lilting Irish accent. An umbrella being shaken. In came Horse, followed by a tall young gentleman in a sodden overcoat and wearing a clerical collar: 'Mr Kane, this is Father Flanagan...'

Kane rose from the table and extended his hand: 'How do you do, Father.'

'Mr Kane, I presume. I should first of all apologise for being early. I was nearby and caught in this inclement weather...'

Kane smiled: 'No apology required, Father. But I am afraid that the need for your attendance has been somewhat overtaken by recent events...'

The priest looked disappointed as Kane continued: '...you see, the case - the one in which we required the translation - will not be proceeding tomorrow due to circumstances beyond our control.'

Kane noted now that the priest's disappointed face was, in reality, looking beyond him – through the window and out into the storm outside.

The young priest smiled: 'You'll forgive me for feeling a bit like Mary and Joseph when they were told: 'There's no room at the inn…"

Kane laughed: 'Forgive me, father. Let's take that wet coat from you and pour you a nice, strong cup of tea.'

***

Fifteen minutes later, Kane, Horse and Father Flanagan were sitting around the fire, enjoying hot tea and toast with the priest drying his sodden coat on the fireguard. Kane sipped from his teacup: 'Well, I apologise again, Father...'

'Believe me, your home is a welcome refuge on a wild night like this.' The priest finished his tea. 'But I wonder, could I have a quick look at that parish register? It would be a nice memory of the auld fella.'

Kane got up, retrieved the court papers and handed them over to the priest. Young Flanagan looked puzzled: 'Well, I regret to say - this is not in my uncle's handwriting. Far too neat!'

Kane explained that these had been copied from the originals by a professional copyist. The priest read through the papers and smiled: 'Ah! It does indeed *sound* like the old man, now that I read them. It was his practice to record - how shall I say it - the more *problematic* entries in the sacred tongue. Keep them away from prying eyes.'

Kane nodded over to Mr Horse: 'My man Horse here thought that there might be some flowers in there somewhere.'

The priest nodded: 'Very perceptive of you, Mr Horse. Herbs and flowers. The Old Father loved his garden, that's for sure. So, you are right...'

Horse smiled.

'...and wrong.'

Horse frowned.

The priest continued: 'Certainly, at first blush, they may look like flowers, but some are, in fact, the proper names of the various parishioners. Look: 'Marigold O'Hara'. - 'Marigold' is not a flower here, but a good old Catholic name.'

Kane sat back in his chair: 'Well, father, in our case, I suppose we should find a 'Rosemary Daisy' Thomas and, as I recall it, her mother's name was 'Violet', but I don't see...'

The priest pointed to the page: 'No, sir. 'Violet' is here alright. Here. 'Hyacinthum' - that's the Latin name for 'Violet'. This is the entry for her death here.'

Kane nodded: 'Yes - she died in childbirth...'

Young Father Flanagan studied the page and shook his head: 'Not according to this, sir. It says here that the cause of death was '*a viride languorem*' - a 'Green Sickness'...'

Kane frowned: 'What about the birth of Timmy Thomas?'

The priest looked at the papers again. He ran his finger down the page. He smiled and looked up: 'Ah! Found it. Birth entry – but no related death of mother. A boy child: 'Nomine Timothus Thoma'. And the boy was born...the day *after* the death Violet Thomas.'

Kane shrugged: 'But that is not possible...'

There was silence in the room for a moment. It was broken by Horse; 'So, if the woman 'Violet' is dead before the boy Timmy is born – who is the boy's mother?'

Father Flanagan ran his finger across the page: 'Yes, that would be – hah! The herb and flower: 'Aposplenos' and 'Bellis Perennis..."

The priest smiled and looked up - to be confronted by two puzzled faces: 'Of course those are the Latin names. It would appear that the person who gave birth to the boy Timothy, was a lady with the Christian names... 'Rosemary…Daisy'...'

*****

Chapter Twelve

'Of course I knew that, sir. Do you take me for a fool?'

Parliament House. As Kane was getting dressed for court that morning, it struck him that one definition of the word 'futility' might be: a court hearing that was not going to happen before a judge who did not want to hear it.

The solicitor, McAdam continued to bellow: 'I do not see how this…this purported discovery is important to the case...'

Kane took a deep breath: 'That a gentleman should be induced to propose to a woman who has a secret - and illegitimate - eleven year-old son, Mr McAdam, I would think is obvious...'

'Oh – stuff and nonsense!' McAdam seemed to get redder and redder: 'Just get us out of this confounded mess. The case is dead. Just see if you can avoid being landed with the expenses, sir. We've invested enough in that girl.'

And now Kane was aware that someone was motioning over to him. Jim Sim, still dressed in street attire, was waving his silver-topped cane to attract Kane's attention. Kane walked over and joined Jim Sim at the fireplace. Sim was smiling, but held up his hands: 'Edward - do not be mistaken - I may be smiling, but I am not gloating...'

'I appreciate that, Jim.'

'I understand that your Rose has withered on the vine. Sorry, chum, but I did try to warn you about those old church papers. Now, Edward, I take it that you will be conceding the expenses of the case?'

Kane shook his head: 'I'm afraid not.'

Sim raised his eyebrows: 'A novel approach. You raise a case doomed to failure – and you expect the other side to bear the costs? You do remember that it's Lord Lambert today?' Kane gave a rueful nod. Sim shook his head and left to get gowned up.

Kane stood before the fire for a moment, looking around the crowded Parliament Hall. Busy today. Other Advocates walking up and down the great Hall in pairs, discussing their cases, proposing resolutions. *No resolution for Rosemary Daisy Thomas here. I wonder what will happen to her? And the hapless Timmy...*

Across the great Hall, sobbing into her mongrel again, sat old Mrs McAdam. Kane walked over. 'Mrs McAdam?'

The old lady looked up: 'Oh, Mr Kane, the pity of it...' and immediately burst into tears again.

Kane spoke gently: 'I suppose that this whole thing must have come as something of a shock to you, madam.'

Mrs McAdam dabbed her eyes: 'Oh, no, Mr Kane, we knew about it all along. I knew about Rose's mother, Violet. She was a good woman, but weak. After her husband died, she required to take in lodgers. Some of those men were of abandoned character. And one night, one of them crept into Rose's room and...and...'. The old lady burst into tears again.

Kane nodded: 'I see...'

'It wasn't Rose's fault. She was a child of fifteen. They planned to pass off the child as Violet's child. But then Violet got sick. She died on the Monday. Rose told no-one and delivered the child - on her own - on the Tuesday. She told people that her mother had died giving birth.'

'But she must have told the priest, Old Father Flanagan the truth.'

'Oh, Mr Kane - Rose is a good girl. A good Catholic. She would never lie to a priest, sir.'

Kane experienced an odd tightness in his chest and he realised that he was suddenly feeling heart-sorry for young Rosemary Daisy. A child requiring to give birth to another child. And alone. Mrs McAdam continued: 'And that is why you are so solicitous of her, madam.'

The old lady looked away: 'I never had a daughter, Mr Kane.'

And then a shout from above as Kane's case was called: 'Rosemary Daisy Thomas versus Thomas Tack.'

***

'Lord Lambert is *not* happy…'

His Lordship's Clerk was speaking to Kane and Sim in the courtroom. He had been instructed to conduct a preliminary 'chat' with both Counsel. Apparently, his Lordship was feeling somewhat 'indisposed' this morning and wished his time on the bench to be as brief as possible.

'And so, Mr Kane, his lordship assumes that you will not be disputing the expenses here, Mr Kane.'

Kane looked at his feet: 'I'm afraid I have my instructions.'

The Clerk considered this for a moment, then: 'So you wish me to inform his Lordship that you are not proceeding with your case and you wish to argue that you should not bear any of the *considerable* expense incurred by the other side?'

Kane nodded. The Clerk was silent, then volunteered: 'Did I mention, Mr Kane, that this morning, his lordship asked why there was a gang of workmen in the room using sledgehammers - and I required to inform his lordship that the sound so vexing him was, in fact, the ticking of the mantel clock?'

Kane said nothing. The Clerk strode away.

Enter the Macer, ceremonial mace over his shoulder. Then, Lord Lambert shuffling across the floor. The old judge bowed - and immediately clutched his temples with both hands, as if to stop his head from falling off. And then he sat - or to be more precise - collapsed into his chair. All present bowed in return and sat down. The old judge's eyes were closed. He said nothing. To all intents and purposes he might have been asleep. But far from it. One eye began to open. And then the other. The total effect reminded Kane of a lizard on a hot rock. The judge, as if blinded by daylight, peered around as if to identify where he was at that moment. And then he looked down at Counsel. The lizard's tongue licked its parched, malevolent lips: 'Mr Kane?'

The Advocate stood up. But before Kane could open his mouth, the courtroom was filled with an almighty clattering. The sheer volume made the judge throw himself back into his chair and clutch his temples. And then, emerging from nowhere, two small dogs appeared and began running around in circles, round and round the clerk's table. Yapping and yelping (loud) and barking (louder), the sound of the nails of their paws scrabbling as they scratched across the wooden floors.

The old judge - in an act of uncommon speed, given his fragile condition - jumped out of his chair and made for the door. Followed off by the Clerk, who was running now, shouting: 'Court rise...'

Kane was still on his feet. He looked over at Jim Sim. Sim's eyes were agog. The dogs headed for the exit. Kane recognised that one of them was a mongrel - and that animal had now been scooped up and held by old Mrs McAdam. And the other dog, a very small poodle, was now in the arms of another, younger, lady. A pretty lady with red hair. And when Kane looked more closely...it was Rosemary Daisy Thomas.

*****

Chapter Thirteen

And now there was a queer collection of people standing in Parliament Hall: a beautiful girl with red hair; a gangly, earnest (but smiling) young man. An elderly lady, seated in a bath chair - being trundled along by a ginger-haired eleven year-old boy. And a miniature poodle. Such an odd array, that Kane was briefly reminded of the coming attractions of a travelling circus.

Kane spoke to the young lady: 'Miss Thomas, I confess that I did not expect to see you here today.'

The lady smiled: 'Mr Kane, I came to thank you for your help in this matter, and...' she gave a shy glance towards the gangly young man, '...and I am no longer 'Miss Rosemary Daisy Thomas'. I am, in fact...' she held out her left hand for inspection of a wedding band, "Mrs Thomas Tack.'

Kane noted the wedding band proudly displayed on her hand. He smiled: 'Many congratulations, Miss...Mrs Tack.'

The lady looked at the floor: 'I know what you must think of me now, Mr Kane. Now that you have read the parish register...'

Kane smiled: 'All that I see before me, madam, is a respectable married woman.'

'Thank you.' Rosemary blushed. Kane looked at her face. Just as beautiful. But there was something different about her now. Something had lifted. She had become radiantly and serenely beautiful, like a clear blue morning sky when the storm clouds had passed.

'We were married yesterday.'

Kane nodded: 'Very sudden...'

'Not really. Mr Tack...' she looked over at the new groom and smiled again '...my husband, Thomas, had posted the Banns, oh, months ago - before all this unpleasantness set in, and so...'

'Forgive me for asking, madam,' Kane proceeded with caution 'but how has Mr Tack's employer, Old Mr Fergusson, taken the news.'

The recently-wed Mrs Tack sighed: 'Thomas resigned his post last week. The old tyrant Fergusson threw poor Minnie at Thomas one time too many. Thomas put his pens in his case, put Minnie under his arm and walked out of the door. We have been living on his mother's meagre savings since then. But that cannot last, sir.'

Kane noticed that someone was approaching. It was Jim Sim, still in wig and gown, beckoning Kane over to him.

'Sorry to interrupt you, Edward, but his lordship's Clerk is pressing for our return to court. And apparently, the learned judge will *not* hear any argument about expenses. He will simply come on and find them against you.'

'Where is the Clerk?'

'Over there.' Sim nodded towards the fireplace.

Kane excused himself, and he and Sim walked over. The Clerk was not a happy man: 'Mr Kane, you are required to come to court now. His lordship will find against you - no argument - and that is the end of the matter. Do you understand?'

Kane pointed over the great Hall to the newly-married couple: 'Clerk of Court, do you see - over there - that pretty girl holding the dog, and the young chap, arm-in arm?'

The Clerk looked over: 'Yes?'

'Well that is Rosemary Daisy Thomas and that is Mr Thomas Tack. The Pursuer and the Defender in this case. And they were married yesterday. Please tell his lordship: 'The lady shook the tree - and the fruit fell'.' The Clerk looked puzzled. Kane continued: 'His lordship will understand. That is my final submission. No need for further appearance. If he finds against me - so be it.'

The Clerk raised his eyebrows and looked over at Jim Sim. Sim thought for a moment, smiled, then nodded. The Clerk left them.

Kane saw that both his instructing agent, McAdam, and Mrs Morag McAdam had now joined Rosemary Daisy (now 'Mrs Thomas Tack') and the others in the group. Rosemary was holding the miniature poodle, Minnie, in her arms and McAdam's mother was hugging her own precious 'Dash'. Kane heard McAdam say: 'What is going on here? It looks like a blasted dog show...' He noticed Kane: 'And what is happening about those expenses?'

'The judge is considering those at the moment.'

McAdam looked at Rosemary for a moment, then: 'So, you are back, young lady. And what do you expect us to do with you now?'

The tall, gangly young man in the group who had been silent until now stepped forward: 'I'm afraid that you are addressing my wife, sir. If you have any issues, then may I suggest that you address them to me...'

McAdam was silent for a moment and stared at Rosemary. Then he broke into a broad grin and turned to Thomas Tack. He extended his hand: 'Mr Tack, I assume. May I be the first to congratulate you, sir. I am sure that I speak for my mother and myself when I say that we will miss her...'

Old Mrs McAdam now chimed in: 'And young Timothy.'

The boy, Timmy, who had been rocking Thomas Tack's mother's bath-chair to-and-fro (perhaps a little too vigorously) gave a cheery wave over.

Kane had an idea 'Mr McAdam, I wonder if I might venture: Mr Tack here has repeatedly drawn the ire of Old Man Fergusson and has now quit his employment. There can be no doubt about Mr Tack's excellent penmanship (we have seen examples in the papers). We all know how busy you are, Mr McAdam. I wonder if there might be a situation vacant for a clerk in your offices at present?'

McAdam stood and frowned, considering this. Kane, skilled in Advocacy, added: 'And such an appointment would, no doubt, vex his previous employer Old Man Fergusson no end...'

'Haha - you are very persuasive, Mr Kane.' McAdam turned to Tack: 'Is that something that would interest you, Mr Tack?'

Thomas Tack looked suddenly nervous: 'I was a mere Writing Clerk under Mr Fergusson, sir. I hoped one day that I would become a proper Articled Clerk...'

McAdam considered this for a moment, then: 'Can you start tomorrow, Mr Tack?'

'With pleasure.'

'And – of course - with your express permission, sir, may I expect that your wife here,' McAdam nodded over to

Rosemary Daisy, 'will also resume her duties in the cash room?'

Tack looked at Rosemary Daisy. She smiled and nodded back. Tack replied: 'We shall be there as the office opens, sir.'

The new Mrs Tack indicated the elderly lady in the bath-chair: 'But what of your mother, darling. Who will tend to her by day?'

Tack smiled: 'I venture that young Timmy can perform that function.'

Kane had the sudden (and somewhat uncharitable) thought that, having witnessed first-hand the abilities of young Timmy, there might soon be a family funeral. His thoughts on the matter were interrupted by the Clerk of Court: 'Mr Kane, sir, sorry to disturb you. Lord Lambert says that there will be no expenses awarded in this case.'

Kane smiled: 'Please thank him for me.'

The Clerk shook his head: 'I would do, sir. But I fear that he has just passed out....'

*****

Chapter Fourteen

EPILOGUE

Christmas Eve

'Who was that at the door, Mr Horse?'

Horse came into the sitting room, where Edward Kane was at the table, finishing his breakfast.

'It was the penny post, sir. A letter here for you.' Horse handed it to Kane. The young Advocate took his butter knife and slit open the envelope.

'Ah, it's a Christmas card, and an enclosed letter from solicitors McAdam and McArthur...I see it is their new headed notepaper...' He smiled: '...but it is, in fact, a personal letter from Thomas Tack and the fair Rosemary Daisy...' He read out as he read down the letter, '...all is well...Thomas Tack is enjoying his new situation…and apparently they hope to start a family in the New Year and...oh!' Kane stopped reading in surprise.

'What's the matter, Mr K?'

'No, no, all is fine, Mr Horse. It concludes by saying: '...we hope that you will not find it presumptuous but, in recognition of the debt we owe you, Mr Kane, if we prove to be blessed with a boy child, then we promise to name him 'Edward''.

Kane smiled broadly. 'Oh, I cannot tell you how proud that would make me, Mr Horse.' He handed the letter to his manservant.

Horse studied the letter for a moment, then: 'But what about this bit at the bottom of the letter, sir?'

'What bit?'

'The bit what says 'Nothing in this ...com...communication shall be con...construed as a...'

'Give me that letter, Horse…'

Horse handed the letter back and laughed: 'Merry Christmas, Mr Kane'

Edward Kane shook his head and couldn't help but laugh: 'And a Merry Christmas to you, Mr Horse.'

DASH and MINNIE

Edward Kane

and

The Vinegar Valentine

Chapter One

Edinburgh 1851

'Mr Horse - are you feeling quite well? I swear that you have turned a violent shade of purple.'

Edward Kane, Advocate, stood before the mirror in his bedroom, open razor in hand, and was about to start shaving. His Cockney manservant, Mr Horse, had prepared a basin of hot water as usual, but had rather plonked it down onto the dresser. The manservant nodded towards the razor: 'You knows what it's like, Mr K. Some days you just wants to take that razor and slit your own throat with it, sir.'

Kane took the open 'v' razor, closed it, and placed it on the dresser. He nodded toward the old Bible at his bedside: 'I am not certain, Mr Horse, that the Good Book would condone such an act.'

'Well, it worked for old Judas, dunnit? When he kicked the bucket and such. Bible don't complain about that, sir.'

'Yes, Mr Horse. But, clearly, that particular individual had a guilty secret.'

Horse looked at the floor and shuffled his feet.

Kane sighed: 'You have been uncommonly morose for the last two days, Mr Horse. I have never seen you like this. What on earth is it that vexes you, my man?'

Horse said nothing for a moment, then sighed: 'I'll get the breakfast on, sir. That old bacon looks a bit blue, but I don't think it will kill us...'

***

Parliament House. The Advocates Library. The Reading Room.

Kane sat, cup and saucer balanced on his lap: 'In brief, Collins, it is a matter of concern. My man Horse is the picture of misery. He survives all of the horrors of Waterloo and now here he is, talking about cutting his own throat at the breakfast table.'

Kane's friend, Collins smiled and shook his head: 'Given the pedigree of this particular 'Horse', Edward, I doubt that you have anything to fear.' Collins sipped his tea – mischievous now: 'And, in any event, if your manservant were to do such a thing – then who on earth would be there to clean up the mess?'

Their conversation was interrupted by the awareness of the silent presence of the Head Faculty Servant, Manville. Kane looked up: 'Manville?'

'I am sorry to interrupt your merriment, gentlemen, but Mr Kane - you have a visitor in the Hall, sir.'

'Who is it, Manville?'

'I understand it to be a Law Agent who wishes to provide you with a set of instructions.'

A set of instructions! Paid work! Veritable gold dust to the struggling young Advocate. Kane put down his cup and saucer and got up quickly. Manville placed a firm hand on his shoulder: 'I should be grateful, Mr Kane, if you would resist the temptation to run in the Library, sir. It would be not only be unbecoming and distracting to the other Members, Mr Kane, but - and I hesitate to say - it would appear somewhat desperate...'

***

When Kane reached Parliament Hall he looked around. A great number of Advocates were walking up and down the Hall today, dressed in wig and gown, instructed on opposing sides, discussing their cases; nervous litigants stood awaiting news of their legal fates; huddles of solicitors formed circles, gossiping the latest Edinburgh news. And then Kane saw a familiar figure at the fireplace beckoning him over. It was a certain Mr Whittle, solicitor. Whittle was small, stooped and somewhat timid, giving rise to the nickname: 'The Mole'. The Mole had previously instructed Kane - to good effect, it must be said - in the case that had gained notoriety as 'The Parlour Maid Murderer' case.

Kane walked over to the fireplace and smiled: 'My dear, Mr Whittle. A pleasure to see you again, sir'

The Mole doffed his hat. 'And you, Mr Kane, and you. I regret that I require to importune you at such short notice, sir, but the matter appears somewhat pressing for the client.'

Kane bowed: 'I am at your service, Whittle.'

The Mole paused for a moment, then: 'I take it, Mr Kane, that you have experience of Valentine's Day cards, sir.'

Kane laughed: 'Only by repute, Mr Whittle. I myself have yet to receive one.'

'Then you might also have heard of its vile counterpart: 'The Vinegar Valentine'...'

***

'Outrageous! Quite outrageous! I shall go to that blackguard's house and wring his neck...'

Kane held up his hand to stay his client's anger. 'Mr Walker, Mr Walker...you have no proof as yet...it might not even be the gentleman that you are thinking of.'

Wealthy industrialist, Robert J Walker, sat seething: 'Of course it was him. Who else knew? Who's else, sir?'

Kane hesitated slightly: 'Well, that would surely be a matter for...for...well, your lady wife here...'

There were four people in that consultation room, Kane, the instructing solicitor Mr Whittle (a.k.a 'The Mole'), Robert J Walker and Walker's wife, Fanny Eudora Walker. The good Mrs Walker was wearing an enormous colourful hat and dabbing her eyes (somewhat flamboyantly, Kane thought) with an embroidered lace handkerchief.

The industrialist turned to Kane, furious: 'And what are you implying by that remark, sir?'

It took the meek and measured voice of The Mole, to restore order: 'Mr Walker, Mr Walker, Mr Kane was implying nothing. All that he was saying was that it is probably best that we hear directly from your good lady wife about...about this...'. He pointed to the card on the table.

The card had arrived by that morning penny post, addressed to Mrs Fanny Eudora Walker. At first blush, a Valentine, but on examination it was a communication enlivened by a colourful caricature of a dog with droopy ears. The dog was dressed as a lady, and the card declared:

'I've studied cats
I've studied dugs
But I never saw a woman…
With such big lugs'

*****

Chapter Two

The consultation room was silent for a moment. The only sound was the intermittent (if somewhat theatrical) sob of the wronged recipient of the Vinegar Valentine, Mrs Fanny Eudora Walker.

The lady's husband, industrialist Robert J Walker picked up the offending card from the table and studied it: 'And who, in any event, would produce such filth?'

Kane sighed: 'I'm afraid that such cards are widespread these days, Mr Walker. As I understand it, they are known as 'Vinegar Valentines'.' He turned to the sobbing spouse: 'Madam, do you have any idea...'

Mrs Fanny Eudora Walker, her eyes, horizontal slits of misery, squeaked out some words: 'I earned my living on the stage, Mr Kane. Oh – some twenty years ago. In fact, I was quite famous for a time. My stage name was Leonora Strong.' She looked up: 'I'm sure that you must have heard of me.'

Kane had never heard of her, but smiled and nodded. This seemed to cheer the lady, and her delivery became less halting: 'In fact, I once understudied that great artist Lola Montez when she appeared on the stage in London. I played her laundry maid. You will, of course, be familiar with the legendary Lola Montez...'

Again, she looked at Kane. Again, Kane had no idea.

'Of course,' the lady continued, 'I performed a very small role in that production, but the 'Northern Star' newspaper hailed me as 'Northern Star's 'Northern Star''. Fame beckoned, sir. In fact, there was even a feature in The Dundee Courier. But then...then...' and with a histrionic wave of the handkerchief, the lady was in floods of tears again.

Robert J Walker took his wife's hand 'She has been like this ever since the arrival of that blasted card. I require to be at her side constantly now...'

The lady covered her husband's hand with her own: 'Oh you are such a dear.' She composed herself and spoke again to the lawyers: 'The final straw - 'the unkindest cut of all', if you will - came in a touring production of Julius Caesar. I played Calpurnia – Caesar's wife. The problem arose during the funeral scene. You must understand, we were playing that night in the Theatre Royal in Dunlop Street in Glasgow...'

Kane thought to himself: *The theatre. A Glasgow audience. This might not end well...*

'...and when Mark Antony cried: 'Friends, Romans, Countrymen - lend me your ears...' someone in the audience shouted: 'Don't ask us - ask Caesar's wife - thone lugs are enormous.' The play required to be halted at that point...'

'I can understand, madam, that...'

'Oh, my Kane, you have no idea. I defy anyone to speak the immortal lines of the Bard, while the audience is pointing at your ears shouting: 'You don't get many of those to the pound...'

It was difficult to pick up the thread of the conversation after this. Kane looked down at his notes: 'And what makes you think that this gentleman...Richard Burr...is responsible for the card in question. I hesitate to be indelicate, madam, but if your...your...'

Kane struggled with a euphemism for 'big ears' '...if you possess such...such conspicuous features...then surely anyone can see...'

The husband, Robert Walker interrupted: 'You do not understand, Mr Kane. My wife always takes care that those 'conspicuous features' - as you would have them - are well hidden. Hair, hat or turban, sir - she has made an art of concealment. The only other person who has experienced them in any proximity was an erstwhile beau, this Richard Burr character that I have referred to. He was a suitor for a time. My rival, in fact. But when the time came, she spurned Burr and chose me. He travelled abroad soon afterwards. But we are informed that after being abroad these many years, he returned to Edinburgh at the end of January.'

Mr Whittle, The Mole, chimed in: 'And thus we have our suspect, Mr Kane.'

Kane considered matters for a moment, then: 'I will be perfectly honest, Mr and Mrs Walker, I am uncertain that there is any remedy here. These so-called 'Vinegar Valentines' may be troublesome and, in some cases, I dare say hurtful, but I do not think that they are actionable. Also, you may have your strong suspicions, but you have no real proof as to the identity of the sender. Thus...'

Walker looked deflated: 'But, Mr Kane, there must be something...'

Kane picked up the offending card again and studied it: 'It strikes me that what you require here is a detective, and not an Advocate.'

Silence in the room again. Broken only by the scratching of a solicitor's pen, some theatrical sobs, and the sighs of a helpless industrialist.

***

Kane's rented rooms seemed a touch cold and unloved when he came through the door that evening. Removing his hat, coat and gloves, he called into the sitting room: 'Mr Horse, the house is positively chilly again. No coal left, I wager. But fear not — paid work today, enough for...'

But Kane stopped, when he walked into the sitting room and saw that his man, Horse, was sitting in darkness. Kane peered through the gloom at the silhouette sitting at the table. 'You will forgive me, Mr Horse, if I light a candle.'

Kane took the box of matches from the mantelpiece, struck a match and lit the candle in the candle-holder. He placed the lit candle in the middle of the table and then went into the larder. Moments later, the young Advocate emerged, with two small glasses in one hand and a bottle of whisky in the other. He set down a glass in front of his manservant and a glass at his own place. He poured a measure for Horse and then the same for himself. Kane pointed at the glass before Horse: 'Drink, my friend.'

Mr Horse lifted the glass to his lips - and drank the contents in one short swallow. He discarded the glass carelessly. Kane stood up the glass, and filled it again: 'Now, Mr Horse. The truth, please. What is it that ails you?'

Horse shook his head: 'Well, Mr K…you'll never believe it...'

And he started to drink again.

*****

Chapter Three

Edward Kane and his manservant, Mr Horse, sat at the table, glasses of whisky before them. Horse raised his glass: 'Thank you, sir. Much appreciated. I know that I've not been meself the last couple of days, sir. A terrible case of the morbs, I've had.'

Kane smiled: 'I'm sure that whatever it is that vexes you, Mr Horse - we shall find a solution.' The young Advocate raised his glass, as if in cheers, and took a small sip.

Horse continued: 'It's these bloomin' cards, Mr K. You know, the Valentine ones...'

Kane almost choked on his drink in surprise. He took out his pocket handkerchief and dabbed his mouth: 'Oh, Mr Horse, I did not expect you to be so affected by such…such a trifle. Many people do not receive such cards. In fact, I myself…

'No, sir, it's not that.' Horse shook his head, 'I don't know if you've seen the other kind of card, the evil type.'

Kane recalled that morning's consultation where such a 'Vinegar Valentine' had been sent to a lady, mocking her large ears. He nodded: 'I perhaps know more than you suspect, Mr Horse.'

'Well,' Horse reached into his jacket pocket 'the day before yesterday, when I was going through the mail, sir, I found this slipped under the door.' He produced a grubby envelope and handed it to Kane. The young Advocate read the block-capital writing on the envelope 'TO HORSE. A HAPPY EVENT INSIDE'. Kane smiled: 'Well, it looks promising at this stage, Mr Horse. Were you expecting a measure of good news?'

Horse nodded towards the envelope. 'Open it, sir.'

As Kane was opening the envelope, he saw that it contained a card of some description. Horse shook his head. 'It's not me that's expecting something, Mr K...'

Kane studied the card. It was a Valentine, certainly, but it was far from the usual hearts and flowers model. Instead, on the front, was pictured a bird with a long beak, reminiscent of a stork. Hanging from its beak – a basket of what looked like buns. And the words:

'Oh look at what
You've gone and done
For in my oven
You've put a bun'

Kane looked inside the card. No inscription. No signature. He knotted his eyebrows, looked at the illustration again and looked up at Horse: 'I don't understand, Mr Horse, what does it mean?'

Horse sighed: 'A stork, sir. A bun in the oven. And something I've gone and done. What do *you* think, sir?'

Kane thought for a moment. He lifted the glass before him. And swallowed the whisky in a single gulp.

***

Precisely two hours later, master and man stood over the table in the sitting room and considered the list before them.

Ever-methodical, the young Advocate had ordered that his manservant provide a list of possible recipients of Mr Horse's amorous attentions in recent months. The list currently comprised two barmaids, Maisie - the young lady who worked for the coal merchant – three married women, a nun and a woman wanted by the police.

Kane looked at the list askance: 'A nun, Mr Horse? A nun?'

Horse looked sheepish: 'She was trying to convert me, Mr K. But I think I might have sent her the other way, sir...'

'Do you think that she would stoop to the sending of such a communication?' Horse considered for a moment, then shook his head. Kane dabbed his pen in the inkwell and scored through the name. 'What about the others, Mr Horse?'

The manservant looked through the list: 'Well it ain't the coal-yard girl, 'cause I saw her last Tuesday and she never said nothing about this sort of thing, sir...'

Kane scored out the name, 'Maisie'.

'...and the barmaids – it won't be them, sir. They know what they're about. You have to get off before your stop, if you know what I mean, Mr K...'

Kane sighed: 'I am delighted to say that I have no idea what you mean, Mr Horse, but I will strike them off in any event...'. Kane studied the list again: 'So, Mr Horse, that seems to leave three married women and an outlaw...'

Horse stroked his chin: 'The married ladies...Mr K, in my experience, if a married woman is a bit of a wag-tail, sir, then she don't usually send a greeting card afterwards. So, it won't be them.'

Kane scored out the three names on the list and nodded: 'Then that leaves you with one name: 'Madge MacAloon' - the lady who appears to be of interest to the police. Does the card sound like her, Mr Horse.'

The manservant grinned: 'Oh , I wouldn't put nothing past our Madge, sir. A right little minx, she is...'

And their conversation was interrupted by a loud knock at the door. Master and man were still for a moment, then Kane spoke: 'Are we expecting company, Mr Horse?'

Horse shook his head: 'Don't know about you, sir, but the only time you hear a knock like that, it's when it's The Rozzers...'

Kane sighed: 'If by that, Mr Horse, you mean The Police, then I venture that you had better answer the door, hadn't you...'

*****

Chapter Four

Mr Horse had been correct. The loud knock at the door was, indeed, the knock of a policeman. In this case, it was the knock of Inspector Mackintosh of the Detective. Mackintosh had worked closely with Edward Kane in the case of The Parlour Maid Murderer and relations had remained cordial since that time.

"Evening, Mr Kane. I was just passing on my way home and I thought I would pop in, sir, for a wee chat, like.'

Kane smiled: 'You are always welcome here, Mackintosh.' He turned towards Horse: 'Mr Horse, why don't you put the kettle on?'

***

Prodigiously strong tea brewed, 'mashed' (as Horse would have it) and poured into the cups (with the addition of some globby, not-quite-fresh milk), the three very different gentlemen sat around the table in the sitting room. Mackintosh continued his narrative: '...and so, Mr Kane, after you told that lady with the 'Vinegar Valentine' that she needed a detective, she came a-knocking at the door of the Police Office.' He produced the offending card.

Kane nodded: 'I was unsure as to the way forward, Mackintosh. But it is not as if any crime has been committed.' Mackintosh, his face serious, stared at Kane: 'Begging your pardon, Mr Kane. This is Scotland. Everything is a crime...'.

In the course of the conversation, Kane noted that his man Horse had been unusually quiet, no doubt because of receiving his own troublesome card. An anonymous card declaring that Mr Horse was soon to become a father. Kane nodded over to Horse: 'Mr Horse, it strikes me that, since our friend Mackintosh of the Detective is investigating such nuisance cards, perhaps he could be of some assistance to you, my man.'

Mackintosh looked up. He studied Horse's head: 'But, sir, I see no problem with your ears.'

Horse was silent for a moment, then: 'It wasn't exactly my ears that got me into trouble, sir...'

***

Some thirty minutes later, the three gentlemen were hunched over the table, studying the cards. Mackintosh, spectacles in his hand, nodded: '...as I say sirs, we are in luck. It is now obvious that both of these cards were made by the same printer.'

Horse screwed up his eyes: 'But how can you know that, Mackintosh?'

The detective held the bottle-thick lens of his glasses over the left-hand corner of the card with the stork: 'Look sir, it is very faint, but there are three tiny dots or smudges in the top corner there'. He now placed the same lens in the same place over the other card: 'And - the self-same same smudges here. Both of these cards were produced by the same printing press.' He placed his glasses back onto his nose. 'Given the slight defect, possibly an older press no longer in use, but...'

Kane spoke: 'But what, Mackintosh?'

Mackintosh frowned and held up one of the cards: 'But there is no indication on the card as to the identity of the printer.' He stroked his chin: 'If we could only find the printer, then we might find the people who ordered these cards.'

Horse spoke: 'Then we can just do the rounds of the printers and ask if it's their work, can't we?'

Mackintosh put his hand to his temples: 'Oh, Mr Horse - do you know how many printers there are in Edinburgh today, sir?

Horse shrugged: 'Nine? Ten?'

Mackintosh came in quickly: 'Sixty-nine, sir. Sixty-nine...'

'Oh...'

'...according to the post office directory.' Her nodded towards the cards: 'And that does not include the seventeen lithographic printers who would consider such cards to be their own speciality.'

Horse raised his eyebrows: 'Then...'

Mackintosh picked up the card with the stork and studied it: 'Then I wager that by the time you found the printer, sir, that your offspring would be old enough to sign the card for himself.'

The detective stood up and took his hat from the table. 'Still, I'll take the time tomorrow to stop in at a number of the printers on Thistle Street. There's a clump of them there, Mr Horse, and they might recognise the defects on these cards.'

And as he was leaving, Mackintosh nodded down at the list of Horse's female suspects - with all-but-one name scored out: 'And - I hope you don't mind me saying so, Mr Horse, but your friend Madge MacAloon is rumoured to be hiding herself somewhere in the South Bridge vaults. I have repeatedly asked my officers to go down there and apprehend her. But they are too scared. Tread carefully, Mr Horse. Many people enter The Vaults, but a good number never make it out again. Goodnight, sir...'

***

"Madge MacAloon'? Sorry, buddy. Never heard of her. '. The enormous figure of the watchman had to stoop down so that he was face-to-face with Mr Horse: 'Now, why don't you go back to England, my friend, and stop asking questions before somebody here gets hurt?'

Horse held a candle before him, but that provided only the merest pool of illumination into what was going on in The Vaults underneath Edinburgh's South Bridge. Beyond the huge watchman standing before him, Horse could hear the sound of the water dripping down the walls. And somewhere underneath the stench of fish and human excrement, Horse detected the odour of barley and yeast. Someone was making whisky down here. Illegally. And large quantities of it too.

The giant watchman was squaring up to Horse now: 'So - turn around now, my friend, or I'll put my boot up your arse....'

'I'm going nowhere until....'

The watchman stooped down again. He pointed to his crooked, broken nose: 'Do you see this nose? Do you know how I got this?'

Horse leaned in: 'Do you want me to straighten it for you?'

The stand-off was interrupted by a familiar voice. Kane looked up and saw the figure of a woman as it emerged through the doorway. She stood, arms akimbo: 'Billy! Billy - just let him through. I know who this is....'

*****

Chapter Five

Madge MacAloon - wanted by the police and holed up in the South Bridge Vaults - was in tears. But these were tears of laughter. Mr Horse saw one of her golden teeth listening in the gloom: 'Oh, Horse, Horse - you did always make me laugh, my love...'

Horse had broached the subject-matter carefully. Not only because it concerned the delicate question of who had sent him the Vinegar Valentine declaring his soon-to-be paternity, but also because Madge's associates - standing in a circle around them - were likely carrying concealed razors, knives and guns. Sudden moves were not advisable.

MacAloon wiped her eyes with the back of her cuffs and handed back the card. Horse looked up: 'So, it wasn't you then, Madge?' The lady outlaw grinned: 'Does it look like me?' She sat back in her chair and pointed at the card: 'If that ever happened to me, Horse, it's not a card you'd get. It's a knife at your throat.'

Horse stared at the card again and sighed. MacAloon leaned forward in her chair and nodded towards the card: 'So - have you had the second card yet?'

'The second card?'

The lady reached over and stroked Horse's cheek with her finger: 'Oh, my Horse. I've missed you so much. You were always so...so...what is the word I'm looking for?' 'Gullible'...'

***

Mackintosh of the Detective could not hide the look of surprise on his face: 'I'm very sorry to disturb you Mrs Walker. You were obviously...obviously engaged in an important activity...'

Mrs Fanny Eudora Walker, entirely unabashed despite being dressed as a matron of Ancient Rome, sat in her lavish drawing room in Drummond Place. She handed the teacup and saucer to Mackintosh of the Detective: 'Not at all, Mackintosh...'

The lady sat back in her chair and sipped her tea: 'I'm sorry, but you have just missed my husband, sir. However, he will not be too long. We have agreed that he will try to spend more time at home from now on - given the recent events...'

Silence. Then: 'You are wondering why I am dressed like this, Mackintosh?'

'I didn't like to say, madam.'

When Mackintosh had been led into the drawing room, he had been encountered by the sight of the good Mrs Walker dressed in the garb of an ancient Roman matron. In a costume that was now, perhaps, obviously too small...

Mrs Walker beamed: 'I like to surprise my husband, Mackintosh, by dressing in my old costumes. Here you see me as Calpurnia, Caesar's wife. And you will note, the costume still fits me perfectly.'

Mackintosh thought to himself, *Perhaps twenty years ago* - but he said nothing.

The lady leaned forward in her chair: 'As a married man yourself, you understand the importance of keeping passion alive...'

Mackintosh was at the stage of his marriage where he was more concerned with the importance of a good night's sleep. But smiled and nodded anyway: 'I just called in, Mrs Walker, to confirm something. You informed me that Mr Richard Burr, your erstwhile suitor, had arrived back in Scotland last month and was now living at an address in Hanover Street.'

The lady sipped her tea: 'That was my understanding.'

The detective frowned: 'The thing is, madam, I have called in at that address and they know nothing of him.'

Mrs Fanny Eudora Walker put her hand to her breast: 'Goodness!'

***

'Mr Horse, is that you?'

Horse came into the sitting room, somewhat the worse for wear: 'Yes. Just me, sir.'

Kane got up from his chair, holding an envelope in his hand: 'I'm terribly sorry to tell you this, my friend...'

Horse was taking off his coat and scarf: 'Let me guess sir...another card.'

'How did you know?'

Horse pointed over at the card: 'Open it, Mr Kane.'

'But it is addressed to you, Mr Horse.'

'Just open it, sir.'

Kane opened the envelope. It was another offensive card. This time, the message read:

'It's time to shout
'Hip-Hip Hooray'
You've put me in
The Family Way'

Horse held up his hand: 'You don't have to tell me what's in it, sir. It will say something like 'For a mere twenty pounds, this problem will disappear'.'

The young Advocate raised his eyebrows: 'How on earth could you know that, Horse?'

Horse smiled: and shook his head 'Let's just say that I've just been consulting with an expert in the trade, Mr K.'

***

Ting-a-ling! The bell above the door of printers, Geo. Simpson and Son in Thistle Street tinkled to announce the entrance of the weary figure of Mackintosh of the Detective. This was the eighth such establishment of the day, and the last before the detective intended to head for home.

A young man, seventeen or so, came to the front desk, wiping the printers' ink from his stained hands with an oily cloth. 'How can I help you, sir?'

Macintosh took off his hat and went into his (by now, well-practised) speech: 'I'm looking to purchase a Valentine's card.'

The printer nodded: 'I'll just get the tray, sir. You'll see that we have quite a selection.' He took down a tray full of ready-made Valentines. Mackintosh studied these for a moment. No printing defect. This was not the printing press that had created the problematic cards. The detective pretended to look shifty: 'If it's no trouble, my lad, I would like one made...made 'specially' - if you take my meaning...not so much the 'slushy' type, son. Something with a bit more...'

The young printer smirked: ''Vinegar', sir?'

Mackintosh nodded.

The printer, Young Simpson, winked: 'Not a problem, sir.' He patted his pocket: 'But it will cost you...'

'That will not be a problem. Perhaps you have some samples that I could look at?'

The lad nodded. He reached under the counter and produced a tray covered by a cloth. He placed the tray on the counter and tugged off the cloth to reveal around thirty Vinegar Valentines.

The young fellow laughed: 'Don't tell my father, sir - he doesn't approve. But you have to move with the times, I tell him. Now, these are the more bespoke ones.'

Mackintosh picked one up and noticed immediately: spots and smudges in the top left-hand corner. This was the printer who had made the offending cards. This conversation was about to become extremely difficult.

*****

Chapter Six

The printer, Young Simpson continued to delight in showing an undercover policeman his questionable wares.

'I wager, sir, that we have the best cards of this type in Edinburgh. Here is one of my particular favourites. You won't see *this* in the window…' He lifted a card from the pile, with an illustration of a large grey seal:

'Your moustache is expansive
I know how you feel, sir
But those bristles remind me
Of a massive grey seal, sir'

Mackintosh simulated a smile in response. But his eyes were fixed on the corner of the picture and the three, tell-tale imperfect dots.

Simpson was suddenly concerned: 'Is all in order, sir? You look perplexed...'

Mackintosh pointed to the dots: 'A small imperfection in your presses, I think? They do not appear to be on your more regular cards.'

The young printer took back the card and studied the picture: 'Aye, sir. We make these Vinegar cards on one of the old presses when my father is not here.' He tapped his nose in conspiracy: 'The left hand doesn't know what the right hand is doing, if you take my meaning...'

It was now time to make his move. Mackintosh spoke: 'These cards are just the ticket, Mr Simpson. But I was wondering have you ever done something for a lady? A lady with large ears?'

Young Simpson beamed: 'Ha! I happen to have the perfect card for you, sir. And it will be cheaper, because the illustration and verse are done already.' He rummaged. Then: 'Here we are!' And he produced the self-same card that had been sent to the lachrymose Fanny Eudora Walker.

Macintosh studied the card and nodded. *Softly, softly now.* 'And who would order such a thing?'

Simpson tapped his nose again and smiled: 'Well, that would be telling now, wouldn't it, sir!'

Time to come clean: 'Mr Simpson. My name is Mackintosh. Mackintosh of the Detective. I am investigating a case of criminal nuisance sir. A case involving a card made by you. I am asking you now.' He held up the offending item: 'Who ordered this card, sir?'

The young printer studied Mackintosh for a moment. Then he leaned back and folded his arms. The professional sheen of bonhomie evaporated: 'If you're a detective, then you'll have your papers to prove it, won't you?'

Macintosh reached into his jacket pocket. His identification papers had not been required to be produced in the previous seven printers that day. They had been innocent. But now, as Mackintosh was reaching further - and further - into his pocket, he realised that he had left his papers in his other jacket.

The young printer saw what was happening. Cocky now: 'No papers, then, 'Mr Detective' - so you'll be getting hee-haw off me, sir.' He lifted up the tray again: 'I suppose ye'd better get away and get those papers, eh? But I fear, 'Mister Detective', that these doors will be shut when you get back.'

Young Simpson came around the counter, walked to the door of the shop and reversed the sign hanging on the window, so that it now read 'Closed' to the public. He opened the door and motioned for Mackintosh to leave: 'Good day to you.'

It had already been a long day. Mackintosh did not move, but spoke now with a quiet intensity: 'I'll tell you what, son. I'll let you into what happens next. What happens next is that I go back to the Police Office and I get my papers. And then I get a warrant off the Sheriff at Edinburgh. And then I come back with seven police officers. And your doors are shut. So we have to kick them in. And then we seize all your printing presses – all of them, because they might be needed as evidence, son. And you might as well board up the shop windows, because you are not getting that machinery back for a good six months - until the trial...'

The young printer rolled his eyes: 'All this for a Valentine?'

'No, son. All this for cheek.'

The printer Simpson considered his position for a moment. Then he shut over the door. 'What is it that you want?'

'Just two names...'

***

'Maisie? Maisie Cummings?'

Mr Horse stood aghast in the rented rooms of Edward Kane, Advocate as Mackintosh of the Detective disclosed the author of his Vinegar Valentine.

Mackintosh looked up from his notebook: 'The name is familiar to you, then?'

Horse nodded: 'She's the girl from the coal-yard. I spoke to her last week and not a dicky-bird out of her, sir. So...so…' He stood at the window, his eyebrows knotted, deep in thought now.

Edward Kane was sitting at the table, finishing his cup of tea: 'Well, that solves one mystery, Mackintosh.' He motioned over to the list in the detective's hands: 'But did you happen to make any headway with that other card. The one directed towards the diva and the large ears?'

Mackintosh grimaced. Then nodded: 'Hers was different, Mr Kane. More complicated. No name was left with the printer in that case, sir. Some evidence, yes, but it's as if it has all been cut up with a jig-saw and scattered in the air. I am seeing Mr and Mrs Walker tomorrow. Then we shall see what we shall see.'

They looked around to see Mr Horse in the process of putting oh his coat. Kane called over: 'You are going out, Mr Horse?'

Horse nodded: 'I'm off to the coal-yard, Mr K. For a little chat with young Maisie, sir.'

Kane pointed over, wagging his finger: 'Mr Horse, I know you are angry, but remember - do the right thing. You are dealing with a lady here – and a lady in a very fragile condition.'

Horse said nothing. Mackintosh spoke: 'Mr Horse, before you go and speak to the lady in question, perhaps you would like to look at the receipt for your card sir.'

Horse shook his head, but the detective handed him the receipt anyway. The manservant took the paper somewhat reluctantly, but began to read it, following the text down the page with his finger. Then he looked up with a start: 'I don't understand, Mackintosh...this don't make no sense at all...'

*****

Chapter Seven

As Horse made his way into the coal yard, he saw a small boy - possibly ten years old - struggling with a large wheelbarrow full of coal. ''Scuse me, son - have you seen Maisie about?' The boy said nothing, but jerked his head towards the back of one of the mounds of coal. Horse turned the corner and there she was. Maisie Cunningham was helping a group of boys load heavy sacks of coal onto the back of a horse and cart. Cold today. Someone had lit a fire in metal bucket and that acted as a small brasier. Mr Horse stood, warming his hands for a while. The lady finished the task and waved up to the driver of the cart, then stood brushing her hands together. And then she turned around and caught sight of Horse. Knowing what he knew now, Horse thought that he detected a glimmer in her eyes that he was not a welcome visitor. She walked towards him: 'Wasn't expecting you, Horse. What are you looking for? More coal 'on tick'?' She attempted a lascivious smile: 'Or something else?'

Horse nodded towards the cart full of coal: 'You done a good shift there, Maisie.'

She gave a sarcastic smile: 'Some of us have got real jobs, Horse.'

'I must say, my lovely, I was surprised to see you lifting those heavy, heavy bags...'. The lady was about to shrug - until Horse finished his sentence: '...what with you being in your delicate condition and all.'

Maisie Cummings folded her arms and looked at the ground. Then she spoke: 'You got the cards, then?'

'Oh, I got them, my dear...'

The coal-girl looked up and gave a smile that was not a smile: 'Then you know that if you've got twenty pound, then the problem will go away, Horse.'

Horse reached into his pocket: 'Oh, I got something better than the twenty pound, Maisie my love, I got this.' And he produced the sales receipt for the cards. Maisie Cummings looked at the receipt and shrugged: *So what?*

'It's the receipt for the cards, Maisie. I didn't quite get it at first, my love. I'm not a big reader, you understand. And it had to be pointed out to me. Look at the price, my dear. This weren't a receipt for the two cards that you sent to me. The price is for *ten* cards, innit? I wasn't the only bloke to get two cards, Maisie - you was sending them out to four other blokes an' all...'

Maisie Cummings nodded to the receipt: 'Where did you get it?'

'I got it off a detective. And he is on your tail, my girl.'

And at that point, the eyes of the coal-girl began to fill with tears. She started to wipe them away with the palm of her hand, leaving sooty streaks down her cheeks. 'You don't know what it's like, Horse. I've already got a wee one, you knew that. She bides with my mother most of the time because I have to work. But she's not well. And everything is so dear...' She was full-out crying now.

Horse shook his head and pulled a handkerchief out of his pockets. He began to dry the tears on the coal-girl's face. 'Look at you, you silly sausage. You could just have asked for a bit of help.' He reached into his pocket and took out some notes and coins: 'Look here. I'm flush at the moment. Got about thirty bob on me...' But Maisie Cummings pushed his hand away, and to Horse's surprise, it seemed as if she was beginning to laugh through her tears: 'I'm so sorry, Horse - you can put the money away....'

Horse was puzzled and looked into the girls' face. She was holding the handkerchief herself now, dabbing her eyes, and Horse thought that he detected a shy smile emerging. He spoke: 'But if you needs the money so badly, my darling....'. And then it hit him: 'They paid up, didn't they? The other blokes paid up the twenty quid!'

The girl nodded: 'Three of them did. And the other one gave me an envelope with seven pounds, eleven shillings and fourpence - he said that was all he could manage....'

'Blow me, girl, that is a…a bloomin' fortune, that is.' Horse put his hand over his mouth and started to laugh. And Maisie Cummings joined in, laughing through her tears and they now both stood by the burning bucket in helpless fits. When the laughter subsided, Maisie pointed at the receipt in Horse's hand: 'But I suppose that I'll have to give the money back now. If you say a detective is on to me....'

Horse nodded, apparently serious now as he studied the receipt: 'Yes, my dear. This wery important piece of evidence appears to be the only thing what links you to the crime. Oh dear - I seem to have dropped it...' And with that, he took the receipt, crumpled it up and tossed it into the fire.

***

'Detective Mackintosh, I am horrified...'

Industrialist, Richard J Walker and his (erstwhile) actress wife, Fanny Eudora Walker were being briefed by Mackintosh of the Detective about the latest developments in their case. Walker continued: '...horrified that while you have found the printer of that obscene communication to my lady wife, you have not yet arrested the actual culprit.'

Mackintosh fidgeted with the hat on his lap: 'As I am trying to explain, sir, the precise identification of the author of the card remains unclear...'

Walker stared at him: 'I have told you, detective. Richard Burr. Who else could it be? Who else knew of her, of her...unusual assets? My wife's spurned suitor of those many years ago - recently returned to these shores.'

The lady whose honour had been so affronted by the offending Vinegar Valentine sat in silence. Her head - and more importantly, her ears - were covered by an enormous, colourful turban which set off the remainder of her theatrical outfit: that of a Persian slave girl. Except the slave in question here was no longer a girl. And the costume was now two sizes too small. Time had not been kind.

Mackintosh placed his hat on the table, took out a notebook from his jacket pocket and opened it: 'I have very detailed notes here taken from the witness. The printer in question, sir.' He read: '*A maid came into the shop and said that she was on an errand for her master...*'.

The lady of the house, Mrs Walker, broke her silence: 'And what did she look like?'

Mackintosh looked at his notebook and then looked up: '*Middle-aged and fat...*'

Mrs Walker jolted up and gasped 'Fat? Fat???' as if she was the one who had had just been personally insulted. Mackintosh nodded: 'That's what the witness said, madam. Either 'fat' or her clothes were far too small...'.

Mrs Walker sat up in her chair. In her tight outfit.

The detective continued: 'Covered in make-up, he says...'. And when Richard J Walker muttered under his breath: 'Trollop...' - his wife promptly slapped her husband on the arm.

Mackintosh kept reading from his notebook: '*...and she was Irish.*'

Fanny Eudora Walker leaned forward: 'And he was absolutely *convinced* that this maidservant was Irish?' Mackintosh nodded: 'The lad was certain of it. Definitely Irish. He said his grandmother was Irish, so he knew the sound well, he said.' The lady of the house sat back in her chair with what Mackintosh thought to be a satisfied smile.

At that point, the briefing was interrupted by the entrance of a butler: 'I apologise for interrupting, sir, but there is a caller at the back door. The foreman from the warehouse. He is insistent that there is a matter that requires your personal attention.'

Walker sighed: 'Apologies, Detective Mackintosh, I require to spend more time at home these days, so I am afraid that these interruptions are inevitable. If you will excuse me.'

The detective and the lady of house were left sitting across from each other. They drank their tea. It was the lady who broke the silence: 'So, Mackintosh, definitely an Irish housemaid we're looking for now.' Mackintosh didn't answer directly, but nodded over to her: 'You appear to have retained quite a number of your costumes, madam.' Mrs Walker smiled: 'My husband enjoys seeing me in them. It reminds him of when we first met. When our love was new.' Mackintosh smiled and nodded. Silence for a while. Then an unspoken, subterranean joust began 'You must miss the theatre, Mrs Walker.' The lady sighed and nodded. The detective continued: 'All the drama and such. The attention. The dressing up in different costumes. The make-up...'. The lady said nothing and drank her tea. 'In fact,' the detective continued, 'I think you told me that you, yourself, once played a maid, did you not? I wager that you still have that costume.' Mrs Walker smiled over her teacup: 'But I did not play an *Irish* maid, detective. The lady in our case was definitely Irish. The young printer said that….'

The detective interrupted her: 'I beg your pardon, madam, did I say that the printer was 'young'?'

Silence for a time. Mackintosh spoke: 'And it must have been a privilege to understudy the great Lola Montez.' Mrs Walker sighed: 'Every day for a year, sir. Every day, I studied her every movement, every sound that she made.' Mackintosh pressed on: 'Yes. From what I understand, Lola Montez was not her real name.' The lady laughed: 'Of course not, detective, this is the theatre! In fact, she was…she began life as...as...' she stopped herself at that point, but Mackintosh finished the sentence: '...as plain old 'Eliza Gilbert'...' He sipped his tea, '...born in Limerick, I understand. And you spent a whole twelve months studying her.' Mackintosh put his cup and saucer on the table: 'The thing that you have to understand about me, Mrs Walker, is this: I never finished first at anything, but I always did finish. I never finished first at school, but I always finished the work. I never finished first in the race, but I always got to the finish line. It's the way that I'm made madam. So, would you like me to finish this investigation into the card or not, Mrs Walker? Would you like me to get to the very, very bottom of it, madam?'

The lady said nothing and sipped her tea. Robert J Walker strode back into the room: 'I have no idea, no idea why I employ managers to resolve such simple matters.' He rubbed his hands together: 'Now, Mackintosh, have you devised a way forward?' The detective said nothing and looked at Fanny Eudora Walker. After a moment, the lady took her husband's hand: 'Oh my dear, it is perhaps time to let this matter go...'. The husband spluttered: 'But the card...that blackguard, Burr...'. The wife stroked her husband's hand: 'Detective Mackintosh has made it quite clear, my darling. An anonymous Irish housemaid - a needle in a haystack in this great city. The absence of any signature on the card. And the fact that Burr is obviously in hiding - there is no sign of him at the address we thought. Poor Mackintosh has so many other, more important things to be doing. Catching murderers and...and..'. The detective added: '...and fraudsters...' The lady looked into her husband's eyes: 'And you are now home so much more, my dear. I do feel so much safer...'

Mackintosh said nothing, but went on drinking his tea.

***

EPILOGUE

February 14th. Valentine's Day. Mr Horse was sorting through the morning mail. Edward Kane sat at the table finishing his breakfast and nodded over: 'Anything of note, Mr Horse?' Horse studied the envelopes: 'Looks like bills, bills and...more bills, Mr K' Kane sighed, but Horse spoke again: 'Oh, tell a lie, sir, here's a letter that's been slipped under the door. Must have been put there first thing.'

Horse studied the envelope and smiled: 'Ooh, and it looks like a lady's handwriting, Mr K.' Kane frowned. Horse read the writing on the front: 'To Mr Edward Kane, Advocate - Personal'. Of course, it *is* Valentine's Day, sir. Was you expecting anything today?' Kane shook head. Horse began to tear open the envelope: 'Then we'd better have a look, then, hadn't we...'. Horse took out the letter and read through it, his lips moving as he read. Kane called over: 'What exactly is it, Mr Horse?' Horse pursed his lips and shook his head: 'Well, sir - it is from a lady – and, I'm sorry – but it don't look good...'. Kane motioned over: 'Give it to me, please.' Horse shook his head, deadly serious, and handed over the letter. It read:

> *'Dear Mr Kane*
> *I would be grateful to know when I am going to receive the rent.*
> *It is now two weeks overdue.*
> *Yours Sincerely*
> *Mrs Beatrice Thomson (Widow)'*

Kane looked up to see Horse, who was struggling to stifle a laugh: 'Well, sir - it's Valentine's Day and you just got a note from an unmarried woman...although...'

'What?'

'...although she *could* have made an effort seeing what day it was sir. Could have sent you a card...'

Kane smiled: 'With a poem, no doubt.'

Horse thought for a moment, then: 'What about a card with a picture of a top hat, sir and a poem:
'Mr K
If you're a gent
Why don't you pay
Your bloomin' rent...'

Kane laughed and reached into his pocket. He retrieved a coin - a shiny silver crown - together with his last pound note: 'Go down and give Mrs Thomson these, Mr Horse.'

Horse took the money and headed towards the door. Kane had a sudden vision of Horse's extensive list of women.

'And Mr Horse?'

Horse stopped and looked back at Kane: 'Yes, sir?'

'Mr Horse - don't be long...'

*****

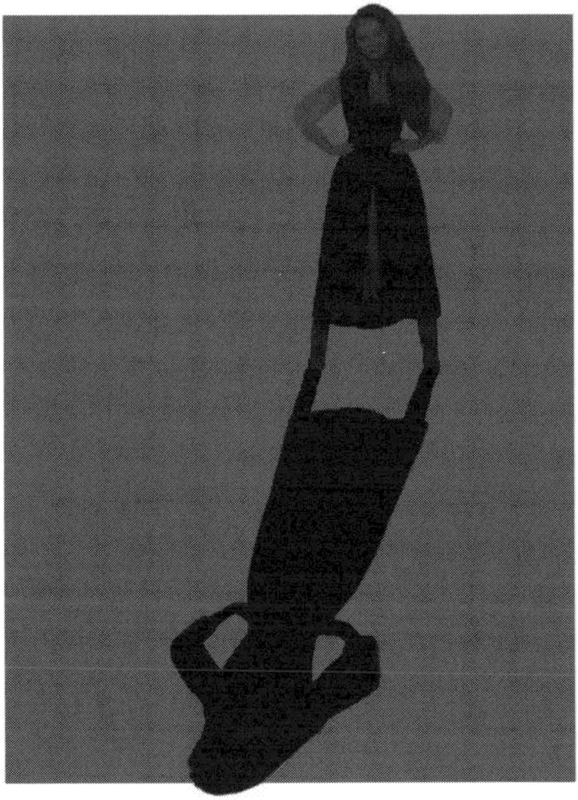

Edward Kane

and

The Innocent Railway

Chapter One

Edinburgh: 1850. Inside the Offices of the solicitors, Stevenson and Rose, Writers to the Signet.

'And what happened to your son?'

'They left him to die, sir. Left him to die like a dog in the street.'

Edward Kane, Advocate, shifted in his chair somewhat uncomfortably.

Mrs Euphemia Campbell, the grieving mother, was sitting across from the Advocate, dabbing her eyes with her handkerchief.

'But he never done anything wrong, sir. I knew my boy. He loved his books. He loved his numbers. He wouldnae have been carrying on. Never.'

The oak-panelled room was filling up with smoke now as the old instructing solicitor, Angus Stevenson WS, nodded and puffed on his pipe. He motioned to the papers on the table before the Advocate: 'As you will see, Mr Kane, the boy was travelling in a railway carriage on the Edinburgh and Dalkeith Railway. Reports are that he started to misbehave. He fell out of the carriage and suffered a blow to the head. His body was recovered the following day.'

The grieving mother gently sobbed: 'The last thing I saw was he went out with his wee pal. And he never came home, sir. And I waited up all night for him, Mr Kane. All night.'

Kane nodded. He had studied the papers. 'What I cannot fathom at this point is why it took so long for the matter to be reported or for the body to be found. Surely, if a child of...'. Kane, suddenly uncertain of the boy's precise age, began to rummage through his papers.

The mother spoke quickly: 'Eleven, sir. He was eleven.'

The old solicitor piped up: 'It happened in the tunnel Mr Kane. The long tunnel at St Leonards. The body was obscured by the darkness.'

Kane sat back in his chair. The law was clear here. And now there was some unwelcome news that had to be imparted to the distraught mother of a dead son.

But before Kane could do that, the old solicitor intervened: 'If I may presume to predict your answer, sir.' Mr Stevenson puffed on his pipe. 'You are about to tell this grieving mother that she has no case. She has no case because if her son - God rest him - was carrying on inside the wagon and he fell out, then the law is clear: if it was his fault, or even partly his fault, then there is no case here. 'The loss lies where it falls', as it were.' he nodded toward the mother. 'She has been told that.'

Mrs Campbell was staring hard at Kane now, as if the duration and intensity of the gaze of a distraught mother could somehow overturn the settled Law of Scotland.

Kane sighed and looked at the lady. 'I'm afraid that your solicitor Mr Stevenson is perfectly correct, madam. Whether the owners of the train - or others - were responsible for the death of your son is only one question in this case. But if your son contributed in any way...' Kane repeated to underline the point '...contributed in any way to the incident, then the law blames your boy entirely for the result.'

There was silence in the room for a moment, while Mrs Campbell closed her eyes. Kane saw her shudder gently as the bad news seeped through her.

Mr Stevenson, the old solicitor, tapped his pipe against an ornate wooden ashtray and broke the silence. 'Well, I am sorry madam that Learned Counsel could provide you with no better answer than a humble instructing solicitor, but...'

The mother opened her eyes. She now looked and spoke like a woman possessed: 'It's all lies. Lies. He was a good boy, my Johnny. And we'll prove that...'

Stevenson interrupted: 'But the expenses alone...'

'I had money saved for my own burial, sir. I never thought I would have to use it for my son. There's still some money left. And I'm going to spend that money, every last penny, until we find the truth, sir. The truth...'

***

The great Parliament Hall was virtually empty today.

At one time, it was the seat of the old Scottish Parliament. But the politicians moved out - and the lawyers moved in. The Supreme Court lawyers, the Advocates. And now the building was used to house the Supreme Courts of Scotland - and the Advocates Library.

The Hall is awfully quiet today thought Kane. Of course, it's Monday. The judges don't sit on a Monday.

Kane walked through the Hall to the entrance of The Advocates Library and began to divest himself of his hat, coat gloves and silver-topped cane. He handed them to a Faculty Servant, thanked him, then enquired: 'Do you happen to know if Mr Collins is in the Library today?'

'Aye, Mr Kane. He'll be in the Reading Room, sir.'

Kane made his way into the Advocates Reading Room. Polished wooden flooring, expensive rugs, plush leather armchairs, wing-chairs and sofas, portraits of past members on the walls and - ahhhh - coffee. Kane looked around the room. A number of Advocates sat, some discussing cases with friends, some reading newspapers, some simply enjoying their smoke and looking out of the window onto George IV Bridge.

And there, at a table in the corner, was his friend Collins, all bookish eagerness and horn-rimmed glasses. Collins was trying to attract Kane's attention, hand raised, finger pointing up, he reminded Kane of an eager schoolboy seeking to be excused.

Collins had called to the Bar with Kane and their friendship had been cemented with a common problem: no work. And no work meant no income.

Kane sat down and the two friends sat among the pipe smoke, drinking coffee and they soon began to bemoan their lack of instruction.

Collins sipped at his coffee: 'Do you know, Edward, my wife required to wake me in the middle of last night. For my own part, I was dreaming of sitting down to a hearty meal of roast duck...'

'Ahhh..' mused Kane '...roast duck...'. He could feel the saliva quicken in his mouth at the mere - if remote - memory.

Collins continued his narrative: 'And when Mrs Collins roused me, she claimed that I was actually chewing at my pillow...'

The friends laughed. 'And no doubt,' smiled Kane, 'corroboration was provided by the presence of a quantity of pillow feathers in your mouth.'

The friends laughed again. And they talked of this and that.

And then the subject turned to Kane's recent consultation. The Advocate outlined the situation to his friend: a young boy of eleven years had taken a trip on the Edinburgh and Dalkeith Railway; he had been misbehaving in one of the railway carriages; as a result, he had fallen out of the carriage; his head had struck a rock and he had died instantly; his grieving mother denied that he would have been misbehaving; she wished to sue someone - anyone - to find the truth.

Collins listened intently, sometimes nodding, but saying nothing. Then: 'Well, Edward, as you have no doubt concluded yourself - and advised as such, I hope - the case is quite hopeless.'

Kane nodded: 'That was my view. I tendered robust advice.'

Collins frowned: 'And you would have stressed to her that any negligent contribution by the chid would exonerate any other party.'

'I made that clear'

'And?'

'And...the grieving mother wishes to expend the last of her life savings in pursuit of the action - against anyone.'

'And so?'

'And so, I suggested that my solicitors should send a brief letter to the rail company reminding them of their general duty to ensure that their wagons are a safe mode of travel.'

Collins shook his head: 'And who, may I ask, is going to pay for such a masterpiece of legal communication?'

Kane was sheepish in his reply: 'The mother, of course.'

Collins sat back in his chair and frowned. He sat silently and sipped at his coffee.

After a few moments, Kane broke the silence: 'If I could spare a penny, my friend, I would tender that penny for your thoughts.'

Collins leaned forward: 'You will excuse me, Kane, for suggesting that - as impecunious as I am - rather than take the life savings of a grieving mother in a hopeless case, I would rather be roused at midnight with a mouthful of feathers...'

*****

Chapter Two

'Pull!'

'It's not budging, sir.'

'Pull harder, man!'

The removal of boots by a manservant can prove to be no easy task.

And the young Advocate, Edward Kane, was being assisted in that process - not without difficulty, it must be said - by a certain Mr Horse.

Mr Horse was something of a singular character. Raised in the slums of London's East End, he had served, while still in his teens - and with distinction - at the Battle of Waterloo in 1815. And it was there that he had acquired the nickname 'Mr Horse' - reputedly bestowed by the Duke of Wellington himself.

Kane and Horse had met when Kane had assisted Mr Horse in what Horse had termed 'a bit of bother' at an earlier juncture. After that, Kane had retained Horse as his manservant. Thus it was that Horse served as Kane's general factotum, servant, cook and - where necessary - his Cockney guardian angel.

The young Advocate, being a person of no great means, had secured a small set of furnished rooms at the top of a tenement building in Edinburgh's Old Town. This was not a fashionable part of the city. The dwelling comprised a sitting room, with the dining table that also served as Kane's work desk; a small bedroom for Kane; a lavatory; a pantry with a sink; and a small recess, where Mr Horse slept at night.

The conditions could not be described as commodious, but the accommodation was inexpensive and served for the time being, as Kane eked out a young Advocate's existence on a trickle of paid instructions.

The Advocate's boots finally removed from reluctant feet and the kettle placed firmly on the fire to provide a nice cup of strong tea, the conversation turned to supper. Mr Horse had already laid the table. Kane raised his eyebrows in hopeful expectation. Any prospect of roast duck was soon dashed.

'Well, Mr K, I was talking to the butcher today, and he says that since you ain't paid nothing for a good three weeks, there's no more grub until you do. Sorry, sir.'

Kane sighed.

'But, Mr K, I had a few scraps of mutton left over from yesterday, sir, so I've cooked us a nice mutton stew, and we can pour that over yesterday's bread.'

Kane sat down at the table, placed a napkin on his lap, bowed his head and, silently, said grace. Being the son of a clergyman, old habits die hard. He was then treated to the sight of Mr Horse emerging from the pantry with a very large pot and sploshing a quantity of the questionable stew into the bowl before him.

And as he ate, he told Horse all about his new - in fact, his only - case. Horse chewed on a piece of yesterday's bread and listened intently. When the narrative had finished, Horse shook his head: 'Sounds like the little monkey got what he deserved, sir. What with him carrying on, and the like.'

'His mother says that he was not that kind of boy.'

'You hear that a lot from mothers Mr K. Usually when their boys are in the Calton Jail.'

Kane nodded as he chewed on a particularly stubborn piece of mutton.

Horse continued: 'And what does the body say, Mr K?'

Kane looked up and narrowed his eyes: *What does a dead body ever say?*

'I mean, sir, are there marks and so forth on the body that tell us what happened?'

Kane - mouthful of mutton - shook his head to indicate that he didn't know.

Horse thought for a moment: 'Then I suppose we'd best go and have a look at it, don't we? The body, I mean. First thing tomorrow. But knowing your delicate stomach, Mr K, best to do that before breakfast, eh?'

***

It's odd - but true - that some people seem unexpectedly and ridiculously happy at their work. Gravediggers have been known to whistle while they work. Street sweepers have been witnessed humming the tunes of Rossini in the course of their arduous toil.

Such an individual was Dr Alistair Stanton. Dr Stanton was a Police Surgeon. His daily tasks would include removing bullets, dressing stab wounds - and examining dead bodies.

The lucky (living) recipient would often hear him 'bum-bum-bum' cheerfully under his breath as he dressed or incised the offending area. And he was the physician who had examined the recently-departed child, Johnny Campbell.

The first thing that Edward Kane noticed on entering the Royal Infirmary 'dead-room' was the strong odour: bleach, was it? Something chemical. But hiding underneath the smell of the bleach, another pungent odour, something that Kane could not quite identify. Something almost sweet. Sweet as a decaying flower is sweet.

Kane wrinkled his nose and looked at Horse.

'It's Death, Mr Kane. The sweet smell of Death. I knows it well from the fields of Waterloo.'

Kane removed the scented handkerchief from his pocket and held it against his nose.

Horse smiled: 'You wouldn't have survived Waterloo, would you sir?'

The rhetorical question was interrupted by the entrance of Dr Alistair Stanton. So cheerful was the good doctor, that he might have been welcoming them to a convivial social gathering.

'Come in, gentlemen, come in. Please sit down. Now - how can I be of assistance here?'

Kane explained that he had been instructed by the mother of the child, the late Johnny Campbell, aged eleven years, and that they were looking at the cause of death.

'Of course, of course, wee Johnny Campbell,' smiled the doctor, 'by all accounts a cheeky wee chappie...'

'Not according to his mother, Dr Stanton.'

'Of course - what else would one expect of a mother.' The good doctor smiled. It was said as more of an obvious statement than a question.

Kane had slept badly that night, in squeamish anticipation of the task before him. But he decided now to grasp the thistle:

'We thought, perhaps...that it might be instructive to examine the body...'

Stanton gave a good-natured laugh: 'You'll forgive me, Mr Kane, for remarking that a lawyer attempting to examine a body would be the equivalent of a physician attempting to persuade a jury not to put a noose around his client's neck. What on earth would you hope to achieve, sir?'

Chapter Three

Mr Horse had remained silent up until this point, but he now entered the conversation: 'Begging your pardon, doctor, but the notion was mine. I saw a lot of death on the battlefield, sir. A lot of people killed in action...'

'And what, precisely, did you expect to find from a child who simply fell from a wagon, sir? Black powder from a musket? Bayonet wounds, perhaps?'

Horse was silent, chastened now. The doctor, realising that his retort had emerged as overly-mocking, softened:

'You served your country, sir?'

'Waterloo, doctor.'

'Then we owe you a debt that is not easily repaid, Mr Horse. And what was your intention in examining the body?'

'I seen a lot of bodies, sir. Every one of them, sir, lying on that field, had a different story written on the body. Sometimes death was long-range, sometimes hand-to-hand.'

The doctor nodded. Horse continued: 'I just thought, doctor, that what with the boy's mother being so, being so...'. Horse struggle to find the word.

Kane interjected: 'Adamant?'

Horse smiled: 'That's the word, sir - 'adamant'. What with the mother being so adamant that this was a little lad who wouldn't say boo to a goose, and all, I just thought...'

Doctor Stanton nodded: 'You are perfectly correct, sir, that every body in death tells a story of what transpired in life. I have examined a great number of bodies where the tale of a dissolute existence can be measured in the number of pock marks on the face - or the sheer size of the liver. But here we have an eleven year-old boy, sir. Not so much a whole Book of Life. More, an exceedingly short chapter. Unfinished...'

Horse nodded. The doctor continued: 'And in any event, any examination of the body is now quite impossible.'

Edward Kane, surprised by this sudden obstructive attitude in the otherwise accommodating physician, before he could contain his surprise, uttered: 'And why not?'

Stanton shook his head.

'The body is no longer here, Mr Kane. Today is the day when the child is to be buried. I thought you would have known that.'

Kane sighed and looked at the ceiling. Nothing was said for a moment, then Dr Stanton opened the drawer of his desk. 'I regret that you have made a fruitless journey this morning, gentlemen. However, I can offer you the closest thing to your request...'. He produced a sheaf of papers from the drawer and examined them. He removed half a dozen papers from the pile and studied them. 'Here we are...'

Dr Stanton laid the papers on the desk before them.

'These are the notes from the post-mortem examination. I would suggest, gentlemen, that anything that you might have hoped to divine from an examination of the child's body may be gleaned from these.'

The doctor then took his pocket watch from his waistcoat pocket, examined it and raised his eyebrows: 'Apologies, gentlemen. You will understand that I have other business that requires my attention, here and at the Police Office, but I am happy that you consider the papers as long as you please. Please treat this study as your own. I assume that you have brought pen and paper. Now - would you like some tea?'

***

As Dr Stanton had predicted, his notes were very full indeed and - for all that Kane and Horse could tell - he hadn't missed a thing. The handwriting was less than clear at points, but between them, Kane and Horse managed to interpret the medical hieroglyphics.

'Child...male...v small frame... post-mortem liv...rig mort......bruising/impression on lower l. chin...shape Fig 1...trauma to head...struck rock?...splayed bruising on the left arm...unlikely to

be fingerprint bruising - too far apart...sustained by rolling action post-fall?...'

Mr Horse frowned: "Fig 1'?'

Kane went through the sheaf of papers: 'I think that the doctor has made various drawings the better to describe the bruising et cetera...'. He held up one of the piece of paper: 'Ah - and here we have 'Figure 1"'.

Figure 1 comprised a rough drawing of a face with a gash on the head and an arrow pointing to an area on the chin, with a circular bruise with ridges inside.

Mr Horse studied the drawing and frowned. Kane left him to it for a while, then enquired: 'So - what story does this body tell you, Mr Horse?'

Horse shook his head: 'I can feel it in me water, Mr K, the story is here somewhere. But we don't know how to read it yet.'

***

It struck Kane later that morning that when there is a scarcity of paid work, then there appears to be an infinite abundance of free time. Thus, did Edward Kane, Advocate, spend the remainder of his day drinking coffee, leafing through newspapers, and strolling across the great Parliament Hall, fully dressed in wig and gown - lest some needy litigant stop him in his tracks and instruct him as a matter of urgency. But all to no avail. *Home, then.*

It was raining now in the Old Town as Kane walked through those narrow, dark streets. And when he reached his tenement, he looked up beyond the darkness and saw a candle burning in his window. Ah, good - Horse is at home. I wonder what's for supper...

***

'Let me take those wet things off you, sir. I've laid out some dry clothes and your overcoat and such on your bed.'

'Overcoat?'

'We're going out, sir.'

Kane was deflated: 'Mr Horse. - I have just returned home after a quite exhausting day of...of...well, doing very little, but you seem to be turning me out of my own front door as soon as I step through it....'

'It's business, sir, not pleasure.'

'And where, Mr Horse, are you suggesting that we find this 'business' at five of the clock on a dark, wet, rainy evening?'

'At the cemetery, sir. I'll get your boots...'

*****

Chapter Four

The New Calton Burial Ground was particularly damp and muddy tonight. Despite the inclement weather, Kane and Horse made their way there on foot. It was Mr Horse who held the purse strings of that household and 'cab fare' would be - in Horse's words – 'a bloomin' waste of good money'.

And as they walked, Horse explained the purpose of their expedition. There were unanswered questions about this case that only the mother could answer. She was still likely at the cemetery. Wee Johnny Campbell had been buried - after payment of the appropriate expenses - at three o'clock that day. Given the time of year, and the weather, darkness had fallen early. The body was young. The body was fresh...

'Grave robbers, sir. There's a fancy name for them, but I can never remember...'

Kane tipped the brim of his hat to keep the rain from his face: "Resurrectionists', Mr Horse.'

Horse looked quizzically at Kane from under his cap. Kane continued: 'These individuals, these grave robbers, they 'resurrect' the fresh body long before The Day of Judgment and sell them on for medical experimentation. And by all accounts, our friends, Mr Burke and Mr Hare had innovated somewhat on the practice.'

'Call them what you like, sir. I calls them 'scum' with no respect for the dead.'

Kane and Horse tramped - respectfully, it should be said - across that muddy, hilly cemetery, until they reached their destination. A newly-dug grave.

Horse crouched down and felt the freshly-dug earth between his fingers. 'This will be it, Mr Kane.'

Kane looked down at the final resting place of Johnny Campbell. Eleven years old...

His reverie was quickly cut short by a furious voice, shouting: 'You! Stand back from the grave. Stand back - or I'll blow your bloody head off.'

And when Kane and Horse turned around, they found themselves confronted by two angry men. And the men were holding shotguns. And the shotguns, held high, were pointed directly at the faces of Mr Horse and Edward Kane.

***

Pouring rain. Edward Kane and Mr Horse held up their hands. Horse spoke:

'It's not what you're thinking here, my friends...'

The smaller man wielding the shotgun barked: 'We saw ye. Aye, we saw ye from the watchtower'. He indicated the round, castle turret overlooking the burial ground 'By hell! The wee boy is no' even buried half a day and you're here trying to rob the grave. Maybe you should join him now, ye scum.'

He raised the shotgun higher, taking aim.

Horse spoke quickly now, pointing at Kane: 'Look at my friend here. Look at how he's dressed. Does he look like a grave robber to you?'

Edward Kane pulled himself up to his full height and tried - albeit, given the driving rain, in a now very soggy fashion - to demonstrate his respectable demeanour.

The small man was unimpressed: 'Aye, there's a lot of money in digging up these poor souls. Yer fancy cloots mean nothing to us. There's still a spade there. I think youse boys should get digging, 'cause we'll likely need two more holes now...'

But before the digging could begin, Horse became aware of a light emerging from the watchtower. Someone else was coming now, holding up a lantern to light the way.

Gradually, the light came down the steep hill towards them, negotiating the vaults, monuments and gravestones, each memorial of stone catching that brief light before being plunged once again into the darkness.

And as the light approached, so did Horse and Kane begin the ascertain the figure carrying the lantern. A large figure? No - a small figure, but bulked out by the encumbrance of petticoats and thick coats in that pouring rain.

As the figure approached, Edward Kane narrowed his eyes, and then exclaimed: 'Euphemia Campbell!'

The grieving mother stood there for a moment and held the lantern towards Kane, her eyes squinting in the darkness: 'Mr Kane? Mr Kane? What are you doing here?'

Kane smiled nervously, then: 'I am happy to answer any questions, madam, but - first of all, I should be grateful if the shotgun could be pointed away from my face...'

***

A roaring fire was burning inside the watchtower now as Kane, Horse and Mrs Euphemia Campbell basked in the light and warmth of the flames. The armed gentlemen had resumed their watch at the top of the tower.

The mother explained: 'You'll have to excuse my brother, Tam and his friend. They're part of The Trades, sir. That's how we came to get that wee burial spot here for my boy.' She looked out of the window into the bleak driving rain. 'And ye'll ken, sir. That's there's still a great deal of trouble. Wi' the bodies being stolen and that...'

The conversation turned to the events that had left her son dead. Mr Horse took the lead:

'You see, madam, Mr Kane here tells me that the last time you saw your boy, he was going out the door with a friend - is that right?'

The lady nodded: 'Aye, sir.'

'And did the friend go onto the train carriage with him?'

Euphemia Campbell thought for a moment: 'I think so, sir. They went out the door together and that's a' they were talking about...' and then, as if realising something, she frowned.

Kane said: 'Yes?'

'His wee pal - Wallace. Wallace Johnson. I haven't seen him since that day, Mr Kane. In fact....in fact...'

The lady knotted her brows.

'Something is troubling you, Mrs Campbell.'

'He wasn't there today, Mr Kane. Wee Wally Johnson didnae attend the funeral...'

The lady thought it through for a moment, then: 'And there was nae sign of his mither or faither either, despite...'

There was silence for a moment, then Kane offered: 'I suppose it was a school day, ma'am.'

Euphemia Campbell gave a hollow laugh: 'Och, that wouldnae have bothered wee Wally Johnson. He's no' the reading and writing type, sir. A bit of a wee scamp is Wally. Him and my boy - they were as different as chalk and cheese, still...'

Mr Horse looked into the fire as she spoke, then: 'And where do you think we can find this little 'scamp', madam?'

*****

Chapter Five

Three o'clock in the morning. Sometimes at that hour, Kane could hear Mr Horse murmur in his sleep in the adjoining room. Very often the babbling related to Horse's experience at the Battle of Waterloo: 'No you don't, Frenchie...heads down, boys, heads down...it's stuck...them poor horses...'

But tonight, the sound was different. Someone was creeping around. Kane sat up at the edge of his bed, took off his night-cap, lit a candle, pulled on his dressing gown and slippers and, holding the candle, made his way into the sitting room.

Horse was standing there, leaning out of the open window. Kane spoke: 'Mr Horse. Mr Horse is all well with you?'

Horse brought his head back into the room. He was holding a jug in his hand.

'Oh, Mr K. I apologise, sir. Did I disturb you?'

Kane put the candle on the table and motioned to the marble clock on the mantelpiece: 'I am more accustomed to you talking in your sleep at this hour, Mr Horse. Not creeping around the house.'

'Couldn't sleep, sir. Thought I'd get up and have a brew.' He held up the jug. 'We still got a drop of milk left.' He sniffed at the milk in the jug. 'It ain't turned yet, sir. Fancy a nice cuppa?'

***

Kettle boiled on the fire; tea properly 'mashed' in Horse's military way (the strength of which tea was notorious), Kane and Horse sat at the table. They heard the clock on the mantel strike four in the morning.

'This case. This bloomin' case! It's like one of them foreign lumps of cheese Mr K - full of holes, ennit...'

Kane sat, his fingers wrapped around his tea cup to keep them warm: 'Oh - I don't know, Mr Horse. It's often the case that the true answer is the most obvious one. A boy of eleven mounts the open carriage of a train. He misbehaves. He falls off. Boys will be boys...'

'Yes, Mr K - but this boy will never grow up to be a man. There's something nagging at me, Mr K. That's why I can't sleep. Something don't make sense...'

'You mean why didn't his best friend attend the funeral?'

Horse nodded: 'They was expecting...what was his name...little Wally and his parents, but none of them turned up. It's all a bit rum, ennit?'

'Possibly, Horse, possibly...'

Man and manservant sat in silence in the semi-darkness around the table, each mulling over the case in his own mind.

'But, there's something else, Mr K. Something else that don't quite fit- but I don't rightly know what it is yet.'

Kane finished his tea: 'We shall have a pact, Mr Horse. We shall put the matter out of our minds until we have had a good night's rest - and then tomorrow, we shall visit the scene. That long, dark tunnel of the Edinburgh and Dalkeith Railway. The place that took the life of Johnny Campbell, aged eleven years.'

***

Bright sunshine. Kane looked around. It wasn't quite a platform, but this appeared to them to be the obvious place to mount the train.

Edward Kane and Mr Horse stood at the side of the train tracks as, periodically, the carriages passed. Kane frowned: 'It all seems rather informal, does it not, Mr Horse? Engines stopping and starting and people appearing to be getting on and off, virtually at will.'

They watched as a family of four, comprising a rather rotund lady being helped onto the carriage by her husband (the large lady in a flurry of groaning and petticoats) being followed by two young sons lugging an outsize hamper.

Horse smiled: 'That'll be them all ready for a nice day at the seaside, Mr K. The sands of Portobello will be just the ticket on a day like this, sir.'

Kane nodded. He recalled that, as a boy, his father had taken him to see that same railway line. But at that time, the carriages were carrying in coal - not people! - from Dalkeith and further afield. And all in service of the magnificent, ever-growing city of Edinburgh. And, at that time, those great wagons were being pulled along the tracks by horses. It all resembled some bucolic scene from a carefree, distant past. And thus the Edinburgh and Dalkeith line was given its informal name 'The Innocent Railway'.

Oh, father, father - what would you have made of this modern age? Kane's father, dead now. How long was it? Kane stood in silence, looking down the rail track into the distance. What was it the Bard had said? *Thou mindst me o' departed joys/Departed never to return...*

The Advocate's reverie was disturbed by the blast of a horn and the puffing of a large steam engine as it chugged past.

Horse looked over: 'You seem melancholy, sir. I'd ask if you've had too much beef - but we ain't seen much of that in the last few days, have we Mr K?'

At this point in his career, a steady income seemed an elusive proposition for an impecunious Advocate and his manservant.

'Well, sir - shall we get on it?'

Kane nodded. Horse began to wave down one of the engines, as if he were hailing a hansom cab. The driver of the engine waved back and the great machine began to slow down, huffing and puffing as it stopped. Horse helped his master onto the open carriage and then mounted it himself.

Kane bowed to the lady and gentleman across from him. They gave only cursory acknowledgement, appearing somewhat evasive. And then, without a by-your-leave, they both got off quickly. But Kane hardly registered this as he sat down. A blue-uniformed rail guard hopped up: 'Where are youse going, gents? Porty will be nice today. Or what about the Musselburgh races? The races are always braw.'

Horse answered: 'Just along to the tunnel, my friend - you know, the big, long one where the little boy fell off last week.'

The rail guard, a lanky fellow in his early twenties seemed to fiddle nervously with his hat for a moment, then tipped it back and waved to the driver to start the engine moving again. And once the engine was in motion, and having taken money for the fares, the young guard examined Kane and Horse with some caution, and then asked: 'You police?'

Kane left it to Horse to reply. Horse was good at this sort of thing: 'No, son. Just friends of the family, like. Just want to know what happened to the poor little lad, if you know what I mean.'

The young guard shook his head: 'Begging your pardon, friend, but the lad was a bit of a pest. At least, that's what they say. Wouldn't give up his seat. And to a gentleman and a lady as well. What the boy was doing in that carriage was naebody's business, I'm telling ye...'

*****

Chapter Six

The day was bright, but when Kane saw the great gaping mouth of the tunnel, it looked to him as dark as death. Inside that great maw, gas lamps created isolated pools of light that punctuated the darkness every few yards.

The engine stopped just before the tunnel entrance. Kane and Horse climbed down onto the grass. The young guard tipped his hat to Kane and Horse below, then motioned for the driver to resume the journey. They stood and watched as the train moved on, the engine and carriage being swallowed by the blackness of the tunnel.

'Well, that young guard was a rum 'un, wasn't he, Mr K?'

'What do you mean, Horse?'

'Wouldn't give us a ticket, sir. We pays the fare - but no ticket. He says that folks don't want tickets because there's some people don't want other people to know what they're about.' He tapped his nose: 'Maybe don't want the wife to find the ticket and see that they've been out for a little ride, if you catch my drift.'

Kane thought for a moment. On reflection, the couple who had been sitting across from them - an older gentleman and a pretty young girl, not quite in that gentleman's class - had avoided eye contact with Kane and had left the carriage perhaps a little too quickly. A clandestine, amorous tryst perhaps?

'All clear, Mr K.'

Mr Horse led the way into the gloom of the long tunnel. They moved along carefully, listening out for the signs of any approaching engines.

They walked on for a few minutes, then Horse stopped and pointed at the wall. 'Here it is, sir.' A very large 'X' had been marked onto the wall with white chalk, with an arrow pointing down. 'This is where the lad was found.'

Kane looked through the gloom at the ground below him. Grass, and stones and mud. No indication that anything had ever happened there at all. Grass and stones and mud. That was it.

Kane drew his walking stick along the ground, leaving a line in the mud. 'Well, Mr Horse, I fear that our visit to the locus has left us none the wiser.' He turned around and saw Horse lighting a match and following the wall towards the entrance, eyes fixed on the grass beneath him.

Horse was silent for a moment, then: 'None the wiser? Oh, I don't know about that, sir. I think it's been a wery interesting trip so far, wery interesting indeed.' They stood in the quivering glow of the match-light. 'But, if you don't mind me saying so, Mr K, I think that now is the time that we'd better go on and find the dead boy's friend - that little rascal, Wally Johnson.'

'Why so, Mr Horse?'

'I don't know if you noticed, Mr K, but the grass from the entrance to here was all scuffed, sir."

'Meaning?'

'Meaning, the dead boy didn't fall out here, sir - he was dragged here. Or at least his body was...'

***

The Cowgate in Edinburgh was hardly the place for a gentleman to stroll on a dark night. On that basis, it was agreed that Kane and Horse should part, Kane returning to Parliament House to examine any scant contents of his work box, and Horse to undertake the visit to the home of Wallace Johnson - possibly the last person to see young Johnny Campbell alive.

It struck Horse that the narrow Cowgate streets were stinking more than usual tonight. And not just with human waste. Maybe it was the dead dog that was lying in the middle of the road, apparently there for some days by the state of the carcass. Horse had been given young Wally's address by the grieving mother and he was now making his way to that tenement building.

When he reached the stair entrance, his path was blocked by a huge object, the outstretched, large - very large - body of a man. Lying on his back, blue jacket covering the face. *Dead?* Horse nudged the shoulder of the body with his foot and heard a throaty moan underneath the jacket. *Ah - dead drunk, more like.*

Horse stepped over the inert inebriate and began to climb the stairs inside the close. *Top floor, the lady said.* Horse made his way up through the darkness, sometimes holding onto the walls at the sides to keep his balance.

Top floor. And now there were two doors. Black door on the left, green door on the right. No nameplate on either door. Pot luck.

Horse knocked on the black door. He waited. Nothing. He knocked again. No answer. But surely there was somebody inside - he could hear a kind of swishing and scurrying. Time to try the other door. Horse knocked on the green door on the right.

A noise from inside. Coming towards the door. And then a voice. The voice of a very old lady: 'Is that you, Patrick?'

Horse hesitated for a moment, then: 'No madam, sorry to disturb you, but I'm looking for the Johnson family.'

The door began to creak, and then, slowly, it opened. Just enough for Horse to see the heavy chain inside that allowed for partial opening. And through the narrow slit, the face of a woman, possibly in her eighties.

'My son, Patrick, telt me no' to open the door of strangers...'

'No need to open the door, madam. I'm just looking for the Johnson family, and their lad Wallace.'

The old lady smiled: 'Is that Wee Wally in bother again? He's a handful, that boy...'

'Sorry to trouble you, my dear, but it was the lad's parents I wanted.'

The lady cocked her head, indicating the wall to her right-hand side. 'They're through the wall from me, son. Is Jessie no' answering the door again?'

'I tried to knock, but...'

'Aye, I doubt she thinks you're the rent-man, so she's no' answering. And them coming intae that money as well.'

'Money?'

'The husband. Drunken sinner that he is. Nae wonder the boy has turned out the way he has, wi' a faither like Jocky Johnson. It's a wonder big Jocky can ever get to his work, the way he drinks. Oh, I hear them shoutin' and bawlin' through the wa', sir. Jocky and Jessie. I doubt he'd been to the races. Again. He'd step off his work at Musselburgh. Mind you, efter that, sir, Jessie seemed to have enough money in her purse.'

Horse nodded. 'And where, madam, might I find Mr Johnson?'

The old lady grinned: 'Well, sir, he's never oot of thone Doric Tavern. But tonight, I'd say - have you looked at the foot of the close?'

Horse recalled having to step over an apparently paralytic body with a covered face at the stair entrance downstairs. He tipped his cap: 'Madam, you have been wery obliging today. Thank you for your assistance. And I wish you a good day, my dear.'

And Horse turned on his heels and began to feel his way down the stairs again, towards the great body lying at the entrance.

*****

Chapter Seven

Police Surgeon, Dr Alastair Stanton, stood drying his hands with a rough cotton rag.

'Mr Kane - you must forgive me, I was not expecting you...'

Kane stood there, hat and walking stick in hand. Horse had been right. There was something that didn't quite add up about this case. Kane had been walking back to Parliament House, but then the idea had come to him in a flash. Thus, he had decided to pay an impromptu visit to the Police Surgeon.

'I am sorry to inconvenience you, Dr Stanton...'

The cheerful Police Surgeon smiled: 'No inconvenience whatsoever, Mr Kane. As you can probably divine from the 'rigorous' washing of the hands, my present task is to ascertain the cause of death of the body in the next room. The word 'rigor-ous' in that context is, of course, a pun - and thus is held to be the lowest form of wit...'

Kane forced a smile and nodded. The doctor continued:

'A lady, possibly in her mid-thirties. Initial thoughts: overdose of laudanum, Mr Kane. All too frequent these days, I regret to say. Fascinating none the less. Would you care to see the body?'

Kane's abhorrence at the prospect manifested itself as a shuddering shake of the head.

'Quite understandable, my young friend. To each his own, I suppose. Now: you wished to speak to me?'

Kane got straight to the point: 'The boy - Johnny Campbell...'

'Of course, the eleven year-old ragamuffin. What of him?'

'That is precisely it, sir. When you previously described him, I believe you used the words 'cheeky chappie'...'

'I possibly did...'

Kane stammered somewhat now: 'And how...how could you establish that from a corpse, sir?'

The doctor smiled and nodded: 'You would be surprised, Mr Kane, the information available from a body, even one so young. Oftentimes it is the absence of distinguishing features that tells the story. For example, with Master Campbell, it was obvious that this was a boy who had been cosseted for a long period, most likely by his mother. The signs were fairly clear in this case: a tad over-fed, no bruising that one might associate with strenuous or sporting activity.'

Kane nodded as the doctor warmed to his theme.

'Also, the clothing tells the same story. Spectacles found in the rear pocket. One of the lenses was cracked. But the thickness of the other demonstrated that this boy had significantly poor eyesight. A little book-worm, perhaps...'

Kane interrupted: 'You will forgive me, doctor, but none of this was in your report.'

Stanton nodded: 'Of course not. The report was an enquiry into the cause of death. It would have been an odd report into a cause of death that narrated a pair of broken spectacles in a child's back pocket...'

Kane nodded. Everything that the doctor said was correct, but...

'Doctor Stanton, I do not gainsay what you have told me, but - and I say this with no disrespect intended - but you have not answered my question, sir'

At this, the doctor began to laugh: 'Oh, Mr Kane, I had, for a moment, forgotten your occupation. The Advocate. The lawyer who asks the penetrating question.'

Stanton himself had been called to give evidence in court many times, principally in relation to likely causes of death. He was not offended by Kane's more direct approach.

'You are correct, sir, that I have not answered your question. How did I know that the lad was a rapscallion?'

Kane nodded: 'That was essentially it, sir.'

'Because, Mr Kane because I was informed thus.'

'By whom doctor?'

'Well, by the police officers and railway guard who brought the boy's body here. But what I find most curious, Mr Kane...'

'Yes?'

'Is why this boy and his fate have become so...so popular?'

Kane narrowed his eyes: 'So 'popular', doctor?'

The doctor put the handkerchief back in his pocket: 'Apologies. I assumed you knew, sir. I was visited by two gentleman this morning asking all of the very same questions that you have. If you give me a moment, I think they left their cards. I'm sure that I've put them in an envelope here somewhere.'

***

Dragging a dead body up three flights of stairs is surprisingly easy. Dragging a body that is not dead, but is dead drunk the same distance is considerably harder, care bring taken not to bang that drunken head on the stone steps. This distinction was not lost on Mr Horse as he walked backwards, holding the mountainous Jocky Johnson underneath the arms and lugging the enormous, unconscious imbiber up the narrow, dark stairs of the tenement building.

Horse stopped for breath on the first floor landing, and gently laid that large body down onto the stone floor. He took the opportunity to have a proper look at his burden. A face shaved this morning by the look of it, so probably fit for work at that time. Has he wet himself? The crotch area was a darker blue than the surrounding trouser. Hands like shovels. A big, big fellow. It struck Horse that Jocky Johnson could probably carry Horse up those stairs - and under one arm, too - with greater ease than Horse was dragging Johnson now.

Another flight to go. Horse exhaled hard. Dead drunk. Dead weight. Horse walked up backwards, lugging the load. One flight to go. *Step up. Step up. Step up...*

And when Horse reached the top, he placed the body once more on the stone floor of the landing. He knocked on the green door.

No reply. Just the same scurrying inside as before. Horse intensified the knock. He started banging now. The door remained shut - but the black door beside it creaked open very slightly and horse could see the anxious face of the old lady who had spoken to him some minutes before. A tremulous voice: 'Is that you, Patrick?'

Horse answered: 'No my dear. It's just me what was talking to you not ten minutes ago.'

The lady stared down at the sleeping body on the stone floor of the landing. 'I see you found Jocky, then.'

Horse nodded: 'Many thanks for your help, madam. I just needs got get him inside now.'

The old lady nodded: 'Well, keep knocking. I heard Jessie not two minutes ago pulling up the pulley.' And with that, she closed the door.

Horse took that as his cue. He banged again on the door: 'Jessie? Jessie? Are you in? I've brought Jocky home...'

Nothing for a good ten seconds. Then Horse heard the sound of a large key turn in the lock. And the door opened. And there, folding her arms, stood the unhappy figure of Jessie Johnson.

*****

Chapter Eight

Mr Horse and an extremely irate Jessie Johnson dragged giant body of Jocky Johnson through the door and they laid him onto a mattress on the bedroom floor.

The wife started to loosen the laces of the boots of her sleeping husband and looked back towards Horse: 'Whit have you done with Jocky's hat?'

Horse said nothing, shrugged, then shook his head. The wife sighed and looked down.

'Roll him onto the floor. We cannae have these breeks on that new mattress. They're reekin' of pish. I'll get them washed, mangled and ironed later. I'll put them in front of the fire and they'll be good for his work the morn's morn.'

They rolled the sleeping giant onto the floor and left him there, now snoring lustily. Jessie Johnson closed over the door.

'Well sir I thank you for your trouble...'

Horse came in quickly: 'No trouble at all ma'am. No trouble at all.'

'Where did you find him?'

Horse thought quickly. Where was it that the old lady next door had said was Johnson's usual drinking haunt?

'It was the Doric Tavern, madam...'

At this, the wife's face grew thunderous, but Horse continued: 'Me and your husband, we had a few in there. I knows Jock...'

''Jocky', ye mean...'

'Of course, I knows 'Jocky' quite well...'

Jessie Johnson looked Horse up and down: 'He's never mentioned you as a crony. And what do they cry you, sir?'

'My name is Smith. John Smith.' This was a lie, of course, but the name was common enough for it to sound true.

'And he was telling me all about the money, ma'am.'

The wife looked nervous: 'The money?'

Horse was flying a kite now: 'The money. The money that came after the little boy fell off that wagon and all. You know - the lad that was with your lad, Wally. At least that's what Jock, er, 'Jocky' said...'

Jessie Johnson interrupted him: 'Aye, well my husband says more than his prayers sometimes.' And then, defensively: 'Any money he has is from his job, sir.'

There was silence between them for a moment. Jessie Johnson eyed Horse up and down, then: 'Well thank you, John Smith for bringing him home. But you must have other things you'd like to be doing now...'

Horse sighed: 'Well, I'm telling you. After lugging that giant of a husband of yours up them stairs, I'm parched. I could well do with a nice cuppa tea. You wouldn't have to worry about no milk or sugar ma'am...'

***

It was a matter of some frustration to Edward Kane that Dr Stanton's notes, while providing a comprehensive analysis of the injury sustained to the chid, had no record of the parties who had brought the child to the good doctor in the first place.

All that Dr Stanton could recall was that the body was delivered by two police officers and a rail employee. He had thought that one of the police officers was called 'Wilson'. Thus it was that Kane made his way to the Police Office beside St Giles Church. To have a chat with this 'PC Wilson'...

***

'And yes, Jocky was telling me all about your little lad - 'Wallace' is it?'

As Horse was about to finish a cup of (indifferent) tea, he was now homing in on his prey.

'Aye, that's right, 'Wallace'.' Jessie Johnson nodded.

'And Jock says that...'Wally', does he call him...?'

The wife frowned now: 'No sir - he'd never call him 'Wally'. That would be common...'

Be careful, Horse, mustn't burst the bubble here...

'Yes, yes - little 'Wallace' it was. I remember now. Little lad - a bit of a little rascal, so I hear...'

Jessie Johnson began to stare hard at Horse. Something had shifted between them now. Some maternal instinct had taken over and she sensed - somewhere in Horse's various faux pas - a threat to her family. She nodded towards Horse's cup: 'That'll be you finished, then Mr Smith. I'll let you out and you can be on your way.'

'And where is your boy, ma'am? It would be a real pleasure to meet him. Heard so much about him from your husband.'

Jessie Johnson stood up abruptly: "You'll no' mind me saying that the boy's whereaboots are nane of your business, sir. Now, if you don't mind, you can get out of my house. You've had your tea. I'll take your cup and I'll see you to the door...'

Horse began to apologise, but Mrs Johnson was having none of it. She snatched the cup from his hand and took his elbow, to raise him (willingly or not) from his chair.

Horse raised the palm of his hands in defence: 'Madam, I apologise, truly, for anything that I might have...'

But his words were interrupted by another voice. An angry one: 'Jessie!'

The angry voice belonged to a giant of a man standing at the door of the sitting room. Jocky Johnson was awake now and everything about him offered the promise of a violent outcome. He barked at his wife: 'Jessie! What's happened to ma breeks? They're a' wet.'

And then his eye alighted on a sheepish-looking Horse, still sitting on the chair: 'And who the blazes are you?'

*****

Chapter Nine

Despite the obvious civility of the Advocate's deportment, despite his fine clothes and obvious gentlemanly manners, Edward Kane, had the distinct impression that the police officers behind the desk were laughing at him.

On repeating his question - 'I wish to speak to Constable Wilson. I do not know his Christian name...' - they began to chortle, none too subtly (and up their blue serge sleeves).

The police sergeant resolved the issue: 'Begging your pardon, sir, but asking for a PC Wilson in this office...you're as well going to Dublin and asking if there's anybody there called 'Murphy'...'

Kane shook his head. He did not quite understand. The sergeant continued: 'We have seven PC Wilsons here, sir: Angus Wilson, Barnaby Wilson, John Wilson Senior, John Wilson Junior, John D Wilson (no relation to either Senior or Junior) Charlie Wilson and Hamish MacLean...'

"Hamish MacLean'?'

"...known as 'Wilson', sir. Now - which one would you like to speak to?'

***

Mr Horse had been throttled before, but - it struck him there, as he was struggling for breath in the Johnson's sitting room - never with such ease.

Jocky Johnson stood, one hand on Horse's throat, lifting Horse off the ground, so that the inquisitive visitor had to stand on his tip-toes. The giant was stooped over Horse now, his nose almost touching Horse's face and Horse could smell the rancid breath of Johnson's consumption of that day's beer and gin.

The giant was angry: 'So what's this with you poking in that neb of yours, eh? Who sent you? I'll crush yer heid like a grape...'

Jessie Johnson joined in: 'He was here tae snoop, Jocky. Askin' a' kinds of questions about the boy...'

The giant stared into Horse's (increasingly blue) face: 'The boy? What has he done noo? Are ye fae the polis...?'

Horse attempted to answer these various questions, but this was proving somewhat difficult with a constricted windpipe: 'I...I...'

Jocky Johnson let Horse drop to the floor and stood over him, waiting for a response.

Horse rubbed his neck, breathed in and out for a moment - to see if the windpipe was still working - then began to answer (in a slightly hoarse voice): 'What is the matter with you, Jocky? One minute, I'm buying you drinks down at the Doric, the next minute you're trying to kill me...'

Jessie Jones, on hearing this location named again, turned her wrath against her mountainous husband: 'Aye! The Doric? The Doric??? I've telt you never to go back there. Thone barmaids...I'm telling ye...thone…thone dollymops!'

Horse saw his chance: 'I assure you madam, your husband was the soul of restraint when it came to Isabel and Rosie ('Isabel' and 'Rosie', the barmaids, had been - at various times - no strangers to the closing-time charms of Mr Horse in that same Doric Tavern).

Jocky Johnson's head was empty of words but he seized on Horse's account to douse the flames of his wife's volcanic ire. He pointed to Horse lying on the floor: 'Ye see! He was there! There was nothing in it, hen. Nothing...'

Horse saw his opportunity. He got up from the floor and brushed himself down. 'Well thank you very much for a nice cup of tea, madam, but I'll be square with you, next time I see your husband in the pub getting scammered, I'll let him get hisself home...'

Both the giant Johnson and his wife seemed chastened by this apparent rebuff and said nothing for a moment.

Time to go

'...so, if you'll excuse me...'. And with a conspicuous exhibition of faux indignation, Horse drew himself up to his full height, gave the husband and wife a short bow, walked out of the sitting room, into the hall, opened the front door, walked into the landing - and then ran down the stairs.

Had Horse not been in such a rush to vacate the tenement, then he would have heard a frail voice behind a door on the top landing asking: 'Is that you, Patrick?'

***

The desk sergeant was confused, but - for the time being, at least - remained polite with Kane: 'So, sir, you're looking for an officer called 'Wilson' but ye dinnae ken whit one?'

Kane gave a feeble laugh: 'I apologise for the apparent confusion on my part, sergeant. I had not expected such a plethora of namesakes in the building...'

The sergeant looked annoyed now - Kane's last sentence was a little too rich for his understanding. He leaned forward across the raised desk and stared at Kane below: 'Maybe you should come back another time, sir, when you ken what you're on aboot.' He indicated all around himself: 'As you can see, sir - we've got work to do here.'

Kane thought for a moment, then: 'I apologise, sergeant. It concerns the child who fell from a train carriage. On the Edinburgh Dalkeith line.'

The sergeant thought for a moment: 'On the Innocent Railway?'

'That's the one sir.'

The police sergeant laughed to himself: 'You'll have a job finding that officer sir - weans are aye falling off those trains...'

'But this one was killed.'

'He'll no' be the first...'

It struck Kane at that moment, that the more that he learned about 'The Innocent Railway', the less 'Innocent' it seemed to become.

The sergeant asked: 'When did it happen? The death?'

'Last week. The boy was eleven.'

The police sergeant looked behind himself and started to shout towards the door at the rear: 'Angus! Angus - get out here!'

At that point, PC Angus Wilson popped his head out of the door: 'Sergeant?'

'That bairn that died on the Innocent Railway...'

'Which one?'

'The one last week - was that on your watch?'

PC Wilson shook his head: 'No - I mind that. It was John and John. They took the wean's body to the infirmary.'

The sergeant turned back to Kane: 'So, sir - you're looking for John Wilson Senior and John Wilson Junior.'

'Thank you. Now - can I speak to them?'

The sergeant shook his head: ‘No, sir.”

Kane raised his eyebrows: ‘And may I ask why ever not?’

‘It’s their day off, sir. Back tomorrow.’ The desk sergeant studied the sheet before him: ‘John Junior will be here first thing tomorrow from seven, and his father starts at two. Do you want to leave your card?’

*****

Chapter Ten

Odd, the things that strike you when you're being throttled. As Mr Horse's windpipe was being constricted, he had had the sudden thought: '*It's after ten o'clock in the evening. Where is the boy, Wally?*' Not in bed. There had been a number of mattresses on the floor of that tenement bedroom where they laid out the sleeping giant - but the other mattresses had been unoccupied. In any event, given the loud melee that ensued, surely a mischievous eleven year-old boy like Wally would have attended - from wherever he was in the house - to watch the scuffle?

It's not too cold tonight, might as well sit at the foot of the stairs and wait. Maybe the lad will turn up...

***

The Advocates Library never closes. The lamps are lit for Advocates all day and all night. Every single day of the year.

Frustrated by his failure to speak to either of the John Wilsons that day, Kane had repaired to the Library, just around the corner from the Police Office attached to St Giles Kirk.

After 10 o'clock now. Very few Faculty Servants on call to take his coat, hat and cane, but still ample (if stewed) tea in the pot in the Reading Room.

Kane sat down on a leather easy chair, reached into his bag and produced the papers from the Johnny Campbell case. He laid them out on the table before him. And of course the envelope that Dr Stanton had given him. In his haste to get to the Police Office at a reasonable hour to find (an elusive) PC Wilson, Kane had stuffed the envelope into his bag and had bid Stanton a hasty farewell.

The envelope was used and stained, and smelled of the same bleach and sweet decay of the dead-room (Kane decided not to dwell upon the possible nature of the staining). He ripped open the top of the envelope and shook out its contents. Two calling cards fell out of the envelope and onto the table. Kane picked up the first one. It read: 'Jonathan Shepherd, Director, North British Railway Company'. The card had the address of an Edinburgh office. Kane picked up the second card: 'John Malcolm, Senior Partner, Malcolm and Company, Edinburgh' with an address in the Edinburgh New Town. John Malcom, it was well-known, was an established solicitor for the great and good in Edinburgh and the keeper of many, many secrets for the old Edinburgh families. Kane had had brief - and not entirely pleasant - dealings with Malcolm during the case of the so-called 'Parlour Maid Murderer'. It was not an association that he was anxious to repeat. But here was the question: if the boy's death had truly been his own fault, then why were a company director and one of Edinburgh's most high-profile solicitors so keen to examine the body?

***

Mr Horse did not own a time-piece, but if the nearby church bell could be trusted, it was just after 10.30 in the evening when young Wally Johnson entered the common stair. Horse had never seen the boy and did not know what he looked like, but what were the odds that it would be a different eleven year-old coming home at that hour? Horse wasted no time and called out: 'Wally?'

Horse had been sitting in the gloom of the stair and the boy had not seen him at first. Wallace Johnson was startled for a moment, then peered through the darkness and replied: 'What?'

Horse responded: 'And what time do you call this, then, son?'

The boy, gangly, assured, with the air of someone much older than his years, answered: 'I don't see what business it is of yours, whoever you are. Just get out my way, mister, or I'll get my da to kick your arse.'

The reality of this prospect was not lost to Horse, and so the spinning began: 'Who do you think sent me down here, Wallace?'

The boy was quizzical and cocked his head to one side. Horse rattled on:

'Your father - my good mate, Jocky - told me to wait down here for you, son...'

'What for?'

'He got pie-eyed and he's lost his hat, he has. He says he wants you to go and get it.'

The boy laughed: 'If he knows where it is, then he can go and get it himself.'

Horse assumed an eminently reasonable voice: 'Ah - but that's the thing. He can't. He's likely left it at The Doric, son.'

The boy gave a sly smile. He knew that the simple mention of that location had caused a great deal of heated discussion in the Johnson household. Horse continued: 'So he asked me to wait down here to tell you to go to The Doric to get the hat back. You know, before your mother - Jessie - finds out that it's missing.'

Wallace Johnson stood, considering the information, then: 'The Doric. Will it no' be shut now, sir?'

'I know the barmaids, son. They'll still be cleaning up. Come on - I'll chum you down...'

***

'Mr Kane? Mr Kane, sir?'

Kane hadn't realised it, but he had fallen asleep in the Advocates Reading Room. Long day. He was gradually aware of a gentle shaking of his shoulders. One of the Faculty Servants was trying to rouse him. He awoke with a very dry mouth: 'Apologies, I was just...ah...just resting my eyes...'

The Faculty Servant nodded: 'Of course, sir.'

Kane looked around: 'I'm sorry, was I snoring?'

'No, sir. You have a visitor.'

A visitor? At this time? Kane looked at the long-case clock that sat against the wall. It was a quarter to eleven in the evening. A visitor? To Parliament House at that time?

'Who is it?'

'I didn't ask, sir. I think that he's a law agent. He asked if I could place something in your box, sir, and I happened to mention that I thought you were here in the Reading Room.'

'Where is he?'

'In the Hall, sir. I telt him to wait at the statue.'

*****

Chapter Eleven

Mr Horse and the boy were now exchanging friendly banter as they headed down towards the Market Street.

'And what was you doing out at this time of night anyway, you little scamp?'

Wally Johnson smirked: 'I was out and and about, sir. Out and about, ye ken. There's things ye see at night that ye never see during the day, eh?' Horse mused that this boy had perhaps seen too much in his tender years...

'Sometimes, sir, I'll get tae watch a gentleman's carriage if he wants to take a lady up a close - if ye ken what I mean. Sometimes, I can get a thruppeny bit, just for keeping an eye out, ye ken?'

Horse laughed and shook his head. He pointed at the boy's boots: 'What about them new boots, young fella? I wager that they didn't come from your collection of thruppenies.'

The boy said nothing, but looked nervous now. Horse thought for a moment, then lied: 'It's alright, son. Your dad told me all about it. The money, I mean...'

This stopped the boy in his tracks. He looked startled for a moment and said nothing. Horse persisted: 'I told you. It's alright. Like I said - Jocky told me all about the money. About how the money came after your friend - what was his name, again - 'Johnny Campbell' - after little Johnny Campbell came off the wagon. Well - you was there, Wally - you know what happened, son...'

***

The great Parliament Hall was dark at this hour, but the lamps had been lit and the open coal fires still had a warm orange glow.

Kane made his way towards the statue of Walter Scott, ghostly in the dark now. He could make out a figure standing nearby. It was old Mr Stevenson, the solicitor from the Johnny Campbell case.

Stevenson peered through the gloom, and when he identified that it was Kane approaching, he tipped his hat. Kane gave a short bow, then smiled and addressed the old solicitor: 'Mr Stevenson. Good evening to you. I apologise for any delay in coming out, but you will forgive me for saying that I was not expecting consultation in Parliament Hall so late in the evening.'

Stevenson nodded: 'Nor I, Mr Kane, nor I. However, I'm afraid there have been developments in the Johnny Campbell matter. They happened at the end of the business day. I immediately sent word to your lodgings, sir, but there has been no response at your door.'

Kane thought to himself, indeed, he had not been at home for much of the day, his tasks comprising the visit to the Innocent Railway Tunnel, attending with Dr Stanton, and then the fruitless visit to the Police Office.

Stevenson continued: 'I will show you a single document, Mr Kane, and that will explain our...'predicament', shall we call it?

Stevenson bent over, opened his briefcase on the floor and produced a sheaf of papers. He handed one of them to them to Kane. Even in the half-light of Parliament Hall in the evening, Kane immediately recognised what this was.

'An Interim Interdict. Granted today. Here in the Court of Session...'

Stevenson nodded: 'Against Euphemia Campbell. As you see, it is an order prohibiting her from conducting any further investigation into the death of her child.'

'But this is outrageous....'

'And yet, it has the force of law, sir.'

Kane studied the document. The allegation was that the grieving mother had been investigating the incident in the tunnel and, in the course of that, she had been making claims that the rail operators, North British Railway Company, were responsible for the death of her son. She was now ordered to stop.

Kane handed back the document, thought for a moment, then asked a lawyer's question: 'And does our lady have the funds to challenge this?'

Stevenson shook his head: 'She has some - if little - left. But the whole process is likely to be ruinous.'

Kane nodded, then: 'Well, Mr Stevenson, I am happy to act for her on a speculative basis and will take no fee.'

'But I am not, sir.'

Kane was taken aback at the abrupt response from a solicitor who had been so accommodating thus far. More importantly, on a practical level, Kane - as an Advocate - was not allowed to take a case unless instructed through a solicitor. And that solicitor had just pulled the rug from under the Advocate's feet.

The old solicitor shook his head: 'Mr Kane, the issue of financial ruin aside, is it not more...more humane, sir, to let this matter wither on the vine now? Mrs Campbell has no prospect of success here. The boy was misbehaving and he paid the price, sir. You said so yourself. Let the interdict stand. Let the boy rest in peace. Let the mother start to grieve properly...'

As Kane listened to the old solicitor's words, he heard the wisdom of many years' practice in the Law. No doubt Stevenson was correct in his analysis of this futile, unwinnable cause.

The two lawyers stood there before the dying fire in Parliament Hall, silent for a moment, then Stevenson continued: 'A copy of the Interdict was also served on my office today, Mr Kane. And it came with a request for a meeting tomorrow. The railway want to draw a line under the whole affair, as I understand it. They wish to meet with you and me...'

Kane remembered his visit to Dr Stanton today and the calling cards of the two individuals who had preceded him: 'And would the parties at that consultation happen to be a 'Mr Shepherd' and a 'Mr Malcolm'?'

The old solicitor could not contain his surprise: 'My word, Mr Kane - how could you possibly know such a thing?'

'Oh, Mr Stevenson - let us call it an educated guess...'

*****

Chapter Twelve

THUD! THUD! THUD!

Mr Horse was pounding on the outside door of the Doric Tavern. After a number of assaults on the door, a woman's voice shouted from within: 'Get awa' wi' ye. We're shut.'

Horse shouted back: 'Is that you, Rosie?'

There was a pause, then the woman shouted back 'Naw - it's Isabel. Who's that?'

Horse smiled: 'It's your favourite Englishman, my dear...'

'Horse?'

'The same, my lovely...'

There was a pause, and then: 'What is it ye want, ye cheeky rascal? Ye ken we're shut...'

Horse leaned in at the door and shouted: 'Lovely Isabel, a wery good friend of mine has mislaid his hat. He thinks he might have left it in your establishment. Distracted by your considerable charms, no doubt, my dear.'

Silence for a few moments, followed by the jangling of a bunch of keys. Then the sound of a large key in the lock. The key turned. The door opened. A head popped out: 'Ye had better come in then.'

Isabel, a knowing twenty nine year-old, full of figure, broad of smile, gave Horse a wry grin and let Horse and the boy through the door. She pointed at young Wallace Johnson: 'And who's this? Likely wan of your wee secret weans, Horse?'

Despite his usual studied composure, the boy looked affronted. Horse smiled: 'This, my dear, is the young son of our friend, Jocky Johnson.' The barmaid laughed: 'Oh - we ken Big Jocky, a'right. He can fair put awa' the beer and the gin. And the amount of money he's splashing about this week. Now, do youse boys want a beer while you're looking for that hat?'

***

The first thing that Kane noticed when he returned to his dwelling was the note left under his door from the concerned solicitor intimating that Mrs Campbell had been interdicted. No need to respond now that Kane had seen old Stevenson in Parliament Hall and had agreed to attend tomorrow's meeting.

The next thing Kane was aware of was of how cold the rooms were. *Of course,* thought Kane, *Mr Horse has been away all of the day - so no fire laid at any point.* The rooms had that air of being chilly and unloved.

Kane took off his hat, and, still dressed in his coat, gloves and shoes, he slumped down in the wing-back chair before the open, unlit fire. The clock on the mantelpiece struck midnight. He undid his bow-tie and could feel a creeping warmth at his back as he sat there fully-clothed. *I'll just rest my eyes for a moment...*

***

Mr Horse raised the drink to his lips: 'Ah, you do get a nice glass of beer in here, don't you, son?'

Horse and Wally Johnson sat drinking at a small oak table at the (closed) Doric Tavern. The eleven year-old boy gave a sly grin and shook his head: 'Nah - I think it's better at the White Hart - you get more froth on the head there.'

Horse and the boy sat at the table, chatting easily, as if they were old friends. Of course, the ostensible reason for the visit to The Doric - finding the lost hat - had been sheer invention on Horse's part. He had a clear agenda: get the boy away from the evasive parents; find out what had happened to wee Johnny Campbell on that train journey; and find out where big Jocky Johnson had got that money. Had the boy been given money to keep his mouth shut about the whole thing? And were the parents spending that money now?

Their chat was interrupted by the barmaid, Isabel: 'Well, my lads, did you find the hat, or what?'

Horse shook his head: 'Neither hide not hair of that head-gear, my love.'

Isabel thought for a moment: 'I was only on the late shift tonight. There's maybe something been handed in earlier. Do you want me to go and have a look ben the back room?'

Hose raised his jug in assent and Isabel repaired to the rooms beside the bar. The boy smiled: 'Ha!! My da's always losing his hat. We thought he'd lost it that day - you know - the day that wee Johnny came aff the wagon...'

Horse furrowed his brow. What was the child talking about? Horse lied: 'Of course, son, of course. Your dad was telling me all about it. What happened again?'

But before the child could answer, a triumphant cry was heard from the adjoining room: 'Found it!' And Isabel came through the door carrying a hat - and a very large hat at that. She held it up for them to see: 'Would you believe the size of Jocky's heid? Look at the size of it. You don't know whether to put it on your heid - or have a bath in it. Here you go, Horse.' She threw the hat in Horse's direction.

Horse caught the hat and placed it down among the empty glasses. Wally Johnson smiled and nodded. This was, indeed, the hat. Horse examined it more closely - was that a badge on the front? And then the creeping, gradual realisation: the marks on the dead boy's arm, like finger marks, but too far apart to be sure, the giant figure lying in the stair entrance with the face covered by his jacket - a blue jacket, the stained blue trousers, the old lady on the landing speaking of Jocky Johnson 'stepping off' his work to go to the Musselburgh races. Musselburgh. A town serviced by the Edinburgh and Dalkeith line. And now, here was his blue hat. With a badge at the front. Part of his official uniform. Jocky Johnson was one of the railway guards on the Innocent Railway.

Horse's thoughts were interrupted by the boy's laughter. 'It's no' the first time that my da thought he'd lost his hat, sir. The last time was when he just flung wee Johnny out of that carriage, ye ken, when that gentleman and that wifey wanted a bit of private time, like...'

And young Wallace Johnson (aged eleven years) drained the beer from his jug.

*****

Chapter Thirteen

'As you will appreciate,' John Malcolm, the railways' lawyer spoke with great deliberation, 'the interdict is necessary to stop your lady from spreading false and injurious stories about my clients.'

Again, the offices of the solicitors Stevenson and Rose were filling with old Stevenson's pipe smoke – and charged with the discussion of the untimely demise of little Johnny Campbell. Except, this time, the railway lawyers were trying to shut down that discussion. Four gentlemen now sat there: on one side of the desk, Edward Kane, Advocate and the old solicitor, Angus Stevenson. And on the other, Jonathan Shepherd, Director of the railway company and his lawyer, John Malcolm. Malcolm continued:

'A written undertaking from your client to desist may be sufficient to prevent the lodging of the Summons here. You have, I trust, already advised her that she has no case?'

It's fair to say that - on close examination - Edward Kane looked somewhat bleary this morning. Roused by Mr Horse from his sleep from a wing-back chair at two o'clock in the morning, and then ushered to his bed - only to be roused again at six a.m. - had left the young Advocate a mite foggy today. The provision of strong tea and crunchy toast (given that the original bread had now attained some vintage) assisted in the process of him being woken up.

And then Kane had sat in bleary silence at the dining table as Horse had relayed the revelations of the previous evening. Discussions turned to Kane's visit to Dr Stanton and the Police Office and it was agreed that they should attend to speak to PC John Wilson (Junior) after seven o' clock that morning. And then, before the consultation, there would be another visit...

Kane shook himself awake now and responded to Malcom: 'Oh, Mr Malcolm, I have advised appropriately, and I trust that you have advised your own client that the truth is a complete defence.'

Railway director, Jonathan Shepherd, could not contain his indignation: 'This is outrageous!'

The railway solicitor, Malcolm, an experienced negotiator kept a very cool head. His voice was smooth and calm: 'You will forgive my client's quite natural outburst, gentlemen. Of course, the truth is always a complete defence, but - and I would have thought it material to your advice - that there would require to be corroboration of these unfounded and wild assertions.'

Kane nodded. Time to hit the railway where it would hurt most: 'I wonder if it might be instructive if I were to outline a hypothetical situation?'

The railways director snorted: 'It is no hypothesis that your client is damaging the reputation of the Innocent Railway.'

Kane held up his hand to placate Shepherd: 'Hear me out, sir. I am certain that any dispute here can be resolved. If you would only hear me out.'

Jonathan Shepherd, director of the railway company harrumphed, shook his head, leaned back in his chair and folded his arms. His lawyer took over: 'Mr Kane, with the greatest of respect to you, sir...'

But Kane pressed on: 'Imagine, if you will, gentlemen, a railway company formed in the last five years or so...'

This, in fact, was the case with the North British Railway Company. Thus the director of that company and his lawyer did not interrupt. Kane continued: '...a company keen to extend its line further into England...'

The railways lawyer, Malcolm, said nothing, but he and his client, Shepherd, exchanged a look, then: 'Continue...'

Kane continued: 'But, of course, to do so, such a plan would require Royal Assent, would it not?'

Nether Shepherd nor his lawyer replied. Kane continued: 'My understanding is that Her Majesty the Queen would, herself, require to approve of that. And it is well-known that our beloved monarch recoils from the mere suggestion of scandal, does she not?'

Malcolm and Shepherd remained silent. Kane smiled:

'However, it is an unfortunate fact that some rail lines - heaven forfend that it should be yours - are plagued with peculiar difficulties. It is an open secret that the practice of not issuing tickets on some railroads is an invitation for the users of those lines to engage in, how shall I put this - immoral activities...'

At this point, Shepherd stood up and began to rant: 'How dare, you, sir. How dare you...'

Kane was cool in his reply: 'I simply posit a hypothesis, Mr Shepherd. If, indeed, the hypothesis bears no resemblance to the, er, 'Innocent Railway', then I fail to see why you are should be so vexed, sir.'

The lawyer, Malcolm, gave his client a sharp look, and with an even sharper motion of the head, indicated that Shepherd should sit down and be quiet. He turned to Kane: 'Continue, Mr Kane.'

'And Let us say that one day, an employee of a railway company, a railway guard - let us call him - hypothetically, of course - 'Jocky Johnson' - agrees to allow his son and a young friend - called 'Johnny Campbell' perhaps - travel in one of the carriages. And he takes tuppence ha'penny from young Johnny for his trouble.'

There was a different kind of silence in the room now, as the hypothetical narrative began to take on human flesh. Shepherd and Malcolm said nothing, but they were now listening intently.

'And soon into the journey - in a long, dark tunnel, an older gentleman and a young lady - and I use the word 'lady' very loosely here - flag down the train and enter the carriage. And the older gentleman indicates to the guard that he would appreciate a measure of privacy in the darkness of that long, long tunnel. And so, the guard tells the two young lads to vacate the wagon. The son complies, but the other lad - young Johnny - being a particular individual, and despite his young age - sits, arms folded, insisting that, having paid for his journey, he is entitled to remain within the carriage...'

The railway director, Shepherd, began to shake his head slowly from side-to-side, muttering under his breath: 'Preposterous...'

'...and the gentleman - in frustration with our particular young lad - takes his cane and pushes the handle - rather like this...' Kane took his walking stick and pressed the brass handle against his own chin to illustrate, '...with some firmness, it must be said, to induce the boy to move. But with no success. And so, in a flash of anger, the guard, Jocky Johnson - a giant of a man - grabs the boy by the arm and throws him - like a doll made of rags - throws him out of the wagon. And so the train moves on...'

Shepherd and Malcolm sat. And said nothing.

*****

Chapter Fourteen

There was silence in the room for a moment, then the lawyer, Malcolm smiled: 'Well, Mr Kane, I had no idea that you had such a talent for fiction, sir.'

'If only it were fiction, Mr Malcolm, if only it were...'

Jonathan Shepherd, who had remained silent during the narrative, now stared at Malcolm, blinking hard now, a look of panic on his face. Malcolm remained collected in the face of any revelation: 'Mr Kane, I can only repeat our more than generous proposal: your client puts a halt to her conduct and we shall draw a line under the matter...'

'The truth will out, Mr Malcolm...'

'Then the Summons will be served and the action will begin.' Malcolm laughed: 'I hardly think that your client has the means to defend it.'

Kane leaned back in his chair: 'I have agreed to represent her for no fee, Mr Malcom.'

The railway lawyer shifted in his chair now: 'Then we will move that she must find some form of guarantee for the expenses of the action...'

Kane smiled: 'Caution? Against a Defender? Oh, I can see it now, Mr Malcolm. The North British Railway Company employing the full force of the law to silence the grieving mother of *yet another* child who perished on that Innocent railway. It all promises to be quite a spectacle. You know your Bible, sir. The meeting of David and Goliath. And the sympathy is never with Goliath...'

Malcom furrowed his eyebrows and thought for a moment, then: 'When you say '...yet another child...who perished...'?'

Kane leaned forward: 'Not my words, sir. That will be the evidence of the police officers who have retrieved quite a number of bodies, as I understand it, from that same…'Innocent' railway. If you wish to verify this, simply go to the St Giles Police Office and ask for a PC Wilson...'

Kane looked over at Jonathan Shepherd. The railwayman had that look of someone who had recently taken a blow to the stomach. Shepherd did nothing for a long moment, and then he looked at his lawyer and gave a nod of the head. Malcolm gave a small nod back and turned to Kane: 'And what is it that you want, sir.'

It was at this point that the old solicitor, Angus Stevenson, spoke: 'Mr Kane has taken the liberty of asking the boy's mother to attend. She is waiting outside, Mr Malcom. Better, I think, to hear from her in person.'

The fight had gone out of messrs Shepherd and Malcolm and so they did not resist coming face-to-face with the grieving mother. After a measure of cursory introduction, the lady was asked for her terms:

'I've been thinking a lot, sir and I'll tell ye what I want. I want a proper burial for my boy. Somewhere nice for the bairn. We'll bury him again - but at the Bairns' Knowe. I used to take him up there walking when he was just a wee skelf of a thing. I mind, he would climb among the stones...'

The railways lawyer nodded. The Bairns' Knowe or 'Children's Hill' was a beautiful burial spot at the Kirk of St Cuthbert. 'I am sure, madam, that we can come to some form of accommodation. The boy's remains can be moved with all due respect and deference.'

The mother continued: 'And I want an angel. A big, marble angel. Wan that will still be there in a hundred years, sir, so that fowk will look at it and say: 'Here lies wee Johnny Campbell...''

Malcom nodded as he wrote down the details of the settlement. The mother spoke on: 'And another thing. When my time is done here on this earth, sir, I want to lie beside him. And you'll pay for that as well...'

***

'I don't know why you're looking so glum, Mr K. You done good, this morning - wery impressed I was.'

Later that day, back in their less-than-commodious set of furnished rooms, Kane and Mr Horse unpacked the doings of the morning.

'You got that widow everything that she asked for, sir'

Kane sighed: 'But I'm afraid that I let it slip that I was prepared to do all of that work for nothing, Mr Horse - so we do not feature in any of the agreed expenses. It appears that we are just as impecunious as we were before.'

'But you done the right thing for a grieving widow, sir - so bully for you, Mr K!'

Kane smiled and nodded. 'Dare I ask, Mr Horse, is there anything in our larder that could possibly be employed to create the illusion of an appetising dinner?'

Horse laughed: 'In actual fact, sir - we got a nice bit of duck in there. 'I thought we'd have a nice roast...'

Kane blinked in surprise: 'Roast duck? Roast duck? Mr Horse - where on earth...?'

'That gold watch and chain of yours, sir. I went and pawned them...'

***

EPILOGUE

Of course, she still thought about him every day. A particular boy, he was, little Johnny. Euphemia Campbell smiled. He loved his books, you know. Maybe one day he would have been a gentleman. Maybe if...maybe...

Tomorrow was Sunday. She would take flowers to the grave. Lilacs. Lilacs for her wee boy. And she would sit for hours under the great angel and listen to the trains in the distance. *Here lies Johnny Campbell.* And she would dream in the gloaming until it was time to leave. One day, when it was all over, they would lay her there. Lay her beside her wee boy, their names carved together in stone. And they would lie there together, perfectly still, in the centre of the beating heart of that great city of Edinburgh.

*****

Mr Dickens

and

The Tale of Ebenezer...Scroggie

23rd June 1841 - Edinburgh

It was well known that Mr Charles Dickens was a famous author, but as he was being followed by what sounded like a murmuring crowd, he felt more like a fox on the run.

Ducking into nearby Advocates Close, and hidden now, he let the crowd pass, muttering 'It's Mr Dickens! Mr Dickens!' as they rushed on by.

Dickens waited until he felt that it was safe, and then climbed gingerly up to Edinburgh's Royal Mile.

The street was crowded now with the bustling life of Scotland's capital. Market stalls lined the pavements as tradesmen and barkers announced their wares to the throngs of passers-by.

Horses and carriages were forced to a halt as a tiny brave apprentice - no more than 10 years of age - bumped an enormous cart of fish over the cobbled road.

Dickens walked on, still finding his way. Passing Fleshmarket Close, a lady - aged somewhere between 15 and 99 - smiled at the author. Teeth missing, she reminded him of a drunken pirate. He found himself detained as she held on to his lapel. Tightly.

'Ooooh, nice material, ma dear - but you look lonely...'

'Thank you, madam, but I am very well provided for.'

Dickens yanked his lapel from the lady, made a courteous bow, then proceeded across the Royal Mile.

Outside St Giles Cathedral, his attention was attracted to a small boy - who was spitting on a heart-shaped flagstone near the great square.

'Hello, my fine fellow...'

The boy looked the author up and down.

'...could you tell me - where is Parliament House?'

'Eh?' returned the boy.

'Where the courts are, young fellow.'

As if he were flipping a coin, the boy jerked his thumb towards the area behind the cathedral.

The author nodded his thanks - 'A pleasure to talk to you, my buck.' - and made his way towards the courts.

***

Inside the great Parliament Hall, the courts seemed just as crowded and chaotic as the streets outside.

The lawyers, Advocates with horsehair wigs, bow-ties and inky-black gowns paced up and down the great hall, discussing their cases, nodding, grimacing, gesticulating, striking bargains.

At the side of the hall, in an alcove above the crowd, an elderly judge cupped his ear to hear one Learned Counsel, who was trying to holler his submissions above the din.

Dickens fumbled in his pocket and pulled on a gold chain, retrieving his fob watch. 1.45pm precisely. Good. He was not late for the meeting.

And then across that great crowded hall, a thunderous voice rang out:

'Dickens! My dear friend, Charles Dickens! Wonderful to see you, my dear friend. Wonderful!'

Looking for all the world like an inflated giant crow, dressed in black robes and a horsehair wig on his head, Patrick Robertson, Advocate and wit, waddled across the floor. In his left hand, he held a bundle of papers bound with pink ribbon. His right hand was extended to the author:

'You see, sir, that my place of work resembles no less than a circle of Hell. But let us repair to somewhere cooler - an unlit fireplace...'

The two gentlemen stood before one of the great fireplaces in Parliament Hall.

'You will note,' quipped Roberson with a twinkle in his eye 'that the fireplace is carved with figures from the work of William Shakespeare. I have often remarked, sir, that if your fame continues to grow, then we may have to erase those carvings and, in their stead, insert images of Mr Pickwick!'

Dickens laughed heartily: 'I fear, Mr Robertson, that my readers would not take kindly to a creation entitled: 'Little Nell, the Moor of Venice."

'And one day, sir, I wager' smiled the Advocate 'there shall be a Dickens Museum!'

'Then I shall be long dead, my friend - and gratefully so.'

The two friends stood by the unlit fire and watched the busy legal world go by.

The conversation turned to work in progress.

'Yes, the completion of 'Barnaby Rudge' is pleasingly in hand, and I have already begun the argument for a new pamphlet.'

The Advocate looked skeptical: 'A new pamphlet, sir?'

'Yes. A pamphlet that will illuminate the plight of "The Poor Man's Child"'.

Robertson was silent. Dickens studied the Advocate's face.

'Mr Robertson, your demeanour perhaps indicates that you do not approve?'

'Oh, I approve heartily, sir. But only in respect that such a pamphlet will be extremely useful in providing plentiful kindling for fireplaces such as this.'

'I must beg to disagree...'

'I marvel that you, Mr Dickens, an author of genius, an author who causes us weep tears of joy or sorrow over your every creation, that you should imagine that a mere pamphlet could reform the minds of men...'

'Sir...'

'Your Christian charity does you credit, my friend. But the Lord himself has decreed that the poor will be with us always. That is the natural order of this world.'

Dickens was silent now.

The Advocate smiled: 'On the other hand, if you were to use the power of your imagination, sir, your stories, your God-given ability to touch the hearts of men, then...'

Before he could continue, suddenly, and high above the din of that great hall, a small window was thrown open and a tiny man began to call out the next law case.

The ample Advocate clasped the bundle of papers to his girth and, again, took Dickens' hand.

'And with that, I fear, my dear friend, I have my cue to enter a different stage. Now, Mary has been enquiring after you all of this week. When will you be joining us at Drummond Place?'

***

Restless, Dickens pushed his way down through the busy streets and down the Royal Mile.

Walking, always walking. Sometimes, when at home in London, he would walk those city streets for hours on end, for miles, forever restless, always observing, always noting, storing away life moments for future reference.

The day began to fade on Auld Reekie as Dickens walked and walked through the great city.

Down, down along the streets of that old town and among the tenements, when his attention was caught by letters of gold inscribed on a building - the very house of John Knox, he was told:

'Luve God abuve al and yi nychtbour as yi self'.

He smiled to himself and walked on aimlessly.

He walked down further, until he reached the gates of an oddly-shaped building. A church perhaps?

Before the gates sat a girl of no more than 10 and her brother, younger and smaller. The girl smiled at Dickens and put out her open hand:

'Mister, mister - have you got a farthing? Have you, mister? It's for my brother. He cannae speak, sir.'

Dickens looked up: 'What is this building, child?'

The girl laughed: 'You're no fae 'roon here, are ye sir?'

Dickens' ear heard the music, but not the sense.

He frowned and craned his neck towards the child: 'I beg your pardon?'

The child retreated quickly, suddenly fearful now, as if she expected an imminent beating.

'Sorry, sir. Sorry. Ah never meant nothin' by it. It's the Kirk, sir - it's the Canongate Kirk.'

Dickens stood by the gate for a moment and took in the shape of the building. His concentration was broken by the child's voice: 'Ye want to see the deid people, sir?'

'Sorry?'

'The deid people at the back - ben the graveyard. The graveyard wi' a' the gravestones. Ah ken a' the deid people here...ma granny learned me...she learned me ma letters as well, if ye canny read the stones, sir. Can you read? Because ah can. Ah kin read the stones for ye.'

Dickens thought for a moment - then clapped his hands in delight: 'Very well, young lady, we shall make a tour of the dead. You as my guide. I will be your Dante and you will be my Virgil...'

The child pursed her lips: 'Naw, sir, ma name is Jenny. Jenny McDuff...'

Dickens smiled and motioned towards the graveyard: 'Then, lay on, McDuff!'

***

It was still light enough for Dickens to take in the view and read some of the headstones and monuments.

Up and down the uneven grass, the girl and her silent brother led him through the well-trodden points of interest:

'And here's the stone for Adam Smith, sir. A' the folk want to see it, but I dinnae know what he done, sir.'

Dickens studied the monument to the great economist. Carved at the top of the monument and peering out of the stone, was a ghostly, grey head, the beard of which looked all the world to Dickens like a grotesque door-knocker.

'Adam Smith. Do you know why this man is famous, child?'

The girl thought for a moment.

'Eh...is it because he's from Kirkcaldy?'

The tour continued:

'And this, sir, is the stone for Robert Fergusson. Ma granny says he was a poet, but he fell doon the stairs and went aff his heid.'

Dickens smiled: 'And that, my child, is a pithy - and entirely accurate - summation of the great poet's demise.'

Finally, the child led Dickens to a small, coffin-shaped memorial standing by the wall of the church:

',,,and this wee coffin is where they buried wee Davy Rizzio, the dwarf - the wee backle that would dance fer Mary Queen of Scots hersel...'

Dickens shook his head and sighed:

'I very much doubt, my dear, that they would bury such a notorious sixteenth-century Catholic in the graveyard of a Protestant church!'

Jenny stood - arms akimbo - then pointed to a sign on the wall: 'It's wrote doon here, sir - oan the wa' o' the kirk itsel and you're sayin' it's no' true. Better no' let the Meenister hear ye!'

And there it was. The plaque on the wall:

'TRADITION SAYS THAT THIS IS THE GRAVE OF DAVID RICCIO...'

And then came the rain.

The author looked up at the sky and pulled on the collar of his coat.

'Well, I am afraid, Mistress McDuff, that our delightful - if somewhat morbid - excursion must come to an end.'

He motioned to the silent child beside the girl.

'You appear to spend your existence in the open air, my child. What do you do when it rains?'

The girl looked blankly for a moment, then:

'We get wet, sir.'

The rain intensified, and darkness was falling quickly now, as they headed towards the kirk gates. But Dickens' eye was drawn to some letters on a nearby gravestone:

'Mean Man'

He stopped and re-traced his steps.

'Mean man?'

'Are ye a'right, sir?'

He had to blink through the rain and the fading light now:

'Extraordinary - that a gravestone should carry such a grievous message for Eternity...'

He was taking to himself now: 'And of all places here. Here - among the Scots - famous for their...their...'frugality', to be designed for all time as 'Mean Man'...this must be the advertisement of a shrivelled soul...a terrible thing to carry to eternity'

The rain was falling in sheets now. Dickens looked down at the gravestone. On each side stood the children. Young Jenny looking up, puzzled, her hair flat now against her head as the rain came pouring down and her mute, nameless brother standing silent, impenetrable as the rain. The children stood there motionless, waiting for him, fading in the rain, like blurred images of ignorance and want.

''Mean Man'...the emblem of a life surely wasted...'

Jenny was shivering now: 'Can we go now, sir?'

'But the name! The name of this shrivelled soul...'

Dickens began wiping the dirt and rain from the lettering of the stone and, as if unearthing a buried artefact with each word, he read aloud: 'Ebenezer...Lennox...Scrooge!'

'Sir...sir...the rain...'

***

Later, before a roaring fire in the White Hart Inn on the Grassmarket, onlookers may have been surprised to see world-famous author Charles Dickens treat two children to steaming hot stew and warm ale.

He looked up from his notebook:

'Better?'

'We're nearly dry, sir. Thank you for the food, sir.'

'A fitting reward for an excellent tour of the illustrious dead.'

The author looked down and began to write again.

Jenny was somewhat fearful, now:

'Sir, sir...can I just say...'

Dickens looked up: 'Yes?'

'That last stone, sir, the last gravestone, 'the Mean Man' you cried it...'

'Yes?'

'It wisnae 'Scrooge', sir, it was 'Scroggie."'

'I beg your pardon?'

'Ebenezer Scroggie, sir...I read it masel, sir. And ma granny kent him.'

Dickens looked disappointed. With an almost theatrical flourish, he took his pen and scored through the name he had recorded in his notebook, and spelled out 'Scroggie'.

‘And...’ - the wee girl looked up, sheepishly.

‘And what?’ - the author, agitated now, raised his bushy eyebrows.

‘And...and...I'm no' sure, sir, but...’

‘But what?’

Jenny looked down at the table. ‘I'm no' sure, sir, but this might be the best bowl of stew ah've ever had sir. Thank you, sir.’

***

Granny McDuff was furious. Wee Jenny and her brother cowered before her. In one hand, Granny held a leather buckled belt, and in the other, she was holding up a silver shilling to the light of the candle.

‘If I find out you've stolen this, ma girl, I'll take you across my knee...’

Jenny was insistent: ‘Naw, naw, granny, I've telt ye, it wis the graveyard and then the White Hart and the stew and then he just gie'd us the coin. An' that was that.’

Granny MacDuff gave the girl a suspicious eye: ‘And what did he want in the *graveyard*?’

No answer. The old lady paused for a moment, then: ‘Are you still a good girl?’

'Aye.'

'Did you show him the stones, like I learned you?'

'Aye. I showed him the Adam Smith and the wee backle and a' that...'

'And he gave you this?'

'Aye. He was very taken with the stones, Granny, very taken. And he even went intae a dwam once he saw the 'mean man'.'

'The 'mean man'?'

'Aye, the 'mean man' - Scroggie.'

Granny MacDuff stood perplexed for a moment, and then she put her hand to her mouth to stifle a laugh.

'What are we going to do with you, lassie? Ebenezer Scroggie wisnae a 'mean man' - he was a 'meal man' - a corn merchant. That's what it says on his gravestone - a 'meal man''

Jenny feared the belt again: 'Honest, granny, ah wisnae sure...it was dark...it was rainin'...naebody could read nothin'...'

***

OCTOBER 1843 - London

Implacable winter weather. It was late now, as Dickens looked out into the October rain from the window of his study.

Edinburgh seemed like a dream now. Work on the pamphlet was finished and he had promised his publisher another short work to be ready before Christmas.

The study now seemed icy cold. Dickens rang the bell for the maid to come up and prepare the fire. No response. He looked at the long-case clock against the wall. Almost midnight. Of course, the servants had been dismissed for the evening. He had quite lost sight of the hour, immersed as he was in his own imagination.

Shivering now, he put a long comforter around his neck - but to no real effect.

Nothing else for it but to build a fire himself.

As he knelt by the fireplace, memories, unwanted memories chilled inside him.

Twelve years old. The officers coming for his father. No food for the house. No coal for the fire. *When will it ever end?*

Kindling. He needed kindling. He got up from the fireplace and went to the chair beside his desk to find any discarded newspapers. None. But there on the desk was the stack of printer's proofs of the pamphlet he had just completed:

'An Appeal to the People of England, on behalf of the Poor Man's Child.'

Dickens stared at the pamphlet. The room seemed even colder now. Kindling?

Kneeling down, he began to rip the pamphlets apart and lay them into the grate of the fireplace. There would be 'plentiful kindling' from the pamphlets. Dickens smiled. In his mind, he had a vision of the enormous, jocular Advocate in that great Edinburgh hall, teasing him and predicting the fate of the pamphlets - and now here they were: kindling. Kindling that would ultimately go up the chimney, like a nine year-old sweep.

And now he was placing wood around the grate. And now, time for the coal. Coal enough, but where are the tongs? No sign. *Borrowed for another fireplace in the house, I wager.* Dickens picked up pieces of coal between his finger and thumb and placed them around the grate. His stared at his fingertips, black now, and rubbed them together.

And he was a child again. Warren's Blacking Factory; the rotten floorboards; the decayed staircase; the dirt; the rats; the endless working day; the black boot polish on his fingertips. Some stains never fade.

But there was always hope, wasn't there? Moments of kindness in the darkest of places. Even in that blacking factory, amid the dirt and decay, another child had always shown him kindness.

Time to light the fire. Reaching into the desk of his drawer, he took out a small box of matches, shook them and then knelt down again. He took out a match and struck it, the flame hissing into life. And now those kindling pamphlets were lit, and the pamphlets caught the wood, and the wood caught the coal, and the coal began to burn.

And what did he see when he looked into those flames? The memory of that gigantic, jolly figure in Edinburgh spreading good cheer; golden letters glowing on a building: 'love your neighbour as yourself'; two children standing in a graveyard, in the driving rain, harmless against the world that would not protect them; a ghostly face, like a doorknocker; the gravestone of a 'mean man' taking that name into all of eternity with him. When will it all end?

Had it always been thus? Would it never change? Two thousand years ago, a child born into the muck of a stable or the ragged children of London's East End. What could be done?

Maybe the Advocate was right. Maybe it was only stories that touched the hearts of men.

Dickens sat down at his desk. He opened his writing ledger. If he could only reform the heart of 'mean' men like Ebenezer Scroggie, then there would always be hope. Perhaps the encounter in the Edinburgh graveyard had been no accident. Perhaps it was for the dead to show the living the true meaning of Christmas.

His pen hovered over the page. Then, with the scratch of quill on paper, he began to write:

'Stave One...Marley's Ghost...Marley was dead: to begin with...'

Dickens looked up from the paper and smiled. And worked on into the night...

*****

Thanks to…

The usual gang: Colin, Douglas, Mike and Gordon - as Advocates go, not a bad bunch.

Alistair Johnson - Faculty Librarian Extraordinaire.

Sandy McCall Smith - for unstinting support and encouragement (since 1986!).

Alan Young @ The Scotsman - since 1817 - (the newspaper, not Alan).

The wondrous Catherine Salmond (@The Herald) for getting our Edward 'out there' at the very beginning.

Iain Livingstone at Scottish Print - for ironing out the bumps and making the process of formatting/printing/publishing look SO easy.

Andy Baker at Number 7. So, I looked up 'good neighbour' in the dictionary and…

Printed in Great Britain
by Amazon

32826785R00196